ROGUE

Chapter 1

Artificially intelligent alarm clocks are the worst. They know your weaknesses, your pet peeves, they know just how to push to ensure you get out of bed on time. While I loved Ivy, she annoyed the ever-loving crap out of me whenever she woke me up.

Arianna, get out of bed right now, or I am going to turn on every light in this room and blast the most atrocious upgrade jingle I can find. Don't make me turn on the air conditioning!

I groaned, pulling the comforter further over my head. Ivy's bossy 'mom' tone was far too close to the tone my actual mother insisted on using every time she spoke to me.

Ugh... I threw the covers off as dramatically as I could manage, eyes struggling to adjust to the soft glow Ivy had set the room to. My room stayed nice and warm, regardless of Ivy's threat. She knew how much I hated climbing out of the splendidly warm covers as it was.

Good morning sunshine! Ivy's voice rang out, painfully cheerful in my ears.

I could see her blurry form in my right eye, spinning in delight at another mediocre day.

She prattled through her morning checklist, something so mundane I wished I could fall back asleep while sitting on the edge of my bed. *Heart rate stable, breathing normal, metabolism slightly elevated. I'm adding extra calories to your meal plan today* Ivy declared happily.

I couldn't help but smile. Maybe if I held off until dinner, I would get a slice of cake or something equally chocolate based, to make up for the missing calories. Though, with my luck I would be stuck with a nasty calorically dense mush instead.

She continued through her usual routine, spouting off the weather for the day, advising me to bring a windbreaker. Apparently, there would be a cold front rolling in this afternoon. Ivy phrased it as a suggestion, but the outfit designed to fit the conditions of the day came sliding out on a tray connected to the closet.

I guess if I didn't really want to wear what she had picked, I could actually go into my closet and pick something else out, but Ivy always had excellent taste. Today she picked out a pair of comfortable blue jeans, a thin soft long sleeve shirt and a light jacket, in my favorite color, green.

I chuckled, noticing Ivy had matched her avatar's outfit to mine, the only change being the color of her jacket, which was purple. Why on earth would an AI need a jacket, I would never know, but Ivy liked to look good, even if I was the only one who saw her.

The thought of Ivy's meticulous avatar brought me back to my early middle school days, when suddenly everyone was altering their AIs. Ashley, my best human friend, had come over alone for once. Usually, her brother Sam went wherever she went, and the three of us had been close since elementary school. But for some reason, she had insisted on coming over alone, which was enough to warrant the full attention of both me *and* Ivy.

Ash had come stumbling into my bedroom, panting slightly, Ivy having let her in through the front door's security system, looking flushed and red faced. Even in middle school, Ash had been gorgeous, adored by all our classmates, but I didn't mind. She got the attention, and I got to hang in the background like I wanted.

She had sat on my bed, breathing hard. I had never seen Ash at a loss for words, so I kept my mouth shut, waiting, Ivy flitting back and forth across my field of vision, expecting the worst.

Ivy always expected the worst.

Ash took a steadying breath, avoiding my eyes.

She picked delicately at a seam running down my plush bedspread and said, "Hey, Ari."

I stared at her, confused. "Hey Ash." Ivy stopped her fluttering. Ash took another breath and finally looked me straight in the face. She had looked so serious at the time that my stomach had clenched nervously.

"Ok, so you know how we can change our AIs, like their clothes and stuff?"

I nodded confused, the knots in my stomach unclenching slightly.

"Ok, well, I found this tutorial on the Feed that showed how to play with your AI's settings, and I found out you can change a lot. . ." She trailed off, a blush creeping down her face into her neck.

I hid my hand under a pillow, typing to Ivy.

Ivy, what the heck is she talking about?

Ivy responded by shaking her head a bit too aggressively. Did she not know, or did she not want me to know?

When I didn't immediately respond, Ash went on, "Well, did you know you can change the gender of the AI into whatever you want it to be? And the voice and everything? Not just their outfits, but like the whole thing?"

Her voice took on a breathy quality, waiting for me to catch on. I stared back at her, puzzled, and she huffed an exasperated sigh, irritation overcoming her embarrassment.

"Ok, fine." Ash began moving her hands gracefully through the air, her eyes looking somewhat distant as she expanded her own field of vision. "Open your private feed. I'm sending you a capture of my massively improved AI."

There was a faint *ding* in my head and a small indicator flashed in my left eye, alerting me to a new message.

Ivy was on it before I even moved a finger, pulling up the image, her face taut with unexpected anxiety. When the image popped up Ivy doubled over in laughter, tension erased by pure unadulterated joy.

"His name is Benjamin." Ashley said quietly, blushing.

I stared at the image. It showed a muscled tan male with dark hazel eyes and sweeping blond hair. He looked like he had just come from the pool, wearing swimming trunks and sandals. His jaw was square and sharp, and as my eyes trailed down his never-ending abdominal muscles, I had to swallow hard. I didn't even know a person could have that many muscles.

Ivy minimized the image before I could start drooling and shook her head, eyes full of mirth. Ash was also giggling now, perfectly manicured hands covering her mouth, making my face bloom with heat.

"You should hear him talk, too. His voice is so deep, and he has this accent, just ah." Ash grabbed a pillow and fell backwards onto the bed dramatically, the picture of a perfect swoon. "It makes those annoying morning checklists so much more fun to listen to, actually it makes everything the AI says more fun to listen to."

Ash smiled deviously. She had always been ahead of me with this type of stuff. She already knew how to do her makeup perfectly, dress perfectly, and had started liking boys when I still thought they smelled. Don't get me wrong, I could see why having an AI like that would be fun, and at the time I had blushed furiously, imagining how I could make one look and sound like Derek, a boy in our class.

Don't even think about it, Arianna. You know perfectly well I like myself the way I am. I'm not some toy to be played with. It was like Ivy could read my mind. I swirled my fingers through the air in response.

Ivy, I would never! You're different, and I love you just the way you are. Plus, I doubt I could change you even if I tried.

Ivy had winked at that, neither confirming nor denying my ability to have an actual effect on her avatar body.

"So," Ash bounced excitedly on the bed. "What are you going to do to your AI? I want to see it!" Ash's question caught me so off guard and I had responded without thinking.

"Oh, Ivy doesn't want to be changed. She likes the way she is." Ash stared at me skeptically and I clamped my mouth shut, instantly regretting what I had said.

"What do you mean, she doesn't want to be changed? She is an AI. She isn't a real person..." Ash spoke as if I wasn't quite understanding the significance. "I know you um, really like her and all, but you should try it. Maybe you'd like your own perfectly designed AI more?"

She and Sam had been around long enough to know that the connection Ivy and I had differed from most people with their AIs. They knew Ivy was also not your typical AI, and they usually didn't question it. Still, I couldn't believe I had said that. I usually avoided talking about Ivy at all costs, but the sight of Ash's new, seriously hot, AI had my brain all muddled.

Nice one, Arianna. Ivy had frowned, her tiny arms crossed. She wasn't really mad, more like concerned, but still I had messed up.

Ash had left shortly after, disappointed that she could not convince me to change my Ivy. I thought things might be tense the next day when we saw each other on the auto-rail, but she had plopped down next to me, immediately gushing about how she had changed "Ben's" voice again.

Smiling and laughing alongside her, I noticed how her brother Sam remained deep in the game he was playing on his field of vision, completely ignoring us, a blush threatening to creep up his neck into his face at any moment. I remember wondering exactly what he had changed his AI to.

Ivy snapped her virtual fingers in front of me, bringing me back to the present, and I wished for a moment I was back in middle school, dealing with middle school troubles, rather than starting my senior year of high school.

Ivy ran through my messages from friends who are just waking up as well. Ashley wanted to know if I had heard anything from Derek lately, and I realized that I hadn't heard from him in the last week. Sam wanted to know if I did my Technology summer project yet, and Jordan was posting all over the place how she caught an "actual cold" and won't be in school for at least a month.

I let out an audible groan as Ivy flashed up an image of Jordan wrapped up in at least twenty blankets, looking pathetic. Catching something as rare as a cold was scary, what with the constant health monitoring of our AI chips, but I could guarantee that her AI had already alerted the authorities and she would receive a cure-all pill soon. She may be out of school for like a day or two, and then her AI will have to have a software update to make sure it missed nothing as bad as an oncoming illness again.

Honestly, I am thrilled you two are no longer friends. She is a dramatic one.

I couldn't help but laugh at Ivy's huffy tone. She usually kept her comments on my friends to herself.

Ivy moved on, reminding me to pay extra attention to the back left molar on the top row of my teeth. The enamel was weakening, and I could be at risk of a cavity if I wasn't careful. I rolled my eyes, knowing she would sense the motion, and walked to the bathroom. I know this constant monitoring is supposed to be a blessing, but Ivy was so naggy in the mornings.

Throwing my clothes on, I checked my hair one last time. It sat dark and straight across my shoulders, as usual. I minimized my field of vision, to get a clear look at my face in the mirror. My skin was still slightly tan from running in the sun all summer long, but my dark blue eyes looked dimmer than normal. I had barely slept last night. I thought as a senior I would shake the first day nerves, but here we were.

I shook my head and ambled into the kitchen. A note was displayed on the fridge from my mom's AI, wishing me a good day at school. I was certain that she set an autotimer for her AIto leave me notes because it was the same note at the same time every day, even during the summer. I used my palm to swipe it across the screen into the little trash can on the monitor, focusing on my approved list of breakfast options.

I settled on a classic; oatmeal with brown sugar, apples, and a glass of juice, 426 calories. Ivy noted the calorie intake and stored them in my file for the day. I could have opted for pancakes and whipped cream, one of my favorites, but I want to save my extra calories for later, still aiming for that chocolate cake. The fridge distributed my breakfast and juice, along with two capsules.

I grimaced, looking at them, and Ivy chimed in, her tone only mildly chiding.

Arianna don't make that face. Take your pills. They're just vitamins, they don't even have a taste.

I stuck out my tongue; I don't care what they say in the advertisement, the stupid pills always left an awful taste in my mouth. Pinching my nose, I grabbed the pills, threw them down my throat and chugged the glass of orange juice, hoping to wash away the taste. Ivy flashed a ticking clock in my face, pushing me to eat faster.

"Yes Ivy, I see the time. Thank you for being oh so punctual, as always," I grumbled back to her. She stuck out her tongue in response, mirroring me. She was right though; I was definitely going to be late.

I ran out of the house, grabbing my backpack on the way out, which contained only the thin sleek tablet we use for homework and reviewing lessons. Most people didn't carry a backpack anymore, but I liked the comforting weight of it on my back. I made it down the street, sprinting to the platform just as the auto-rail pulled up.

Cursing under my breath, I earned a glare from Ivy at my 'foul' language. I knew there was no way we would make it through the gate and down the platform in time. I didn't even have my ID badge ready for the spindles. I was going to be late to school on the first day of senior year. How fitting.

"Ivy, I could use some help. Please" I tried to whisper as quietly as I could while all out running, not having the time or the coordination to type a response to her. Ivy crossed and uncrossed her arms patiently.

I told you to get up earlier. She snipped at me, irritated by my sass earlier.

"Come on, I don't want to be late!" I was almost to the spindles.

You promised me we would stop doing this. Her tone was serious, and I nodded gravely.

By doing this, she meant all the times I asked her to manipulate the Grid, for lack of a better term. I wasn't sure what she did, only that Ivy could take control of pretty much any system connected to the Grid given enough time. Not that she would. She wouldn't do anything she thought would put me at risk, which, turns out, was pretty much everything. But this, manipulating a train spindle, this was child's play. She was just being stubborn because of the last prank Derek, Sam and I had pulled.

I slowed down, resigned, and was about to reach for my bag when the spindle flashed green, allowing me to pass without touching my ID. I laughed in relief and Ivy couldn't help but crack a faint smile and my excitement. She wouldn't admit it, but she loved the way I was always impressed with her abilities, even the small ones. I sprinted through the closing compartment doors, barely missing the edges.

-

Chapter 2

It is impossible to miss the school's compartment in the auto-rail. It's bright yellow, a cliché throwback to when students used to be carted around on buses. Now it just looked tacky next to the other sleek silver compartments. The seats of the school compartment were all made from thick brown leather and were stiff and uncomfortable.

The other compartments on the auto-rail were filled with people traveling to and from the city. The silver compartments contain sleek black leather recliners and smooth stainless-steel tables for executives, while the duller compartments at the back of the auto-rail had faded cloth seats, which were crammed so close together, you wonder how they breathed all squished together like that. Those compartments were for people who work in the manufacturing factories. The school compartments separate them, like a shiny yellow caution sign, making sure neither group crosses over to the other side.

Ivy sent a brightly colored arrow into my field of vision, pointing to the left, showing me were Ashley and Sam were sitting. Ash was bouncing up and down, waiting for me to make my way over to them, while Sam stared down into his lap, a small frown etched onto his gentle features. I squeezed over to them, storing my backpack above me in my designated bin, and sat down, bracing for Ashley's intense morning energy.

"Can you believe we are seniors?" Ashley squeaked excitedly. She bounced us both on the seat, to hyped to keep still. Sam rolled his eyes, moving to a seat across the aisle. Clearly, he had dealt with an amped up Ash for too long this morning.

"Thank the Grid, only one more year in that miserable soul-sucking prison." Sam's voice was barely above a whisper but held an unusual amount of emotion. His eyes glazed over again; hands moved deftly in front of him.

His face was set in a neutral mask, blonde hair spilling over his forehead, partially hiding his eyes from view. According to his stats online, he was going after a new record in Zombie World VI, but I knew those stats were fake.

Sam hated gory first-person shooter games. He was probably playing the newest instalment of Ancient Dynasty Boyfriend, a boyfriend simulation game that he and I both loved. It had come out last week and I had yet to get my hands on it. I eyed him enviously, a faint blush coloring his cheeks as he studiously ignored me.

I glanced away, not wanting to draw attention to him. I have no idea why he puts up a front, especially with Ash, but that wasn't my business. I scanned the rail casually and Ivy shook her head, eyes twinkling.

I already checked. He isn't on the auto-rail. I thought he didn't like taking the auto-rail anyways.

I discreetly moved my left hand, nodding absent-mindedly at the flood of words coming out of Ashley's mouth. I was faintly surprised she remembered to take a breath between sentences.

I know, he almost never takes the auto-rail. I laughed, hoping Ash thought it was at something clever she said, and continued typing. *And when he does, it never means anything good. Remember the last time? I thought for sure he would be given a lifetime ban.*

Ivy tried to look stern, but failed miserably, laughing at the memory of Derek's last auto-rail prank. At least he never involved me in those ones, Ivy would like him a lot less if he jeopardized my transportation rights. It was like they had an unspoken rule. Anything too risky, Derek kept to himself, in return Ivy let me help with his less outlandish schemes.

I was hoping he would be here. I haven't seen him in days. He has been weirdly secretive lately, and it's making me nervous.

You'll see him soon enough, Ari. I'm sure everything is fine.

Ivy's tone was soothing, and I nodded in response to both her and Ash, who was asking if I was feeling alright. Ash had noticed that I was checked out and her eyes were staring intently at me, a hurt look on her face. I pushed Derek out of my mind and focused on Ashley, giving her my full attention, making sure my responses were as animated as hers. I have no idea how she maintains this level of energy, and by the time the auto-rail slid screeching into the school's platform I was exhausted.

We pushed our way off the rail, fighting nervous freshman who looked weirdly small. Were the incoming freshmen always so baby faced?

I scanned the crowd, which was a challenge considering I wasn't the tallest person in the world. All 5 feet 4 inches of me craned over the throng of people on the platform. It was useless. Thankfully, Ivy took pity on me and flashed a green arrow to the left. She had found the AI signature that belonged to Derek and pointed into the thickest part of the crowd. I should have guessed; Derek always drew a crowd.

I squeezed Ash's hand to let her know I was taking off. She nodded vaguely in my direct already surrounded by her own admirers. Sam had wandered off as well, most likely to find a bench away from the crowd so he could focus on his field of vision in peace.

There was one advantage to being small, it was easy to weave through the thick crowd. The front of the school wasn't usually this busy, but everyone had gotten to school early since it was the first day back from summer break. Student's mingled, eagerly waving to friends, while others absent mindedly ran into people, deep in their fields.

I turned sharply to the left, splitting up a couple deeply invested in a public display of affection and there he was.

Derek caught my eye immediately and winked, a dimple showing as he smiled. My heart fluttered erratically. A small group of googly eyed girls surrounded him, and I stifled a groan. This would be so much easier if we just went public. Then, maybe I wouldn't have to fight off all the bad boy savior types who had absolutely no idea how "bad" Derek really was.

I fought my answering smile, and paused a few steps away from Derek, crossing my arms defiantly. I was senior now. I refused to be seen as one of Derek's little lovesick pets. Ivy nodded her approval in the corner of my field of vision, taking the same stance as me. His smile slipped away, a brief look of confusion flashing across his dark eyes, before being replaced by a soft smirk.

Derek pushed off the bench, making his way to me, much to the disappointment of his adoring fans. I stifled a laugh as their faces slipped from stunning smiles to irritated grimaces. I almost asked Ivy to snap a pick, but then I remembered, I didn't care. Not that much at least.

"Hey charming, how was your ride in?"

Derek's voice was lower than when we had first met. In fact, there wasn't much about Derek that hadn't changed over the last 4 years. He was significantly taller than me now, almost breaking 6 feet. His shoulders were broad and muscled, but not from sports or lifting. Derek was fit because a remarkable number of his pranks involved moving heavy objects and running, so much running.

I stared up at him, temporarily forgetting how to speak. He smirked again, showing that dimple of his, eyes sparkling. Those eyes though, they had not changed one bit, and neither had his confidence. He exuded it with every movement, which explained the constant crowd around him. He drew in people like bees to honey.

"That good, huh?" He chuckled softly. Ivy stifled a laugh, and I almost told her to shut up. Sometimes I forgot I was the only one who could hear her.

"It was fine. Having fun with your little ducklings?" Trying unsuccessfully to keep the bitter edge from my voice. I focused intently on my hands instead.

A soft pressure pushed on my chin lifting my face. Derek's eyes danced, causing my stomach to clench. I couldn't stop the smile that spread across my face. This was a smile only I knew, one that spelled trouble, but I didn't care. It was mine.

Derek's finger slipped from my chin as Ivy groaned dramatically. She also knew what that look meant, and she was not nearly as thrilled to see it as I was.

The warning bell rang loudly, encouraging students to make their way inside. In approximately three minutes an additional bell would ring, threatening all stragglers to move it. I took a step forward, following the heard of students headed towards class, but a gentle tug at my wrist stopped me.

I looked down in surprise. There was a hand holding mine, pulling me back away from the crowd.

An actual hand, holding my hand.

I glanced down in shock at the five fingers entwined with mine, slowly letting my eyes travel up the tanned arm they were connected to, past the frayed sleeve of a badly worn shirt and up to a dangerously beautiful face.

I clenched my jaw to keep it from popping open, Ivy let her own fall for me, in as much shock as I was. Derek was holding my hand. In public. Granted, in the minute I had been staring up at him, most of the students had made their way away from us and towards the entrance of the school, but still, there were plenty of people close enough to see Derek DeSoto holding my hand.

Derek's eyes danced again. He was tugging my hand back to keep me from following the crowd to home room. Just as he opened his mouth an annoying high-pitched giggle cut through the air to my left.

Derek's face shuttered as he dropped my hand, all traces of humor wiped away. My hand burned from the unexpected loss of contact, and I turned to face whoever had interrupted us, hoping I looked as pissed as I felt.

"Oh, I'm sorry, did I interrupt something?"

Christy plastered a false look of remorse on her face, eyeing Derek up and down like a predator. Delilah, a smaller junior with a killer sprint time, stood next to her awkwardly.

Christy was captain of the track team, and even though I felt like punching her in the face, I didn't feel like facing the consequences all season. I was slated to win the tri-city tournament this year and I wasn't going to let her ruin it.

"Of course not, what's up?"

I kept my voice as even as possible. Ivy flashed an old picture of Christy up and began drawing unflattering images on it. I tried not to laugh, but my face must have given me away because Christy's eyes narrowed angrily.

"I just wanted to make sure you were coming to practice today. I've got a killer workout planed, wouldn't want you to fall behind."

Christy's voice was sugar coated acid, and her eyes never left Derek. He glanced at her briefly and she flashed him her most brilliant smile, twirling a lock of her hair around her finger. My cheeks flushed crimson as hot anger bubbled in my stomach. I knew Derek, Christy was definitely not his type, but it stilled irritated me that girls openly flirted with him, especially girls like her.

"I can't wait to see your new distance times, Ari! I saw your Feed posts over the summer, you PR'd like 3 different records! No one can out pace you now. I'm sure you'll win tri-city this year!"

Delilah's sincere voice was like a calming balm. Christy turned to glare at her, and she shrank back, unsure of what she had done wrong. I couldn't help but smile. I had spent all summer working on my 5-mile and 8-mile times. I was going to crush everyone this year.

"Thanks, I'll be there, don't worry Christy."

I flashed a smile at the two of them as the tardy bell rang loudly. It was time to go, or we would all be late. Christy glared openly at me, then turned to face Derek again. She batted her eyes like a deranged butterfly and smile seductively at him.

"You can come too, Derek. I always love having people watch me run."

I thought she might lose one of her synthetic lashes if she continued blinking so fast, but Derek turned, giving her his full attention for the first time. Christy preened under his gaze.

"Sorry Chelsea, but I'm busy today."

Christy's face went from white to red to purple in an impressive display of colors as she realized what he had called her. I choked on a laugh as Derek grabbed my hand and pulled me towards the front of the school.

I grinned down at our entwined fingers. Derek was not one for public displays of affection, and he might be doing this just to piss off Christy, but I didn't care. This was the second time he had held my hand in public. Senior year was already a hundred times better than I thought it would be.

Chapter 3

Derek dropped my hand again as we entered homeroom, but not before he gave it a reassuring squeeze that sent my heart racing again. Sam waved us over, rolling his eyes at the ridiculous grin plastered on my face. I couldn't help it. Sam would just have to deal with it. Today was going to be a great day.

I slid into my seat next to Sam, Derek plopping down on the other side. Derek and Sam immediately pulled up their fields of vision, tuning out poor flustered Mr. Davidson's welcome back lecture. Sam didn't need to pay attention to ace his classes, and Derek could care less what he learned in school. I on the other hand, needed to at least pay some attention to get the marks I needed.

I didn't really care about my grades. I cared about the choices that came with having high grades. The higher your marks were in school, the more choices you had when it came time to track into a career. The others may not care where they wound up for the rest of their lives, but I wanted as many choices as possible. Especially since I still had no idea what I wanted to do with my life. The thought that in one year I would be forced to decide made me want to puke.

Mr. Davidson's voice slipped into a dull rhythm, challenging the students to stay awake as he droned on about the creation of the AI microchips. We had gotten this lesson in some variation every year, and taking notes was the only way I could keep myself from slipping into the half-asleep coma most students had succumbed to.

"Artificially intelligent microchips were designed to save our species. After the bio-war, our population declined rapidly. Birthrates crashed, economies crumbled, and nations floundered."

Even Mr. Davidson sounded exceptionally bored today. After three years with the same homeroom students, I bet he was as eager for us to graduate as we were. I could have had Ivy record the lecture for me like most students did, but there was something relaxing about typing up notes the old-fashioned way.

"City-states built up walls, and international communication ground to a halt. It was a dark time for humanity. Then the Founder brothers developed the first AI. They named it Kronos after the King of the Titans. While Kronos was far less advanced than the AIs in each of your chips, it was the basis of all modern AI technology."

Derek made a disgruntled noise and I tensed automatically, hoping he would stay lost down whatever rabbit hole he had fallen. It wasn't unusual for him to question and needle everything our professors said in class. He liked to argue everything. At first it was entertaining, watching the professors studder and fluster at his probing questions, but lately it was kind of exhausting. We all just wanted to get through our classes and be done with school. I understood his need to challenge the information being shoved at us, but at some point, wasn't it just easier to nod along?

I glanced at Ivy, wondering if she was on red alert as well, but her avatar bobbed idly in place. She was probably off on the Grid somewhere looking up something. I always wondered where she went and what it looked like, but she laughed when I had asked changed the subject.

"AI technology has allowed humanity to stabilize, to gather together once more in beautiful cities like ours. Thanks to the Grid system which covers the city like a protective blanket, and the interconnected rails which extend Grids from city to city, we are once again a global community."

Mr. Davidson's words faded into the background as I braced myself for Derek's sharp interruption, but it never came. I risked a glance over at him, and all the air whooshed out of my lungs.

His hands were clenched into white knuckled fists on top of his desk, eyes blazing with a fury I had never seen. His already dark brown eyes were close to black, a large tendon strained in his neck beating in time with his racing pulse.

He shook, mostly likely with the effort it took him to hold his tongue, which was odd. Usually, Derek never held back, it was one of the things I liked most about him. His was honest, even about things others would keep to themselves. He was always the first to speak up and out.

I reached over, gently placing my hand over his. He flinched, eyes flickering over to mine, anger seething out of them before he shuddered. He blinked a few times and then it was all gone. The tension, the rage, vanishing like smoke in the wind. His clenched fist relaxed underneath mine as he took a slow steady breath.

"Thanks, Charming."

Derek's breath was warm as he leaned over, pressing his shoulder into mine. He leaned away sliding his hand out from under mine and began lazily typing against the blank desk, a bored look replacing the intense emotion from before.

Half a dozen questions raced through my mind. What the glitch was that about? It wasn't like Mr. Davidson's lecture had been different than any of the other dozen he gave in years past. There was no reason for such a dramatic reaction.

I tried to focus on the rest of the lecture, while sneaking glances at Derek every few minutes, but it was useless. I didn't hear a word Mr. Davidson said and Derek's face remained in an impassive smirk throughout the period, eyes glazed over focused on whatever his field of vision showed him.

I gave up, pulling up my own field of vision. The edges of my peripherals blurred slightly, as my overlays came sharply into focus. Some people liked to crowd their fields with all sorts of overlays; news windows, credit exchange updates, some people even had a Feed window permanently loaded into their field. I have no idea how people get anything done with a constant stream of videos and posts right in front of their face.

I like to keep my field of vision simple. I had a digital clock up in the corner, mainly because I'm perpetually late and thought if might help. It doesn't. There was also a tiny flashing heart tucked into the bottom corner which Ivy had insisted I add after my first panic attack. The tiny heart didn't help much either, but it was interesting to watch, kind of soothing.

Other than that, my field of vision was clear, except for Ivy's small avatar form, which still bobbed idly. Derek's rage filled eyes flashed in my mind and I desperately wished Ivy would hurry up. The look in his eyes made me shudder. I needed Ivy, especially if Derek decided to do something foolish.

Chapter 4

Ivy returned as homeroom was ending. I had given up on listening to Mr. Davidson drone on about AI advancements, instead focusing on a pacing workout for after school. If I could just shave off a few more seconds, I could guarantee the top spot on our long-distance relay.

Ivy's avatar swilled slowly in a circle, her face transforming from a broad grin to a concerned frown in under a second. She had examined my vital monitoring system the second she returned and had seen the blip from Derek's weird emotional outburst. Her avatar faced me; eyes concerned.

I swiped away my workout routine, lifting a hand to type a message, eager to tell Ivy everything that happened, when the bell rang catching me off guard. The bell was a revival song, stirring people back to life. Everyone began moving at once, rushing to get out of homeroom and on to their next class.

Sam nodded to us as he filed after the rest of the class. He teased me relentlessly, but he always gave Derek and I privacy when he thought something was going on. He tried to play it off, but I knew he would hound me for details later, far away from Ash who could never know how invested he was in our little romance.

Ivy paused curious. She would have to wait.

I grabbed my bag and glanced at Derek. He was staring down at Mr. Davidson, a cruel smirk twisting his face. I followed his line of sight, hoping Mr. Davidson hadn't seen Derek staring at him like some crazed glitch. Explaining that expression would take some serious creative leaps.

The bell must have caught Mr. Davidson off guard, too. He was standing mouth open, as if mid-sentence. He looked frozen, body unnaturally still, muscles locked rigidly into place. I took a step back, bumping roughly into the desk behind me a chill going up my spine.

Then, Mr. Davidson was moving again.

He turned away from us and walked to his desk, rummaging through one of his draws, as if getting ready for his next class. I shook my head confused. Had I imagined him frozen like that? Derek grabbed my hand and pulled me silently from the class, lips pressed into a firm line.

Derek and I didn't have 2nd or 3rd period together, but he walked me all the way to my class anyway. He was lost in thought, gripping my hand almost painfully as he led me through the halls.

I ignored the whispers around us as we passed other students. Another time this would have been the highlight of my day, possibly my entire week, but Derek's earlier rage and the weird way Mr. Davidson had just stood there, frozen, had officially creeped me out.

I was glad that Derek and I didn't have 2nd period together, I needed to talk to Ivy, even if she told me I was seeing things. Ivy simulated a chair in my field of vision, taking a seat and crossing her legs delicately. She didn't need to sit down, but it was an impressive display of impatience.

When we reached my classroom Derek paused, finally turning to look me in the eye. His face held a mixture of concern and determination, lacking his usually cocky mischief.

My stomach clenched painfully.

I had no idea what was wrong with Derek today. He was all over the place, which was not a good sign. He only behaved erratically like this when he was amped up for a big prank, but we hadn't planned anything lately. It didn't make sense, we always pulled pranks together, relying on Ivy to cover our tracks.

The warning bell rang. We only had about a minute to make it to our next class and the hallways were rapidly clearing out. Derek waited patiently for the hallway to empty, not caring when the late bell rang signaling we were officially late for 2nd period.

When the last student, a tiny lost freshman, scrambled out of the hallway, Derek leaned forward causing my heart to jump.

Was he going to kiss me? Is that why he wanted the hallway to clear out?

It wasn't Derek's usual side, but who was I to argue. Suppressing a sudden wave of self-consciousness, I closed my eyes in anticipation, but his mouth never met mine, instead it slipped past my cheek to brush my ear. His breath was hot causing me to shiver involuntarily as it tickled my ear.

"You saw it too, didn't you?"

Derek's words were so soft I could barely hear them. I doubt they would even register loud enough for an AI to record them, but it was always possible. I shook my head in confusion, did he mean Mr. Davidson?

I opened my mouth to respond, but Derek pressed his finger to my lips silencing me.

"Shh. I can't risk you getting caught so just listen. You did see it. That was a glitch. It had to be, a real glitch. I told you there was something off about Mr. Davidson."

Derek's voice dropped so low, I had to strain to hear him. His finger was still against my mouth as my heart threatened to beat out of control. I wondered what someone would think if they decided to leave class right now. None of this made sense.

Derek paused, breathing hard. I was getting impatient with this game. I hated being confined and the feeling of his finger against my mouth was rapidly changing from cute and mysterious to annoying.

"I'm sorry Ari. I know I promised to let you help with jobs, but I couldn't with this one. It's too big. Too much of a risk. I'm on to something real this time." Derek's voice took on a determined tone, chest brushing mine as he took a deep steadying breath.

We had been pulling small pranks together since we were freshman. Little things like altering the school menu so it served only desert for lunch and releasing test questions during exam week. Thanks to Ivy, we never got caught, but it was still exciting to disrupt a school that seemed to only focus on classifying us before shoving us into meaningless mind-numbing jobs for the rest of our lives.

Derek always let me in on his pranks, 'jobs' as we had coded them whenever we actually talked about them. He was the only person who even remotely knew that Ivy could do more than the average AI, much to Ivy's annoyance.

He didn't know for sure what Ivy could do, but he had guessed quite a bit. She was the reason he was able to step up his pranking to a school wide level, so he stayed quiet and never asked questions about her. It was our unspoken rule; don't talk about Ivy.

This was different, though. Derek had planned something. Something he thought was big, and he hadn't said a word to me. There was no way he would get away with whatever he was doing without his AI tattling on him, without Ivy to cover for him. What was he thinking?

I took a step back, pushing against Derek's hand to speak but he pulled me closer, his grip firm. He rested his head on my shoulder for a moment. He shoulders sank downward and I wanted to hug him, he seemed so tired and alone.

Derek raised his head to look me in the eye and shook it, determination radiating from his eyes once again. He set his shoulders firmly and dropped his finger from my mouth, finally trusting me to stay silent.

"Ari, you need to trust me. If it all goes as planned, I'll explain everything to you, but you can't be a part of this one." His eyes bore into mine until I gave in.

Who was I kidding? I couldn't say no to him.

I nodded weakly, wondering what he had planned, but it didn't really matter. He would get caught, then he would get into trouble. A sick feeling twisted my stomach, but there was nothing I could do. After Derek's little speech about how dangerous this prank would be, there was no way Ivy would let me get involved anyway.

I stared hard at Derek, trying to guess what he had planned, but I had no idea. He looked relieved, and I wanted to laugh, but the sick twisting feeling in my stomach wiped away any traces of humor. Derek flashed me one of his signature cocky grins, but it was forced. A dark tension clouded his eyes.

He leaned forward, placing a quick kiss on my cheek and stepped away. I clenched my hands together to keep myself from touching the spot he had kissed, holding my breath. He grinned again, looking surer of himself and turned to walk away.

"Good luck, Princess."

I whispered the words just loud enough to reach him as he strolled down the hallway. I should have stayed silent, but I needed to say something. This felt too much like a goodbye. He didn't turn around, instead raising a hand briefly to wave behind him.

Chapter 5

It was too late to go into 2nd period without creating an awkward scene, so I turned and headed the opposite direction towards the labs. Inside were several empty rooms students could reserve for study sessions, but they were almost always deserted.

I slipped inside one of the rooms, Ivy unlocking it without a word. I didn't want to ask the front desk for a key and then explain why I was not in class, and for once Ivy didn't question me. She knew I was shaken up and I needed peace and quiet to sort through everything that had happened this morning.

I sat in the back corner of the room, ignoring the table and desk in the middle. Ivy left the lights off, knowing I would prefer sitting in the cool darkness. Plus, with the lights off there was less of a chance I would be spotted out of class. She manipulated her avatar, drifting it to the middle of my field of vision and expanding it so she took up most of my line of sight. She hovered cross legged, patiently waiting for an explanation.

I let my head fall back into the corner and closed my eyes. Where to begin? It only took about 10 minutes for me to fill Ivy in on everything she had missed. She sat quietly, face carefully neutral as I told her about Derek's rage filled eyes, Mr. Davidson's glitch, and then she knew the rest. She had heard everything Derek had said, but it all felt so strange. Like a bunch of puzzle pieces trying to fit together, but they were from completely different puzzles.

Ivy asked if I was certain about Mr. Davidson. I wanted to pretend that I wasn't sure, that I was seeing things, but the memory of him standing, frozen in time was seared into my brain. When I said yes, and she made me describe it again, everything about it from his stance to how long I thought he was frozen. I asked if she thought it was a real glitch, a brain malfunction caused by an AI, and she shook her head concern etched into her avatar's features. She didn't know either.

Glitches weren't supposed to happen. An AI can't take over your brain, can't make you move or say something, that's not how they worked.

AIs, well most people's AIs, were just there to monitor vitals, access the Feed, and help their host whenever they needed it. The only major downside was that it was nearly impossible to sneak out or break the rules. If you tried your AI would report you to an enforcer and that was it. You had to have serious Grid manipulation skills, like Derek and Sam, to get away with anything, or and AI like Ivy, which I was pretty sure was the only one in existence.

I was drained when the bell for 3rd period rang, but I couldn't spend the entire first day of my senior year locked in a study room. Groaning, I hoisted myself into a standing position and grabbed my bag. Ivy scanned for Derek's AI, know I would ask, but found nothing. My anxiety threatened like a monster waiting just below the surface of a lake.

There was nothing I could do about Derek; he had made his choice. If he wanted to leave me out of his ridiculous plan, then he could suffer the consequences on his own.

I couldn't keep the scowl off my face as I entered 3rd period, earning a few baffled looks from classmates I hadn't seen all summer. Sam waited with an eyebrow raised as I made my way over to the empty seat next to him.

"So, did we decide 2nd period wasn't worth it today? Too busy making out in the hallway to grace Bio-Tech?"

Sam took on the low casual voice he used whenever it was just the two of us. He was always more at ease in a small group, and by small he meant 2 people or less. Even back in middle school, whenever we had to participate as a class or when we went to birthday parties, organized by the parent's AIs of course, he always hid somewhere quiet, focused on his field of vision. Everyone assumed he was a shy nerd, which he definitely was, but he mainly stayed away from people because he didn't want them to judge him.

I rolled my eyes at him but refused to say anything. I couldn't help the small grin battling for control over my carefully blank face, thinking about Derek's breath on my ears, the adorable kiss on my cheek. I groaned loudly, drawing a questioning look of several students nearby. Why did he have to pull a stupid prank?

"What, is he that bad of a kisser?"

Sam's voice shook slightly, which he tried to cover up with a quick cough. He attempted a wink, playing it off as a joke, but the tips of his ears turned crimson. I raised my eyebrow at him.

"Wouldn't you like to know."

I blew Sam a kiss as a trail of flaming red skin flushed down from his ears to his cheeks. Not wanting to make Sam too uncomfortable, I quickly changed the subject.

"Derek told he was up to something, but he wouldn't tell me what. I think it is bigger than normal because he wouldn't let me help at all."

I dropped my voice to a whisper, leaning close to Sam, choosing my words carefully. Ivy nodded as I finished. She was great at making sure I didn't trigger other AIs by saying something careless. Luckily, over the last 4 years of hanging out with Derek, our little group had developed a sort of code.

Sam's face, still flushed from earlier, paled slightly. He shook his head trying to process this news. Class was starting, Language Arts this time, cutting off any chance of further discussion.

It was easy to talk and mess around on your field of vision in Mr. Davison's class. He was anxious and flustered most of the time, and never seemed to get the hang of anything tech based, but Mrs. Abara was different.

She had her room locked down so much that as soon as her lectures started, your field of vision would close automatically, locking you out for the entire period. Even Ivy struggled to work through the restrictions Mrs. Abara had set up in her room. Luckily, most of us had had her for World Literature last year and knew what was coming, but there were a few muffled groans from students who were knew to Mrs. Abara's classroom. I suppressed a laugh at the confused look of the boy sitting next to me, he would learn soon enough.

Mrs. Abara's class was one of my favorites. She had a rich voice that was made for storytelling, and she had a way making me want to try harder. I didn't even like writing, but I never wanted to disappoint her.

I tried hard to focus on what she was saying, but the usual first day syllabus and expectations speech couldn't compete with the rapidly growing list of stupid things Derek could be planning. Each scenario that came into my mind was worse than the last, and before I knew it, class was over.

Sam walked with me to 4th period, staying close to my side. I kept glancing around the hall, looking for Derek's tall form to appear above the rest of the students. When we got to the class I waited outside, while Sam went in to get us all seats giving me a knowing look.

The late bell rang, and I couldn't justify missing another class, so I ducked inside hurrying over to Sam. We glanced at each other, concerned. Halfway through the class, I was convinced that Derek would burst in at any moment. My eyes were stuck in a constant rotation between the door and the digital clock projected on the board. Each minute dragged on until, mercifully, the bell rang once again.

I know you are panicking, and I know no matter what I say you won't focus back on your classes, so I'm recording your lectures for the rest of the day. We can look at them later. I also downloaded a recording of 2nd period someone posted earlier, since you missed that one completely.

It was moments like this that I wished Ivy had a physical body, just so a could pick her up and squeeze her. Since I couldn't squeeze her in real life, I sent her a video of two little ducks in tiny blue rain boots hugging.

Ivy, I know you know this, but you are an absolute treasure. A gift from the heavens.

Yeah, yeah, I know. Get your lunch before the line gets long.

I looped my arm through Sam's, who looked down at me puzzled at my sudden mood shift and pulled him towards the dining hall.

"I'm sure Derek just skipped class. He skips class all the time, I don't know why I was freaking out so much."

I was talking more to myself than Sam, but he nodded along patiently, already bored of Derek's antics. I was starting to feel like the only thing that connect the two at all anymore, like putty slowly being stretched in opposite directions.

We got to the dining hall quickly, taking a deserted hallway that bypassed the crowded main hall. The line wasn't too long as we entered the large surgically clean room. Everything in the room was either stark white or stainless steel in an over-the-top attempt at cleanliness.

It was the opposite of appetizing, giving off weird hospital vibes that made food significantly less appealing. Most students didn't even bother eating at the cold steel tables, instead heading outside to the benches and tables strew randomly around the courtyard.

I stepped up to the automated machine, Ivy connecting to its signal, transferring over my caloric data as well as the credits needed for lunch. After a second, several options appeared across a screen in the center of the machine. My stomach turned, I needed to eat or track practice would really suck after school, but my anxiety was starting to swell, taking up any empty room I had.

I went for the safest option, a classic nut-butter and jelly sandwich, a fruit cup, some veggie crisps, and a caloric cookie to balance my blood sugar before practice. I stepped to the side as a tray slid out on a conveyer belt.

Grabbing my food, I scanned the rapidly growing crowd. You'd think with all this advanced technology they would figure out how to make the lunch line move quicker, but apparently that wasn't a priority.

Derek was still nowhere to be seen, but that wasn't unusual. He usually brought food from home to avoid the overpriced school lunches. Hopefully he was already at out spot, waiting with a good explanation of why he had skipped 4th period, giving me a heart attack.

Sam picked up his tray and we shoved our way through the crowd, heading for the doors. The sun blinded us as we stepped outside. Sam took the lead, making his way toward the hidden alley between two of the buildings. As freshmen, the four of us had drug a table down the alley, away from the rest of the chaos, and had put it under a beautiful old oak tree.

It was a weird spot for a tree, sort of crammed between the gap between two buildings, and we suspected that the gardeners had forgotten about it long ago. It didn't matter though, it was ours. That spot was the only place on campus we could all be ourselves, even Ash loosened up away from the constantly judging eyes of her pre-exec classmates.

Ash was already sitting at the table when we rounded the corner, bouncing up and down with barely contained excitement. I wondered if that was how she stayed in such great shape, she was constantly bouncing, as if her emotions were simply too big for her to stay still.

Lunch was worse than 4th period. Derek never showed and I gave in and pinged him, twice. He didn't answer. I forced a few bites of food down as Ash discussed her entire morning in explicit detail. Eventually, when I wasn't absolutely shocked that Jessica hadn't done her summer assignments, she asked what was up.

I didn't really know what to say. Derek was being weird, had ditched class, but it wasn't that unusual. I didn't know how to explain that this felt different, and there was no way I could explain what had happened with Mr. Davidson. Fortunately, Sam stepped in.

"She's having trouble in Derek-land."

Ash made a sympathetic noise, patting my hand. "Ari, you know how he is. You should just ditch him." She laughed, only partially kidding. "I could set you up with someone way better. You're adorable. I know a ton of exec boys who would kill to date you."

Ash sounded so sure of herself that I had to laugh. I doubted there were that many boys from her class that were interested in me, but I didn't doubt her ability to coerce them into faking it. She was a force to be reckoned with.

The lunch bell rang, and I lost all hope of seeing Derek for the rest of the day. He had ghosted, and he might be safe for now, but the next time I saw him, we would discuss certain behaviors which were plain rude.

I trashed most of my uneaten lunch, ignoring Ivy's grumblings about missed calories, and threw the wrapped cookie into my bag. I would really need it before practice now. Ash linked her arm in mine, describing several boys she thought were perfect for me from her class, as if we hadn't attended the same school, with the same people, since kindergarten.

As we stepped into the main courtyard, I saw him. I stumbled, feeling transported back to this morning, once again catching a glimpse of his tall frame against the crowd. But this time the picture was wrong.

Derek was walking casually across the opposite end of the courtyard, but he wasn't alone. He was being led, rather forcibly, across the courtyard towards the administrative building. He still had his cocky grin on, but his arms were pinned behind him at a painful looking angle.

There was a man on either side of him, gripping his arms tightly. Derek's relaxed expression looked wrong next to the frightening men beside him. They towered over him, expression blank, arms gripping him tightly. I hesitated, wanting to call out to him. The sight of the men around him froze the words in my throat. They were leading him away from us quickly, but not before Ash caught a glimpse of him.

"Derek!"

Ash's clear sparkling voice rang out, cutting through the chatter of the students around us. Everyone turned to look between us and then at Derek, who had paused at Ash's voice. The men pushed roughly at Derek's back, forcing him forward. Silence rippled through the courtyard as everyone took in the scene, Derek being led away, arms pinned behind him, and the creepy men behind him.

The men must have sensed the tension in the courtyard, because they hurried to pull Derek towards the building and out of sight. It was too late. Half the students in the courtyard were already recording the scene, posting it live to the Feed. Everyone would see this now.

Derek craned his neck around and locked eyes on mine. I held my breath, waiting for something, some sign that he was fine, that everything would be alright. He winked once before he trotted up the steps into the admin building, throwing the men off with his sudden movement.

The late bell rang, causing a flurry of motion as an entire courtyard of students realized they were now late for their next class. Not that it mattered. No one would be learning anything this afternoon now. Derek's capture would be the talk of the school for the rest of the day.

Chapter 6

My afternoon classes were an anxiety filled blur. It didn't matter who was at lunch and who actually saw Derek being led away, enough recordings had made it to the Feed that now everyone had an opinion.

Suddenly everyone was a Derek DeSoto expert, having their own theories about what he had done and where they were taking him. After the third speculation that he was being expelled, Sam finally snapped, anger overcoming his introverted ways.

"Will you all shut it! Some of us are actually trying to learn something."

Sam breathed hard, probably from the immediate regret of opening his mouth, but I was grateful. I couldn't take the wondering.

Mercifully school came to an end, and I was released to track practice.

Christy was in a delightful mood, both icy from this morning and self-satisfied by Derek's latest scandal. I ignored her, consequences or not. I was the only person on our team who could compete at tri-city for long distance, so I mostly practiced on my own anyways.

Our coach uploaded our practice schedule for the day, Ivy automatically modifying it to better push my times. The coach did her best, but Ivy was supreme at analyzing my form and times and had been modifying my training schedule since freshman year, when I started taking running seriously. I had placed first in our league since, but this year I wanted to shatter the long distance tri-city records. Every single one of them.

Trying to push Derek out of my mind I lined up at the starting line. Ivy flooded my head with my favorite running playlist. I could barely feel the vibrations in my temples as the bass pumped in time with my heart.

My field of vision expanded into race mode. Ivy had configured this one to optimize my running performance. Slightly above my line of sight was my race clock, which counted lap splits and my overall time. In the bottom left corner was the time of my closest competitor, which Ivy hijacked using the Grid location system, completely legally of course. My pulse rate was in the bottom right corner. Ivy also digitized any race map, a bright green arrow guiding me through the twists and turns of long-distance courses.

The last feature was my favorite and had taken me years to convince Ivy to configure. While I was racing, Ivy would blur out the edges of my field of vision, narrowing my focus dead ahead to reduce distractions.

For most people this would be dangerous, but with Ivy watching the entire race and everything around me, it was perfect. All I had to focus on is moving my legs and the arrows in front of me, Ivy took care of the rest.

Ivy flashed a countdown in the center of my field. Three, two, one. I sprang forward, ready to leave this day and everyone else behind. Music blaring, I focused on pumping my arms in time with my legs, breathing steadily.

The first few laps were slow, a warm-up, but as I rounded the bend for lap 3, I turned up the pace, slipping into a zen only running can give me.

My little purple heart simulator beat quickly, but at a steady pace, smoother than my normal anxiety driven pulse. I slipped into a trance of pumping legs and arms, breathing carefully regulated. I could usually run for hours at this pace, but after a few laps thoughts of Derek invaded my mind. They forced their way through the cracks, throwing off my rhythm. I pushed my pace faster, closer to a sprint, breathing hard. Ivy monitored my stats closely, always making sure I didn't push it too far and hurt myself.

I ran and ran and ran, desperate to outrun my own thoughts. As I ran my thoughts shifted from Derek to my father, a rabbit hole I try frequently to avoid. I started running because of him. Because when he disappeared, I gained a crippling anxiety that only running, and Ivy, could make a dent in. I guess, in a way, it was his fault I was such a good runner now.

I pushed the thought out of my head, upping my pace again. Now was not the time to take a trip down memory lane.

Ari, watch it. You can't sustain this pace. You still have 10 laps to go.

I ignored her. She would lecture me later, but today my thoughts were faster than normal, and if I was going to get any peace, I would have to be quicker, to move even faster.

I ran, narrowing my vision onto the lap counter, barely even looking in front of me. I had run this track so many times I could run it with my eyes closed. Only 9 laps to go. Where were they taking Derek?

8 laps left. What had he done this time?

7 laps. I needed to move faster.

6 laps. People had stopped their own workouts to stand and watch me run. I could barely see them.

5 laps left. My breath was ragged, heart rate becoming uneven again as I pushed past my limit.

4 laps. What if he finally pulled a prank they couldn't just let go?

3 laps. What if he had done something serious, something worth really punishing him for?

2 laps. I couldn't breathe, my brain was scrambling for both oxygen and a new thread of thought.

Final lap. I ran faster than I had ever before. People were cheering, thinking I was going for a personal record. I wasn't. I was desperately trying to outrun the fear that had been creeping up on me.

As I crossed the finished line, I doubled over seeing stars. Ivy lowered the volume of my music, but I didn't notice. There was only one thought going through my mind. What if they *corrected* Derek?

Coach Garison came over to pat me on the back as I fought for air. Her touch was a shock, bringing me sharply back to reality. Several of my teammates were standing around, awestruck expressions on their faces. I straightened, arms on top of my head still fighting for breath.

"Arianna, that was amazing! You must have worked hard this summer."

Even Coach Garison sounded a bit shocked. I glanced around, noticing Christy's sour expression, but she wasn't the only one who seemed irritated by my run. A few other long-distance runners were shaking their head in resignation, shoulders slumped.

"If you run like that at tri-city, you are definitely going to break some records."

Normally a compliment like that would have me glowing, but I was still reeling from the thought of Derek being corrected.

"Thank ... you" I managed between breaths. Coach looked skeptical at my lackluster response wandering away to yell at the rest of the team to get back to work.

"Ivy, what was my time?" I asked breathing slowly coming back to normal, not bothering to type my question.

That was quite a show, Ari.

Ivy's voice was a mixture of pride and irritation. My time must be good for her to take that tone, but she didn't like it when I ran frenzied like that. I tried looking for it in my field of vision, but she had already wiped it.

You PR'd again. You just ran 4 miles in 23 minutes and 46 seconds. Less than a 6-minute mile. That's 73 seconds faster than your last PR a few weeks ago. She hesitated. *What happened?*

If I had the air, I would have burst out laughing. Less than a 6-minute mile? I had pushed all summer and I still hadn't broken that pace. Now we knew. All it took for me to set a personal record was the fear that one of my best friends, and potential boyfriend, would be corrected.

Derek.

My typed response was short, but I knew she would understand. Anxiety is what pushed me to run, and apparently anxiety was what made me faster. Now I would really be in for it. I doubt I could reproduce those times without something major happening again, but Coach Garison would expect that type of performance regularly.

I groaned, setting off at a slow jog around the track to cool down. I cut practice early, knowing coach wouldn't care after my little performance.

I grabbed my bag heading for the auto-rail. My head was still buzzing as I watched the city slide by, so I got off a few stops early to walk. I got off early most days, dreading the silence of home. When mom wasn't working late, she was in her home office, working some more.

It hadn't always been like this. We used to be closer, but dad's disappearance had changed her. She was colder now, so hyper focused on work that it felt like she had forgotten I even existed. The only time she really paid any attention to me was when I messed up, failed a test, got caught pulling a prank with Derek, then she was more than willing to lecture me on how I was ruining my life.

As my house came into view, I thought about going on another run. My thoughts were dark, my brain a hurricane. Clearly practice hadn't helped. My legs were tired, the muscles already tightening from the overexertion earlier, and I doubted Ivy would approve another run. I would probably just end up cramping and hurting myself anyways. There was definitely such a thing as too much running.

Irritated, I slid my palm against the door. No one was home, thank goodness. The house was dark and cool, and my stomach grumbled, protesting my half-eaten lunch. I didn't bother turning on the lights, and Ivy left the dim, sensing my mood. I swirled my fingers gently, getting Ivy's attention.

Ivy, would you add an anxiety med to my dinner. I'm all wound up. I don't think I'll be able to sleep at all tonight.

Ivy looked worried but nodded. She paused, drifting slowly through my field of vision.

I'm proud of you Arianna. You ran well today. And it's alright to be anxious, you went through a lot this morning. Hopefully you will see Derek tomorrow and you can get some answers from him, but I'm happy that you are willing to take your anxiety medication. You don't have to manage all of this on your own. If you want to talk, about anything, I'm here.

I smiled faintly. Ivy tried so hard to fill the gaps. To be my friend, to be a parent when I needed one, a doctor, everything. I would be lost without her.

A tray slid out from a compartment in the wall next to the panty. I took it, not bothering to check what was for dinner. I ate quickly, barely registering the food, swallowing the small white pill when I was done. I had to move fast now; these things worked too well. I would be out cold in less than 30 minutes, and I still needed to shower.

I scrambled with the shampoo, ignoring the half dozen messages from Ash and Sam. I bet they wanted to talk about Derek, or at least Ash would. Sam was probably wondering if I had started my math homework, which I had chosen to ignore. They would all have to wait. I was officially done with today.

I had just changed into my pajamas when the medicine took over, forcing my eyes closed. I didn't fight it. I knew I would spiral out of control with worry over Derek all night if I did, and there was nothing I could do about it right now.

Sleep overtook me, wiping away a collage of images; a corrected zombified Derek, my mother face red, screaming at me with oddly blank eyes, my father patting me on the head after a game of hide and seek in the woods, and then nothing.

Chapter 7

I woke up slightly dazed, trying to blink the sleep from my eyes as Ivy ran through her morning checklists quickly, sounding rushed.

Good you're awake. You're already late this morning. I let you sleep a little longer, but you'll need to hurry now.

"Thanks for the extra sleep. I needed it." I responded sleep scratching my throat as I drag myself out of the covers.

Halfway to my closet a tidal wave of memories from yesterday hit me like a wave. Everything seemed to move in slow motion. I needed to get to school. Now. I rushed to my closet, picking clothes at random.

Snatching them from the tray, I ran into the bathroom, attempting to change and brush my teeth at the same time. Wiping the toothpaste from my hair, a testament to my extreme coordination, I sprinted from the bathroom to the kitchen groaning from the tightness in my legs. Ouch, I had pushed it too hard yesterday.

I appreciate your sudden commitment to being on time, but you don't need to rush that much, Ari. Ivy's amused voice tinkled through my head.

I punch random items into the fridge, swallowing my immunity pills in one go. Grabbing a bran muffin and banana, I sprinted out of the house, not bothering to check the mirror before running out the door.

I made it to the platform with time to spare. A lot of time to spare. I stood anxiously picking off bites of muffin, waiting for the rail to pull up. Ivy bobbed quietly, a skeptical expression on her face. I could count on one hand the number of times I had been early for the auto-rail over the last 4 years.

When the rail finally slid screeching into the station, I was bouncing on my toes. The doors were barely open when I pushed my way through, scanning for Derek, Ashley, or Sam. I didn't see Derek, but my heart dipped only slightly. I hadn't expected him to ride the rail today, anyways.

Ash was craning over her seat waving furiously. I squeezed down the aisle taking the empty seat in front of them, dropping my bag and twisting around to face them both. Sam looked serious, face tight in concentration as he typed away, clearly searching from something on the Feed.

Ashley was harder to read. It looked like she was concerned, but there was an oddly excited vibe coming off her. She looked like she was trying as hard as she could to be serious but couldn't quite suppress all of her energy.

Ari, we need to talk, something weird is going on.

Ivy's voice was stressed, but before I could respond Ash was grabbing my hands, half pulling me over the seat.

"Ari, have you checked the Feed today?" She asked quickly, words tumbling together. Sam's eyes flicked up to meet mine for a moment before returning to his typing.

"No, I overslept and haven't had time to do anything this morning."

I partially lied, kicking myself for not checking the Feed while waiting for the auto-rail. I had spiraled down the rabbit hole of possibilities instead of looking for something real. My heart rate jumped erratically fearing the worst.

"Is there anything about Derek?" I asked Ash and Ivy, knowing she would pick up the question too.

That is what I was trying to tell you. Ivy began again but was cut off by Sam this time. Ivy huffed, irritated by the fact that no one else could hear her talking. She hated being interrupted.

"That's the weird thing. There is nothing on the Feed from yesterday. Nothing." Sam's voice was hushed. He paused waiting as the words sunk in.

"But the video! That should still be in the top school Feeds, it was too dramatic to just disappear." This wasn't what I had expected at all. People rarely messed with the

Feed, and once something was on the Feed it was almost impossible to get rid of it completely.

"I know! Way too many people had recordings out too! It doesn't make any sense." Ashley rushed before Sam could respond, proud of her own assessment of the situation. She looked at me, doe eyes large and concerned. She was worried about how I would react, but it was clear that she was hyped from the drama of it all.

I glanced at Ivy, waiting for her to add in her thoughts, but her avatar was suspended, face blank. She had gone to the Grid to double check that all the video copies were actually gone. Ivy had a knack for finding things that were usually hidden from the Feed.

"I've checked every site I know. The only thing out there right now about Derek are speculations. People are still chatting about what they think will happen to him or what they think he did, but the videos from yesterday have all been wiped." Sam looked up; worry etched across his face. If someone took the time to wipe the Feed of every recording from yesterday, things were a lot worse than I had thought.

Ivy's avatar swirled in a circle indicating that she was back again.

It's true. The copies have been wiped, and professionally. There is no trace of the video, which means whoever did the wiping had upper-level access to the Feed and the Grid.

Her face reflected the same worry Sam's had, the three of us realizing the severity of the problem. Ashley was still focused on the scandal, not realizing what this could mean for Derek. My heart rate climbed, fear flooding icily through my veins, collecting in a block at the center of my chest.

They wouldn't correct a teenager, right? They almost never corrected minors; it was frowned upon. Derek would be fine. He probably got in major trouble, but he would be alright if he just kept his head down and laid low for a while. I would make him lie low.

My thoughts continued to roller coaster from complete and utter fear to being convinced that things would be just fine. Ash looked at me concerned and gave my hands a reassuring squeeze. I knew she wanted to talk, but thankfully she stayed silent for once, focusing on her own field of vision.

My heart clenched. This was supposed to be the year Derek and I became official. Last year things had gotten more serious and during one of the last pranks we pulled, we had kissed for the first time. I remember him looking at me breathlessly as Ivy had manipulated the school's security system using a key-code Derek had swiped, to wipe out the standardized test scores we had taken the day prior. Derek had wanted to protest the unfairness of tracked testing.

"You know they use these scores to manipulate us, to herd us into futures we don't really want, from data they claim proves our aptitude."

Derek was seriously attractive when he waxed poetically, and I had stared mutely at him unable to form a response. He had looked at me something shifting in his eyes, a darkening which had sent shivers down my spine causing my stomach to flutter.

He had grabbed my chin gently, stepping towards me in a dark office at the back of the school. He tilted my head ever so slightly and leaned in to kiss me. Our lips had touched for half a second when the lights had flickered in warning. The security system would be up again soon, and we had to get out of there.

That prank had caused one of the biggest fights Ivy and I had ever had. Another weird effect of having an AI different from anyone else's, no one I knew had ever had a fight with their AI. Ivy's anger had been astronomical, hating that I essentially tricked her into sabotaging the school's records, the most criminal offense I had ever asked her to do.

On the other hand, I knew she had flared the lights early, ending what should have been the most perfect first kiss ever. We didn't speak for two whole days. Those were the loneliest days I had experience in a long time but eventually we forgave each other, promising to be honest with each other, if I swore no more criminal activities.

I glanced at Ivy, hoping she would be willing to help me now.

Ivy, can you ping Derek's signal?

I already did, he appears to be heading to the school. He is traveling on a different auto-rail though.

A wave of relief washed away most of my anxiety. He would be at school today. Whatever he had done, whatever trouble he had gotten into, he would still be at school. We could talk, he could tell me what the glitch he had been thinking and then we could move on and enjoy our senior year together.

Can you message him, send him a funny face or something?

A small pool of anxiety sat deep in my stomach. I wasn't nearly as stressed out, but I couldn't shake the feeling that this wasn't over.

Done.

I waited impatiently for a response. Nothing. Before I could even ask, Ivy confirmed that the message was successfully delivered. Minutes ticked by, still nothing. I stared out the window of the auto-rail as the city drifted past. Anxiety filled visions of Derek danced in my mind, all the way back to the first night we hung out. I groaned, pressing my head against the cool glass, thinking back to that awkward summer night.

Chapter 8

The first time Derek and I hung out was fairly embarrassing to think about. It was a long time ago, but the entire event had been one big crush-fueled nightmare. I had always known about Derek, had seen him over the years growing from an obnoxious child into a slightly less obnoxious, but far more attractive teen. Derek always seemed to chase trouble. He actively pursued situations in which he could rile as many people up as possible. While I stuck within my perfect goody-goody bubble, I had to admit, trouble looked good on Derek.

By middle school, I had convinced myself I was in love. It didn't matter that by then Derek had built a reputation of being a school nuisance, or that he would probably be threatened with a correction at least once by high school graduation. No, none of that mattered to me. I was convinced that if Derek and I were together, I could bring him back down to some semblance of decency; I could level him out.

The only problem was that Derek did not seem to know I existed. He was nice enough, and I swore he had even winked at me before performing some ridiculous dance atop the teacher's desk in 6th grade. (When Ivy had offered to show me, the playback recording of the whole thing, I had refused, not wanting to know the truth.)

By 8th grade, I was desperate to get his attention somehow. Ashley and Sam knew I was crushing, and Ash immediately became my compatriot in the 'attract Derek' scheme. Sam had blushed crimson and then made a show of rolling his eyes, dramatically playing his video games whenever the subject came up from that point on.

A week before we 8th grade started; I came up with a plan. We were going to have a midnight picnic at the park close to their house. Ash had laughed when I told her about it sitting cross-legged in my bed, but Sam, sitting in a chair at my desk, had been so shocked he had paused his game, turning to face us.

"What about the curfew?" he asked incredulously.

"Are you kidding?" I joked back at him, mildly irritated that they had not swooned over my intensely romantic idea.

"Curfew isn't even a thing. It's more like a suggestion. Kids break curfew all the time. Nothing happens. It doesn't even trigger an alert from your AI unless you go too far from home. We are only going to the park." My confidence grew with every reassurance. I smiled triumphantly at them both, but Sam gave me a smug gotcha look before responding.

"Oh yeah, ok well what about the security systems? You know your mom won't let you out of the house that late, and the second you reach for that door handle every alarm system is going to go off." He flicked back to his game, fingers flying across an invisible keypad as if that ended the discussion.

I remember looking at Ivy bobbing gently in the right corner of my vision, but she was already shaking her head like she knew where I was going with this plan. She always seemed to know where my thoughts were headed.

"Don't worry about the security systems. I can handle them." I said the words tentatively. For years I had kept Ivy's abilities to myself as much as possible. I hid them from everyone, even from Ash and Sam, but Derek was a risk I was willing to take. I would just have to come up with a good enough cover.

Ash and Sam turned to look at me, both with eyes slightly wide. They knew something was different about Ivy and I's connection, about Ivy herself, but they had decided long ago to leave it alone, I didn't want to tell them, and they didn't want to know, and we were all perfectly fine with leaving it at that.

Arianna, what are you doing? You know I can't just 'take care' of all those security systems! Ours is fine, I know the systems in the house, but I don't know theirs. You are going to give away too much, Ari. Is this boy worth it?

Ivy was working herself up, growing larger until she blocked the right half of my field of vision. I worked my hands slowly, trying not to draw any attention to myself as Ash and Sam continued staring blankly at me.

Ivy, please. I know you can do it. Please please please, just this one thing, and I promise I will listen to you all the time. Whatever you say! I'll even try those stupid breathing exercises you always want me to do.

Ivy shook her head but shrank slowly back to her normal size. She folded her delicate arms in protest but did not comment again. I took this as a yes and pressed on before I lost Sam's quickly fading attention.

"Trust me, alright? I got this." I kept my voice steady, even as excitement threatened to spike my pulse.

"Sam, you know Derek. Can you invite him?" I could see Ivy rolling her eyes, almost exactly in sync with Sam, who knew this request had been coming. Sam was friendly with Derek, in a "people who had played sports together as littles," kind of way, but they were not close anymore.

"Ari, you know we aren't friends like that. It's going to be weird." Sam groaned in distress. For the second time that night, I threw out my most pleading voice, smiling as brightly as I could.

"Sammy, please. You know I can't do it. That would be way too obvious. This won't work unless you ask him. Say you don't want to be the only guy or something. Come on." Sam grumbled something about it still being obvious under his breath and turned back to his invisible screen.

At first, I thought he had returned to his video game, his fingers hovering mid-air, but then he turned to me and asked, "So when exactly are we doing this picnic?" and I knew I had won.

"Wednesday!" I squeaked, bouncing on the balls of my toes.

Sam returned to his typing, and with a swipe of his hands, looked back at me.

"Done. You owe me for sending the most awkward message I have ever sent. 'Hey Derek... Ari really likes you and doesn't have the guts to say it so will you please come with us on a midnight picnic... oh and don't worry about getting out of your house's security systems. Ari says she will take care of them. K see you.'" Sam mimed typing and sending a message, using a high mocking voice.

"You did not say that!" Ash's voice hitting an impressively high octave in protest.

Her face was already turning a shade redder than normal, embarrassed for me, but I knew Sam was joking. He had more tact than that, despite his grumpy attitude. Ash turned to me with a desperate look.

"Ash, he's joking." I grabbed her hands, shooting Sam an exasperated look. He shrugged and went back to playing his game.

I sat on the bed next to her, the soft plush comforter warming my bare legs. I grabbed a pillow and hugged it to my chest, slowly coming down from the excitement of finally having a plan in motion. Now I just had to figure out the rest.

An hour later I poked Ash to get her attention away from her field of vision saying, "Ok, this is actually happening now. What should I wear?" I looked at Ash with her typical perfect makeup, cheeks contoured, and eyes lined, not a hair out of place in her tight bun. She had on dainty jean shorts with lace trim and a pink camisole top. She looked stunning, and she wasn't even in high school yet. I shook the envy from my head and tried not to dwell on my non-existent curves and faded t-shirt.

Ash lit up with my question. She had been begging me to let her do a make-over all summer. I had politely declined. Wasting time playing with shadows and pallets of eye color didn't sound fun to me.

Ash sprang off the bed with uncontained excitement and went straight for my closet. She opened the door to the massive walk-in space, not bothering to contain her sigh of envy. Not that the closet was even remotely full of clothing. Barely half the space was occupied with my collection of faded anime shirts, jeans of various colors, and maybe a formal dress or two for when mother paraded me around her high-rise colleagues. Still, this closet was the stuff of dreams for Ash; Ash and Sam's house was on the smaller side, in a different district of town than my obscenely large and stupidly luxurious house.

We only had this house because the tech company my mom worked for paid for it. She had risen high enough through the ranks after my father left, that we had left the neighborhood where I grew up, just a few houses down from Ash and Sam, and moved closer to the city center with all its obnoxiously bright lights.

An unimpressed grunt quickly replaced Ash's sigh of envy. "Come on Ari, you are killing me. Please, just let me take you shopping. You know your mom will let you use her credits, and you are desperately in need of a wardrobe change." I shook my head resolutely, there was no way.

"Fine. I'm sure you have something decent in here." Ash said, mostly joking, as she made her way towards the back of the closet. A half hour later, Ash had assembled a decent outfit, somehow finding a pretty light blue shirt mixed in with the tees and a non-ripped pair of shorts.

At 9pm, Ash and Sam left for the auto-rail station. They did not want to draw any attention to themselves by breaking curfew, especially before really breaking curfew the next week. Ash had promised to ping me every day. Thankfully, it was Saturday and I only had to wait a few more days before the big event. Sam had begrudgingly promised to screenshot any replies from Derek and send them to me as soon as he got them.

My mom hadn't been home when they left, but that wasn't unusual. I guess she figured an all-knowing Artificial Intelligence chip attached to your brain was a good enough substitute for a parent. Maybe she was right. Things were a lot better at the house when it was just me and Ivy.

Chapter 9

By 8pm Wednesday evening, we had everything ready to go, and I was pacing my room in small tight lines back and forth. I had started the breathing techniques 15 minutes ago just to keep Ivy happy; she had done a lot for me today.

Ivy had successfully worked her way into Ash and Sam's home security system. Turns out, it was much easier than she let on, considering how complex our own system was compared to theirs. 'Child's play' she had declared proudly. She wouldn't be able to connect to Derek's until we actually got to his house though, since we had never been there before.

Ivy also manipulated the house's food storage system to force it to produce snacks, or what would pass as snacks. It only spat out a few apples and a bag of health crisps, something supposed to resemble chips, but instead tasted like a sad vegetable-based version of cardboard.

Apparently, the house was running low on food. It normally wouldn't be a problem. Food was delivered automatically and would be restocked later tonight, but that didn't help me now. Ash and Sam couldn't get more food out of theirs at all, so the apples and veggie-cardboard crisps would have to do. Maybe no one would remember the picnic part?

Normally I wouldn't have been so nervous, even with the security breaking and curfew skipping parts, but Sam had messaged that there had been no response from Derek yet. I was resigned to follow through with the plan, but I was losing hope Derek would join us.

At 10:45pm, two things happened simultaneously. First, my mother walked through the door, the house chirping "Welcome home Ms. Salvante" and second, Sam messaged, saying he finally got a response from Derek. I desperately wanted to look at the message, but I had to deal with my mother first. If she came in here and saw what I was wearing and that I had attempted to put makeup on, she would die from shock, and she would know something was going on.

Ivy was on it, and before I could move, she had the lights in my room dimmed. I tiptoed over to the door and shut it as gently as possible, then sprinted to my bed and pulled the covers over. Ivy turned the lights off completely and played the LoFi playlist I listened to while sleeping through my wall speakers.

A few minutes later, I heard the door open and tried to keep my breathing as even as possible. I heard a brief sigh of relief, as if she was thankful I was asleep, so she didn't have to deal with me.

If she bothered to glance around at all she would have seen my fully packed backpack on the floor, clothes strewn around the room, and my computer was still up and running, none of which would have been out if I had truly gone to bed. Cleaning my room before bed was my nightly ritual. Having everything in its rightful place made it easier for me to sleep, but I doubt she would know that.

Less than a second later she closed the door, not bothering to be nearly as gentle as I had been. Ivy's avatar bobbed silently the second she dimmed the lights, as she monitored my mother's moves through the house's security cameras, just in case. When the door closed, she reappeared, her mouth a thin line.

The coast is clear. She is heading straight for her room. I thought you said she wasn't coming home tonight. Things will get more complicated if she wakes up while you are out.

Ivy's face slipped from a line into a frown as she recalculated the risk of tonight's escapade. I swirled my hand to type a response, not wanting to risk speaking out loud in case my mother walked back down the hall.

It's fine. I honestly didn't think she would come home. She never comes home on Wednesdays, but it's too late to back out now. Ivy rolled her eyes at this, clearly disagreeing, but I typed on. *We are doing this alright, plus you know she'll never check on me again. She already did her motherly duty of checking on me once.*

Luckily, the bitterness in my words didn't show as much in writing, but Ivy still got the drift. Her hard look softened ever so slightly.

I checked the clock, 11:00pm. It was now or never. I needed enough time to make it to walk past the auto-rail station to catch an automated cab. The trip would take almost twice as long, and we needed time to get to Derek's. Derek! I had completely forgotten the message Sam sent. Scrolling back, Sam had sent a screenshot of Derek's reply.

Never pegged you as a rule breaker... feeling glitchy, Sammy? Fine... I'm in.

My heart kicked in double time, and I held my breath, hoping Ivy wouldn't notice. I couldn't help but catch the use of Sam's nickname, Sammy. Only Ash and I used that nickname. It didn't matter though; we were going to be late.

Ivy bounced back into view, looking somewhat breathless, which is odd for an AI, considering they don't breathe.

Ok, go now Arianna. She's already in bed. She must have had a rough day. I've already got the cams looping an image of the last few minutes, but it'll only run for 3 minutes, so get a move on.

I shoved a pillow under my blanket to make it at least look like a human shape was there, grabbed the backpack, and cracked the door. Ivy was right. The lights were already off down the hall, so I snuck into the hallway and slowly shut the door.

2 minutes and 30 seconds.

I glared at Ivy's image in the corner of my eye where she had thrown up a small timer ticking alarmingly fast. Why had she made the loop so short? I'd have to ask later.

I tiptoed as quickly as I could down the hallway to the front door. My hand reached for the door, but I hesitated an inch above the handle. The timer ticked down.

Arianna, it's fine. I disarmed the entire house, hurry. Don't you trust me?

She looked up at me, or whatever she saw from her digital vantage point in my brain, questioningly. I grabbed the handle firmly and pulled the door open. Of course, I trusted Ivy, I trusted her with my life.

We made it across town in record time, getting to Ash and Sam's house right at 11:40pm. That would give us about 10 minutes to get to Derek's place, but Sam had assured me it was only a few blocks away from their house.

Ok Ari, message them. Tell them the same thing I told you. They have 3 minutes to get out of the house before they trigger the alarms. They don't have any interior cameras though; it should be easy for them.

I typed the message and sent a copy to both Ash and Sam, just in case. Ash sent me a googly eyed smiley face while Sam only sent a thumbs up. Now we waited. I sat on the curb in front of their house, trying to keep my breathing controlled.

A few seconds later, we heard footsteps on the path. I looked up, heaving a sigh of relief as a tense Sam and Ash ran down the path from their house. Both were breathing hard, as if they had run a race, rather than snuck silently out of their house.

"Our dad got up to get a drink," Sam said flatly as a way of explaining their disheveled state. "We barely missed him coming up the hall."

Ash let out a high-pitched giggle which had a painfully screeching quality to it, like when an auto-rail hit the brakes too hard coming onto a platform.

I looked back and forth between them and checked the clock. 11:45pm—we needed to move to make the midnight meeting time.

"You guys alright? Ready to go?" I tried to be as gentle as possible while trying to get them moving. Sam looked to Ash, who took a deep breath and then nodded. "Alright Sam, lead the way."

Sam did not look ready to lead the way at all, but he turned and started walking down the dimly lit street, anyway. There were streetlights every so often, which created blinding white spots we avoided, favoring the pitch dark in between.

I looked around in shock. We had walked maybe ten blocks, but the change was dramatic. The houses had gone from small, but clean and tidy looking, to run down and almost sad. We stood in front of a home that could not have had more than a single bedroom. The paint on the front door was long faded, and there was no yard; just a collection of weeds randomly dispersed among the bed of rock. I felt an instant wave of guilt knowing people lived in these conditions when I lived in a giant house in the city center. I would have bet that we had more unused rooms in our house than were in this entire house, and I was certain Derek had siblings.

I swallowed past the hardness in my throat, swirling my fingers to message Ivy, when a soft cough froze me to my core. Ash squeaked and immediately covered her mouth, looking terrified, and Sam let out a surprisingly detailed stream of curses under his breath.

"Derek, you scared the glitch out of us," Sam whispered, stepping towards the chain-link fence surrounding the house. Derek chuckled softly and pushed off the fence, grabbing Sam's outstretched hand and pulling him into one of those weird bro hugs where they slap each other's backs aggressively, Sam's cheeks flushing under the light of the streetlamp.

Derek was already taller than Sam, his skin tanned from the summer sun. His dark brown hair matched mischievous eyes that seemed to reflect the light. Wearing a faded black t-shirt and dark black jeans he blended in with the night.

"Hey man," Derek's voice had gotten deeper over the summer, sending a chill up my spine.

"Hey Ash, did I scare you?" There was a hint of mockery in his voice which made it difficult to decide whether he was playfully teasing or just being a jerk. Ash blushed crimson and coughed once, trying to cover her embarrassment. Then Derek turned to look at me. His gaze drifted up and down, like he was just now seeing me for the first time.

"Sam said you put this party together. I never pictured the perfect angel Arianna breaking so many rules." His voice was skeptical, questioning.

I opened my mouth to speak, but my mouth went dry. It seemed like all the moisture which should have been in my mouth, had been sucked down to my sweating palms. I swallowed hard and tried again.

"How - how did you get out of your house? I mean, how did you get past your security system?" The question was out before I could think. I had no idea why I asked that of all things.

He let out a chuckle. "I should ask you the same thing. I bet a fancy place like yours has one heck of a system." His eyes glistened, hinting at a guess that was probably not too far off the mark.

Ivy cursed, something I wasn't even aware she could do. Her favorite costume wings were beating quickly, eyes dark, pulling everything she could find off the Grid while assessing the situation.

Thankfully Derek continued, "Luckily for me, this house is barely even connected to the Grid, and the alarm system, if you could even call it that, hasn't worked properly in years. I doubt I could get it to trigger an alarm if I tried."

My head spun, realizing he had played us. He didn't even need us to come break him out; he had just wanted to see if we could do it, and I fell right into his trap. Derek walked casually toward me, past a stunned Sam and a slack-jawed Ashley. He brushed past me, not quite touching but close enough that the force of our bodies repelled slightly against each other, creating an illusion of touching. I stood frozen. Ivy looked pissed, and once he had passed, he cocked his head slightly, speaking in that low voice of his.

"Well, are we going to just stand here or are we going to have ourselves a midnight picnic?" In that same joking but not joking tone.

Sam jogged to catch up with him, and Ash grabbed my hand, spinning me around and pulling me along with her since I had yet to move. She was determined to not let him get the upper hand.

We trekked slowly back to the park near Ash and Sam's house, dodging the pools of light, or at least the three of us dodged the light. Derek drifted from lamp to lamp, like a moth in search of a resting place. He would pause, tipping his face up to the light, mouth open as if he could suck the brightness down into his soul.

He spun around in one and caught me staring at him. He smiled showing a hint of a dimple and spun around again. His weird mannerisms only made him more attractive to me. He was so different than everyone else.

Eventually, we made it to the park and Ash pulled Sam away towards the swings. We had already discussed it. Ash would take Sam away so that Derek and I could be together; alone. I tried to shoot a look at Ash that said ABORT, but she smiled slyly and dragged a disgruntled Sam away.

Derek ambled in the opposite direction towards a small plastic playground with the metal slide. This thing looked like it could have come straight out of our history movies. I stood still for a moment, unsure what to do.

Arianna, don't you dare back out now. This is exactly what you planned this entire night for. Woman up and get over there!

My mouth opened in shock at Ivy's words. Ivy's avatar bobbed slowly, face going blank as Ivy left to survey the surrounding Grid. Now I truly alone, or as alone as I would ever get. I steeled myself and stepped forward to follow Derek to the playground. He had made his way up the monkey bars and was standing atop the second level by the slide. I stopped at the bottom of the slide, staring up at him.

"Rapunzel, Rapunzel let down your long hair." I called in a chirpy fake-deep voice, praying he got the reference. Things were going to get very awkward if he didn't play along.

Derek smiled a ghost of a smile and called back in a breathy, high-pitched feminine voice, "Why, prince charming, I seem to have misplaced my hair. You'll have to find another way up."

I stared at the monkey bars; finger strength had never been my strong suit, and instead moved to the bottom of the slide. Since this was a smaller kid's playground, the slide was only about seven feet off the ground, so with me standing at the bottom and him at the top, we were maybe 10 ft apart. Plenty close enough, I congratulated myself. Certainly, closer than we had ever been before.

Derek cocked his head to the side again, realizing I was not coming up to him. Before I could blink, he had pushed himself down the slide and, apparently misjudging how close I was to the bottom, slid straight into me.

I let out a loud "oof" as his legs hit my shins and the rest of him came straight after knocking me on my back and the wind out of me. I gasped for a second, sucking air in as Ivy avatar swirled into view between the stars in my eyes, looking at me worriedly.

"I'm fine, you can go away." Ivy took off again with an irritated huff as I rolled off my bag and put it beside me.

"Do you really want me to go away?" Derek had landed beside me, limbs sprawled around. His voice held an uncertainty I had yet to hear, lacking his normal confidence. I hadn't realized I had said it out loud.

"Sorry, I was talking to Ivy. I mean my AI. She felt me fall and was checking in, I mean checking up on me to make sure I didn't get hurt..." I let myself trail off from the rambling path I had been on. I had learned over the years that most people didn't have as attentive AIs as I did. Derek raised an eyebrow at me.

"So, Arianna, how did you get out of that top-notch house of yours? I know your mom works for Tech, so there is no way your house isn't buttoned up from top to bottom. Did you have a glitch?" The abrupt change in conversation left me speechless. There was no way I could tell Derek about Ivy or what she could do. Where was he even going with this?

"A magician never reveals her secrets."

I had meant for this to come out confident and smooth, but it came out glitchy, sounding a bit like a kid lying to their parents. I let out a resigned sigh, a bit on the loud side, and cringed. This was not going well.

Derek propped himself up on an elbow and looked over at me. I was immediately grateful for the cover of night, hoping it kept most of my flaming red face hidden.

"You know, I think there is more to you than you let on. You're different. Why else would you risk breaking curfew just to go to the park?" His voice was distant, as if he had started talking to me and then faded out into himself, like he forgot he was speaking out loud. He chuckled to himself and lay back on his back.

"Fine Ari, you can keep your secrets for now."

My heart threatened to burst with his praise, or with what I thought was praise, and when he used my nickname, I almost swooned. Which, I immediately realized was one of the stupidest things I had ever thought in my life. We were silent for a time, but it was a comfortable silence, one which was completely unexpected.

"Do you know any of the constellations?" Derek asked suddenly. I turned my head towards him, again surprised by the abrupt change in conversation. I shook my head, and then realized he couldn't see me in the dark, so I said, "No, not really, do you?"

"No, not a single one." He stated it so blandly that I had to laugh. What a strange person. We settled into somewhat of a rhythm. Brief spans of silence, and then as if he couldn't take it anymore, a random outburst from Derek, whether it be a question, comment, or just a random fact. He could never take the silence for longer than a few minutes.

Eventually, we heard approaching footsteps, and I swore I heard an irritated sigh from Derek as I sat up. Ash and Sam seemed to be arguing about something, but they fell silent as they got closer, trying to find us in the dark. Ash spotted us first with a hopeful questioning expression on her face.

"So, what happened here?" She asked lightly, teasing. She raised her eyebrows at us both sprawled on the ground side by side.

"Rapunzel wiped out the prince." Derek responded matter-of-factly leaving both Sam and Ash looking confused as I chuckled. Ivy popped back into view; our alone time was up.

Arianna, you need to get home. It's getting late and we have already pushed this too far. Say your goodbyes.

I hated when she used her mom's voice on me, but I knew she was right. It was well past one in the morning, and we had already gotten extremely lucky. I struggled to my feet; my limbs stiff from laying on the cold earth for so long. I reached for my bag, laughing again.

"What's so funny, prince charming?" Derek asked, stretching as he stood. I held the bag out to the three of them.

"The picnic... well, I couldn't get much food, but if anyone wants a bruised apple, I've got two of them, and a crushed bag of veggie cardboard."

Ash and Sam had both looked excited about the prospect of food, but when they heard the options, they shook their heads no, faces crestfallen. Derek held out his hand for what I guessed was an apple. I dug my hand into the bag, feeling for a mushed apple, then handed him one. He took the apple, not seeming to mind the mushiness, taking a big bite.

"Thanks for the apple, charming. It better not be poisoned." He winked and turned on his heel heading into the darkness.

"Um, bye," Ash called after him, irritated by being left out of the joke. Derek raised his apple in response, not bothering to turn his head, and disappeared into the night.

"What the hell was that about, prince charming?"

Ash turned on me since she had not gotten a response from Derek. I smiled and gave them both a brief rundown of the evening as we headed back towards their place. Ash seemed thrilled by the end, but Sam didn't look convinced. I left them at their walk, waiting for Ash to messaged me a thumbs up, then took off towards home, once again hailing an automated cab. Ivy was silent on the ride home, and so was I, each lost in our own thoughts.

Ivy came out of her silence to start the three-minute timer when we arrived home, but I didn't need it this time. I was inside the house, stripped and in bed in under two minutes, both mentally and physically exhausted from the evening.

Arianna? Ivy asked tentatively as my eyes drifted closed.

"Hmm," I mumbled back at her.

Sweet dreams, was all she replied. I had tried to ask what was wrong, but the only thing I remember was waking up the next morning to Ivy, once again complaining that I had overslept my alarms.

Chapter 10

The lurching of the auto-rail as it halted at the next stop pulled me back to the present.

Ashley's voice cut the air, a forced whisper containing thinly veiled hysteria.

"Listen to this. Jessica just pinged me that Derek got flagged yesterday for aggressive thoughts or actions. She said that she heard the administrators were only going to update his normal AI, but his chip caught him thinking violent thoughts and flagged him as dangerous to others. She said now they had no choice, that they had to correct him."

Ash clutched my hands, squeezing the life out of them, eyes wide in shock. She fully believed Jessica's story and was waiting for me to have a massive panic attack. I would have had Sam not burst out in a condescending laugh.

"Ash, you are a complete glitch. You know as well as anyone that the chips can't read your mind. Your AI can't read your thoughts unless you say every single one of them out loud, like you seem to always do. We have taken so many classes on this, don't be stupid. Jessica is just a gossip. She's an airhead. I bet her AI has to remind her how to breathe and walk at the same time." Sam dismissed her, looking casual, but I could see the tension in his eyes.

This thing with Derek had really gotten to him. Usually, he wasn't that aggressive towards Ashley.

She huffed back into her seat looking offended, but it took all of two seconds for her to refocus on some other piece of gossip she found on the Feed, trying to distract me as much as possible. I put myself on autopilot, nodding and laughing when she expected it, as I lost myself in the thought of Derek and the correctional AIs. Whenever someone dared to bring it up in school, our teachers always said that you could come out of a correction and go back to a normal AI if you behaved, but I have never seen someone come back from one before.

For the most part, the only people who ever got corrected were so strange already that nobody really knew them or noticed much of a change.

People generally spoke about the whole correction process as more of a myth or a scary bedtime story used to keep kids in line. I distinctly remember my mother yelling at me, after finding out I had failed a coding test, that she would send me off to be corrected if I didn't get my act together. Ivy had been more pissed off by that remark than anything I had ever seen before. She left for a bit. She never told me where she went. In fact, she never tells me where she disappears to when her avatar isn't on my screen. I've always assumed she went on the Grid.

Derek wasn't like the others who had been corrected. They were all on the fringe. He was smart and funny, and so good looking. I looked up at Ashley and Sam, wondering if either of them was as concerned as I was, but they weren't looking at me. They were both still lost in their bickering back and forth.

I couldn't picture Derek as one of those corrected zombies. Nobody knew why, but something about the correctional AI made the person who was corrected seem almost out of focus. You could barely get two words out of them, let alone a full conversation. They just sit there staring into space. It was always kind of creepy.

I needed to see Derek, to speak to him myself. Hopefully, this whole thing was just a nasty rumor that he would laugh off when we get to homeroom. You never know, Derek may have even started the whole thing himself as some sort of prank. Either way, it was my mission to get some answers as soon as we got to school.

I checked my field of vision to see if Ivy had found anything about Derek, but her avatar was bobbing idly, face blank, leaving me to stare aimlessly out the window instead.

The auto-rail slowed as it made its way through the city, stopping at several of the tall steel high-rise buildings. You could barely make out the large conference rooms and offices through the massive holographic advertisements. Some of them were twenty stories high, advertising the latest software upgrades for your AI or some new tech-gadget for your home, designed to make your life that much easier.

The current advertisement was for a new brand of vita-cure gummies. Apparently, daily vitamins and an AI monitoring your health 24/7 wasn't enough for some people. Instead, people were willing to fork over bundles of credits for any supposed cure-alls. I shook my head, slightly disgusted by the way the advertisements constantly flashed and changed across the building's windows. I wondered what city skylines used to look like before they became an extension of your screen.

Ivy's avatar swirled slowly as Ivy returned, a frown etched across her face.

I don't like this. They rarely wipe the Feed for petty things like a minor correction. There are firewalls all over the Feed right now, and I can't trace their source without some serious effort. I don't want to leave you for that long. I want to investigate this, but it will have to wait until tonight.

You're such a mom. I'm fine. I want to know what is going on. You should check it out.

Ivy paused and thought for a moment. This was another one of her abilities. Normal AIs were stuck with their humans all the time. I had found this out by accidentally mentioning Ivy's absence to my mom once in 6th grade. She spit out her coffee and grabbed me so hard by the arms I immediately took it back. I'd never seen her so tense before. But Ivy can come and go as she pleases. She doesn't enjoy being gone for long, and she never really tells me where she goes, but I know she uses the Grid to find things, kind of like a car driving down a street. Ivy shook her head no. She didn't want to risk being gone when we got to school.

We paused at an executive station for a moment as some techs stepped off the rails, dressed in their expensive suits. They rushed from the auto-rail towards the high-rise buildings as if they were already late for the most important meeting of their lives. Their endlessly stoic expressions made their life seem monotonous. Most of the kids in my school wanted those jobs for the money and the prestige, but I didn't know, it didn't look like much of a life to me.

I watched them turn into ants as the rail sped away towards our school. Anxiety built in my chest like a balloon slowly filling with air, taking up all the space between my ribs, expanding more and more until I was sure it would burst.

The little pink heart indicator flashed a warning, and I immediately started my breathing exercises. The auto-rail slowed again, and Ivy expanded slightly with a knowing expression, as if she was saying, see, this is why I didn't want to leave you. I tried to smile back at her reassuringly. Everything would be fine once I saw Derek and made sure that he was okay.

The auto-rail squealed as it came to a stop in front of the school station and we pushed our way out of the compartment, Ashley still ranting about something trivial, me still pretending to listen. We made our way through the throng of students milling around the front of the school, and I casually let my gaze wander from person to person, looking for Derek. Nothing. No broad tanned shoulders, no wisps of dark hair always sticking out in that causally messy but incredibly hot way of his. He was nowhere to be found. The bell chimed as the last auto-rail rolled in, signaling the start of the day.

Ash squeezed me to her, as if we would never see each other again, and ran towards her building. She may act like an airhead sometimes, but Ashley was incredibly talented when it came to selling anything. Literally anything. She would graduate and eventually go work at the top of one of those shiny advertisement buildings, riding the same auto-rail, but sitting in those sleek, modern compartments. I wondered what she would look like in a suit. Probably fantastic.

Arianna, you need to get moving.

I looked around, realizing how few kids remained in front. Several bored looking kids dragged their feet towards the right wing of the school. They headed to the vocational side of the building, though technically it wasn't called that. Everyone knew that if you failed your exams, they sent you there to learn the ins and outs of factory production. If you were lucky, you would end up as a line manager or a foreman. If you weren't, you ended up stamping out tiny metal parts for the latest tech gadget.

The middle building, my building, along with Sam and Derek, was made for students that could swing in-between. Students who had just enough potential to eke out a life doing a job considered mildly important by society, but not enough to run a tech company or make a real difference.

Some people became teachers, barbers, enforcers, and secretaries for the tech companies. They were all supposedly "important" jobs, but they had little pay and even less prestige. A history teacher a few years back had said this used to be called the middle class, and to me, it just felt like another dreary future. I didn't like any of the options set in front of me, but this was my senior year and I needed to pick a path soon, and hopefully keep Derek from falling completely off his.

Sam made his way over to meet me. He had scored one point below the pre-executive level and Ash never let him live it down. He would still become an executive, just like her one day. But for now, he was the one tutoring me through these courses to test the highest I could for the exams at the end of the year. Those would determine our jobs for the rest of our lives. No pressure.

Sam looped an arm through mine, a silent reassurance that whatever we faced in homeroom today, we would face it together. My heart thrummed an off-kilter tune as we walked towards the class. I paused at the door, too nervous to go inside. Ivy had indicated that Derek's AI signature was already in the room, but how he would behave was a complete mystery. We entered the room and Sam nudged me, a slight intake of air my only warning. A lone figure sat in the last row at the back of the room.

It was Derek. He sat with his arms folded across his desk, staring towards the front of the room, the dull blank expression on his face telling us everything we needed to know. Whispers and the sounds of fingers tapping on empty desks filled the room, word already spreading across the school of the worst possible scenario. Jessica's gossiping nonsense had somehow been true.

Derek had been corrected.

Chapter 11

My grip on Sam's arm tightened, icy fear coursing through my veins. I had no idea what to do, what to say. Several people stopped to glance back and forth between Derek and I, knowing our history. I hoped they weren't recording my reaction right now. Sam sensed my fear, my inability to do anything and patted my hand reassuringly, clearing his throat.

"Hey Derek," Sam half-yelled across the room. He feigned confidence, something he didn't exude on a good day, and I could hear the hesitation in his voice.

Derek glanced in our direction, like he had heard him, but didn't quite comprehend that Sam was talking to him. His eyes to slipped past us like we were ghosts. I felt a chill go up my arms. Sam glanced at me, fear shining through his eyes. Neither of us had every interacted with someone who was corrected. We had only heard stories, a friend of a friend's overinflated recollection. Was there a possibility that Derek there, but stuck inside his own head?

Ivy, pull up my messenger. Send a new message to Derek please.

He hadn't responded to my earlier messages, but maybe since he was back in class, he would be able to now. It would be weird if someone who was corrected could never respond to any messages. How would they communicate?

Ivy frowned but pulled up the messenger screen. I could see Derek's cheesy profile picture in the corner as I moved my fingers through the air over my holo-keys.

Ari: Hey Derek. How is your morning?

I started off easy. A nondescript question that even someone corrected should be able to answer. I hoped he would respond, would give me a sign, anything to indicate that he was still in there. A soft ping in my ear altered me to a new message.

Derek: My morning was fine, thank you.

It was worse than we thought. There was no way Derek had written this message. How was this even possible? Derek should still have full control of himself, even while corrected. Right? Nausea prickled in my stomach, sending shivers up my spine.

This called for more drastic measures.

Arianna, whatever you are thinking about doing, stop it right now. You are going to make it worse for him and yourself. Ivy was back to the motherly tone she knew I hated, and I knew she was right, but this was Derek. I had to do something.

I opened Sam's contact; I needed his help.

Ari: We have to do something, Sam. This isn't right.

Sam flinched as he read my message. His figures shook as he responded, eyes flicking up to where Derek sat, alone. It was pretty easy to have a mostly private conversation through the AI messaging system. The key was to keep your face as neutral as possible and your hand movements slow and subtle. Most people had this mastered by elementary school.

Sam: I know. Don't freak Ari, but what if he really did something bad? What if they corrected him to keep other people safe? There was a tinge of bitterness in the message, but Sam kept his face turned away, not daring to look at me. I shot a message back.

Ari: Oh, shut up, he could really be gone. They might keep him corrected for good or take him away from us!

Sam: You mean from you? He is a rule breaker, he will find a way out of this.

Sam walked towards a desk to the right side of the room and sat down shoulders slumping. Not wanting to draw any more attention to myself, I followed him, turning slightly to keep a clear visual on Derek in the back. Sam sighed, resigned, and sent a message back, face pained.

Sam: So, what's your plan?

Ivy paused mid screen, as if she too wanted to know the plan. I thought for a moment, honestly not knowing what would bring Derek out of his trance. I had one potential idea, and Ivy would not like it. I started typing slowly.

Ari: We've got pull a prank. Something small so we don't get majorly busted, but enough to get him to laugh. If he laughs, we'll know he is still in there somewhere.

Sam: Really, your big plan is to get him to laugh?

Ari: When have you ever heard of a corrected person laughing? Or showing any emotion at all?

I was certain Derek laughing would prove he was still there, that he was alright. And, if he was still in there, he would be able to come back to us.

To me.

Sam: Are you sure about this? We have perfect records this year, and you want to mess that up day 2?

Sam was blatantly looking my way now, mouth set in a firm line. His jaw was square, and I noticed how grown-up he looked. He had come into his own over the summer, despite his introverted ways. Sam was fully aware of the risk he would take if he helped me with this. I smiled faintly in his direction.

Ari: You know they wouldn't stay clean for long. Yes, I'm sure. He would do it for us, Sammy.

I watched as Ivy read my message to Sam, shaking her head in disbelief.

Sam: Alright, so what's the prank?

Sam looked resolute now, firm and decided. I wondered what his AI thought of all this, or if it even though anything at all. We would need to be careful not to trigger it, we needed something good, something funny but harmless. I diverted my message directly to Ivy this time.

Ivy, my dearest, smartest, bestest friend, can you please check the Feed for me? Can you find anything embarrassing about Mr. Davidson?

Ivy swelled in my field of vision, not buying my flattery.

You want to go after your homeroom teacher? You, no we, could get in serious trouble for this, Arianna. I thought we had an agreement.

Sam stared at me impatiently, and I held up a finger, responding to Ivy instead.

Not if we are careful. Just check it. You are faster at this than anyone else. Please, this time I swear it will be the last time. I paused, but Ivy didn't look convinced. *We need to at least try. What if it was me?*

Ivy shook her head.

There is no way it would be you. Fine, I'll look, but no promises.

Ivy's avatar was still and vacant for a moment. When her avatar fluttered back to life, Ivy was trying, and failing, to hide a smile.

You found something?

My heart hammered in my chest as Ivy nodded, still looking amused despite her best efforts. Sam looked at me expectantly, still waiting for the plan. And then a soft *ping*. A media file popped up, and I had to press my knuckles hard against my teeth to keep from laughing.

Ivy, you are the absolute best.

A video looped through my field of vision of a much younger, and much hairier, Mr. Davidson dressed in a hula skirt and coconut bra. He was clearly in one of those holo-vacation hotels where they convert your room to wherever you want to go. He was attempting a hula dance, a serious expression on his face. It was majestic. Sam raised his eyebrows at me, and I put up a finger typing as fast as I could without bursting out laughing.

Ari: Alright Sam, here's the plan. I'm sending you a media file. Can you get it to the Feed under an anonymous account? Tag everyone in class and set it to post as soon as Mr. Davidson starts on attendance.

I sent the video to Sam and watched in delight as he too, struggled to keep his composure. Maybe this wouldn't be such a big deal with another teacher, but Mr. Davidson was so uptight. It was ridiculous to even imagine him dancing around in a grass skirt, let alone the coconut top.

Sam: How in the glitch did you get ahold of something like this? This is going to cause a riot. We are going to get in so much trouble.

Sam had a literal tear in his eye, shaking his head. I glared at him. There was no time to back out. Mr. Davidson was running late as usual, but the classroom was full of students already. Students were openly gawking at Derek, not attempting to hide it when he gave them no reaction.

Ari: We are running out of time. We have to use it. Are you going to do it or not?

Sam: How do you know if I can even manipulate the Feed? You know it's protected. They don't like when people post under anonymous accounts.

Sam's face was turning a light red color. I shook my head again.

Ari: Really? I've seen you manipulate things far more protected than the Feed. Remember when you manipulated the streaming network just to get the latest season of AI Romance a week before it came out? This should be a piece of cake for you.

Sam: That was different! But whatever, I'll see what I can do.

Sam's face was a much deeper shade of red as he typed.

Sam: *You better not tell anyone about that. I don't even watch that stupid show anymore.*

Ari: Sure, you don't.

Ari: Don't worry, your secret's safe with me.

Sam went back to typing furiously under the desk. We had about two minutes before Mr. Davidson would walk in. I spared a glance at the back of the room. Derek was still staring straight ahead with a blank expression on his face. There were usually at least three girls crowded around him by now, vying for his attention. But right now, no one would even glance his direction. I could hear the whispers floating around the room, and there was a solid two desk buffer around him, a visual warning that something was wrong. *Ping.*

Sam: It's done. We better not get in trouble for this.

I smiled in Sam's direction without making eye contact; he was nowhere near as skilled as Ivy, but he was getting a lot better at accessing things he should not be able to.

Ari: That was fast. Did you cover your tracks?

Sam: You know I'm better than that. Not a trace.

Ari: You are too good. You do not belong on this side of the school. I hated to admit it, but I was still grateful that he was here with me.

Sam: True, very true. But what would you do without me?

I could almost hear the snicker in his message as I responded.

Ari: Oh, you know... waste away into nothingness. I looked at my field of vision. Ivy was noticeably quiet.

Sam: Crap, here comes Mr. Davidson. Are you sure about this?

I looked around the room, and back and Derek, or zombie Derek. I nodded my head; we had to do this. We had to see how far this stupid correction had gone. If there was even a Derek in there to save. We couldn't go back now. I nodded to Sam faintly.

Sam: Ok. Sign off so it doesn't look suspicious.

Ari: You got it.

I gingerly typed a message to Ivy.

Would you please wipe our messages?

I braced myself for an explosion, but she just gave me a stern expression and said, *Already done.*

With that, my messenger screen closed, the conversation wiped. Sam really was good at manipulating the Grid. He could probably be picked up for a tech company, if he didn't want to be an exec. Maybe he would go into research and development with that crafty brain of his.

Mr. Davidson walked into the class flustered and bustling as usual. He dropped his papers as he entered the room and they went everywhere, which would have resulted in a laugh if anyone had noticed his arrival. I almost felt bad for what we were about to do, but this was for Derek. It had to be done.

Mr. Davidson collected his papers, composing himself, and walked over to his desk. He worked his way through the attendance list projected on his field of vision, eyes glazed. The stray whispers disappeared when Derek's name was called, and even Mr. Davidson looked up with a curious expression on his face. It was very rare for someone to be corrected, let along to be back in class, and no one knew what to expect.

A dull, mono-toned 'here' came from the back of the room. Muffled tapping sound echoed through the room, as students typed messages to one another. I kept my gaze locked onto the front of the room, resisting the urge to look at Sam for reassurance.

Mr. Davidson cleared his throat awkwardly and continued down the list. When he got to Sam, I looked up and could hear the slight tremor in his voice. He was already feeling guilty, and the video hadn't even popped up yet. Next came my name.

"Arianna Salvante" Mr. Davidson called out.

"I'm here," I answered, hating hearing my last name, most of my teachers just called me Ari like everyone else, but not Mr. Davidson. My last name was well known in an obnoxious way. My parents were once high up in one of the leading tech research companies. In fact, that company was the one to create the technology that was added to everyone's AIs for them to monitor calorie and nutrient intakes.

It was thanks to my parents that our diet was so restricted. That fame only grew when my dad suddenly disappeared when I was in the 5th grade, and my mom moved to a different tech company, this time the ones who worked on the actual AI software. The people who put the 'intelligence in the artificially intelligent chips' according to the company website.

My anxiety climbed as Mr. Davidson pressed on. Only a few more names now. What was taking Sam so long?

I saw the Feed update a fraction of a second before the first fit of giggles broke out across the room. Suddenly everyone was snickering. Some were trying to hide it, but most people were openly laughing, hands clutching their stomachs.

"Excellent moves Mr. D", snickered Todd, a stocky kid a few seats down from me. He barely managed to speak through fits of laughter.

Mr. Davidson froze.

I could see his fingers moving as he realized what was causing the commotion. Someone must have tagged him in the post. He stood frozen in place as he stared vacantly at the video looping through his field of vision.

I hope you're happy, Arianna. I hope this was worth it, because Sam is not as untraceable as he thinks he is.

I sat motionless in the chaos of the classroom, the warning running through my head. Ivy could be such a killjoy.

Chapter 12

It took everything in me not to turn and look at Sam. Mr. Davidson looked like he was going to explode. He began mumbling under his breath, the word *bet* slipped out, and the laughter doubled. I cringed, feeling bad for Mr. Davidson and turned slowly, risking a glance behind me. This was it. There was no way Derek could resist something as funny as this.

He was staring straight ahead, like he had been all morning, but I could see a battle in his eyes. He was at war with himself, that much was clear, but which side would win, I had no clue. The tagged post should have auto populated the message into his field of vision, correction or not.

For an instant, it seemed as if his eyes cleared. They were suddenly bright and gleaming with mischief. He caught me staring and gave me a small smile which left my heart stuttering. He then turned his attention to Mr.

Davidson, who, by this time, realized he had officially lost control of the class.

"Mr. Davidson," Derek's soft commanding voice broke through the commotion of the room in a way that I'm sure our teacher envied. He rolled his shoulders lazily, as if relaxing for the first time in days. His eyes shone, and my heart soared. This was my Derek. It had worked.

"Your form is flawless. I'd give you an 8 out of 10 for commitment, though you might have to downgrade to seashells next time. Don't worry, it'll compliment your trim figure more."

The room went silent for a moment as people spun around to stare in shock at Derek. Then the laughter returned tenfold, becoming so loud we couldn't hear Mr. Davidson's remark as he tried again to regain control of the classroom. Sam and I traded a discreet look of pride, silently congratulating ourselves on bringing the old Derek back to life. Maybe we could turn this whole thing around.

A sharp choking gasp cut through the laughter, silencing all thoughts of happiness, and sending a tingle of unease up my spine. Ivy was instantly on alert, scanning the area for the threat.

I spun back around in my seat to see Derek slumped over his desk, writhing around in pain. He clutched at his hair, pressing his hands together as he tried to crush his head between them. Suddenly no one was laughing.

Everyone turned to stare at Derek once again. The sound faded away as he rocked back and forth once, twice. Almost as quickly as he began rocking, he stopped, freezing altogether. Then slowly he sat up into a rigid sitting position with machinelike precision and stared straight forward. It was so quiet that when air conditioning kicked on in the room next door several people jumped in surprise.

I sat stunned, unable to move. I wanted to go to him, to see if he was alright, but Ivy filled my vision, solidifying enough to block my view of Derek.

Arianna, no. Stay put, or you will make matters worse than you already have.

Her words stung, as if she had slapped me. There was no gentle codling in her voice this time, and I stilled obediently. She continued, her voice a low warning as she shrunk back down to normal size.

Pay attention, watch, and see what has truly happened to him.

I stared intently; it didn't matter if I was obvious now. Everyone else was staring just as much as I was, Sam included.

"Mr. Davidson." A voice rang out, piercing the silence. It had come from Derek's mouth, but there was no way that it was truly Derek speaking. The voice had no emotion, none of the grating roughness Derek's usually had. "I apologize for the insensitive and hurtful comments. I behaved disrespectfully and degraded your authority as the head of this classroom. I apologize to my fellow students as well, for interrupting class and sacrificing crucial learning time. Please forgive me."

My jaw dropped open, along with the rest of the class. It was as if he was a robot speaking a scripted response, and I wondered how artificially directed his response really was. He continued to stare straight ahead; eyes glazed over. The single bead of sweat that dripped down from his hairline was the only indication of the painful struggle we had just all witnessed.

Mr. Davidson cleared his throat once. He looked incredibly uncomfortable, and it wasn't just because of the video loop still streaming on everyone's Feed. He mumbled, "I accept your apology, Derek. Now can we all just move on to the lesson for today. We have lost enough time, now we will be behind tomorrow."

Everyone slowly turned around. There wasn't a moving mouth or hand in the classroom for once. Everyone was in complete shock. My mouth tasted acidic, and I realized it was fear that coated the back of my throat. I was afraid for Derek, and possibly of him.

Mr. Davidson selected the lesson again and the holoboard burst into life. He tried to move on with his lecture, but his voice was pitched slightly higher than normal, a small tremor reminding us of what had just happened. All I could see was Derek slumped over his desk writhing in pain, and then the cold lifeless look in his eyes as he spoke his apology. A glance told me that Ivy was out again, her avatar unmoving in the corner.

The bell rang, herding us on to our next class. Sam and I watched as Derek stood, collected his bag, and walked mechanically out of the room without looking at anyone. People cleared out of his way, but he didn't acknowledge anyone. Sam and I walked together slowly to 2nd period, too stunned to speak.

Derek wasn't in our 2nd or 3rd periods, and by 4th period I was dying to know how he was doing, if there had been any changes, but he never showed up. His empty desk seemed to scream in the room, and a deep despair seeped coldly through my body, threatening to push me into a full-blown anxiety attack. Ivy stayed quiet, silently monitoring my unstable heart rate, her delicate arms crossed with an emotion I couldn't quite read.

Eventually, I found myself at lunch, the only time I really got to see Ashley during the day. She made her way over to us uncontained curiosity radiating from her, then stopped dead when she saw our expressions. I shook my head as Sam filled her in quietly.

He omitted the part where we were the ones who put the loop on the Feed; we both knew his sister could not keep a secret to save her life, or ours. As soon as he mentioned the Feed, her hands flew through the air searching, but she looked back at us puzzled. Apparently, Mr. Davidson's loop had been wiped already, which didn't bode well for us. It meant someone had noticed or was alerted to the incident. Someone high enough to have that sort of Feed control.

When Sam got to the part when Derek glitched, he took a shaky breath before continuing, "He just choked all of the sudden. He slumped over and clutched at his head, rocking back and forth. I thought he was going to have an aneurism right then and there. And then he just stopped, went silent and sat up and apologized" Sam finished looking like he was going to be sick. I knew my face mirrored his. A wave of nausea filled my stomach, Derek's blank expression behind my eyes.

I swirled my hand, to confirm what Ash had said.

Have you checked the Feed? Is it really all gone?

Someone had to have recorded what happened to Derek. Ivy looked up at me with an almost sad expression.

Ari, I already checked. Someone wiped the entire scene out. There is nothing there, not even a trace. It looks exactly like earlier today when you asked to see Derek. The same person probably did it. You need to lie low. Something is going on outside of what we can see.

I didn't like the way Ivy looked; it was beyond nervous, and it sent a rush of panic through me.

"Wait a minute! He apologized?" Ashley practically shouted the question. So much for lying low.

"Shush! Yes, Derek apologized, but it wasn't really like Derek. He didn't sound like himself at all. It was creepy." Sam's voice shook as he shivered. Ash cocked her head in disbelief, unable to picture any form of Derek apologizing to a professor.

"I wonder what caused him so much pain. It was like his brain was exploding or something, and then poof, it was over, and he just turned back into zombie Derek." I mumbled more to myself than anyone else, but Sam still responded.

"I don't know, but whatever happened was not good, and should definitely not happen again." With a single side glance, he let me know he thought we were to blame for whatever had happened to Derek in that room, and I guess we were.

I nodded in agreement. I knew that whatever moment of lucidity we had gotten out of Derek had cost him dearly. This was far worse than I had thought. I just didn't understand how an AI could take over like that. It was obviously the AI talking for Derek when he apologized. There was no other logical explanation for what came out of his mouth.

But that's the thing, AIs were not supposed to be able to do that, to take over someone's body, or else no one in their right mind would want them. I needed to ask Ivy about it later, without so many people on the Grid around us.

The bell rang for us to return to our afternoon classes, and we gathered our things. I realized I hadn't eaten lunch for the second day in a row, not that it really mattered. This was a bad habit, but the thought of food made me cringe. Ivy would get on my case later for not meeting my calorie count for the day, but there was no way I could force anything down without it immediately making a reappearance.

Glancing around I noticed a man I had never seen walking towards our table. He was massive, shoulders broad covered in a terrifying amount of muscle. He had a sharp hostile expression, one that made you want to duck to avoid looking at it. I could tell that his keen eyes would catch and analyze all of our movements, so I held his stare, resisting the urge to get Ivy's attention. His cold, hard gaze sent chills crawling up my spine. I knew in my bones that he was not a good man.

Sam and Ash finally saw him as he strode uncomfortably close to our table. It was clear he was coming for us, and I desperately hoped this had nothing to do with Derek or what happened this morning.

"Who are you?" Ashley questioned boldly. Nothing seemed to phase or intimidate her. It was one thing I loved about her, but it was going to get her in trouble one of these days. Her back was stiff and straight, as if she sensed something off about him as well.

"Ms. Arianna Salvante, Mr. Samuel Richards, I need you both to come with me to the office," the man stated flatly, not even sparing Ashley a glance. My stomach plummeted; I was going to throw up on this creepy man's shoes.

"Hello, I asked you a quest-" Ashley began, furious when the man ignored her.

Sam yanked on her arm to shut her up, and she glared back and forth between the two of them.

"Ash shut it," He whispered harshly.

He tried to shove her in the direction of the other students who were trickling out of the courtyard and back into the school, but she refused to budge. While the man assessed Ashley, I gulped down a deep breath, steeling myself.

"Can I ask what this is about?"

I spoke in what I hoped was a confident voice. I could see Ivy buzzing around my peripherals. She had noticed our intruder, and she obviously didn't like the look of him, which only made me more nervous. The man's eyes flashed cold fury for a half a second, but it was replaced with a blank stare so quickly I couldn't tell if I was seeing things.

"The headmaster would like to discuss what happened during your homeroom this morning. I believe you know exactly what I am referring to."

He looked evenly between us, and I repressed a shudder. They knew what we had done. Sam didn't cover our tracks well enough, or they found our messages somehow. I didn't know how, but they knew.

Arianna, you need to be very careful. Do not step out of line. Do not draw attention to yourself. Play this off as a prank gone wrong, and do not mention me at all.

Ivy spoke low and fast, her voice urgent. I looked into the man's eyes; he was staring intently at me. I desperately hoping he couldn't read the thoughts going through my head.

Chapter 13

I slung my backpack over my shoulders, shoving my anxiety into a box at the bottom of my stomach, and took a tentative step forward. Sam sighed quietly, resigning himself to his fate, and stepped up next to me. Our shoulders weren't quite touching, but I knew Sam was sending me the same message he had earlier. He would have my back, no matter what went down.

I could see Ash open her mouth to protest, but Sam silenced her with a severe look that left her dumbstruck. The man turned his back on us and began walking swiftly towards the main building, not looking back, his feet making clipped noises against the concrete. He was obviously used to people following his orders without question.

We had to jog to keep up, and I could feel Ashley's glare as it bore into our backs. There was nothing she hated more than being left out of the loop, and she had no idea what was going on, or what we were keeping from her. I felt a twinge of guilt, but it was better she didn't know, especially if we were about to get in trouble.

We followed the mystery man in silence down one corridor after another. He led us through the building in such a way that even though this had been our school for three years now; I was completely lost. I realized our school building was far larger than I had thought.

After our fourth turn, the walls changed from a bland porridge color to a stark white, like that of a hospital, or a mental institution. The floors were a stark white to match the walls and the hallway would have been blinding, but the lights were turned low. It gave the entire hallway a creepy horror movie vibe, and I moved closer to Sam instinctively.

We eventually made it to a door which stood out from the others. It was made of a rich, red wood and had a silver name plate towards the top. The nameplate was completely blank, giving no hint of who the door belonged to. I glanced at Sam, and he raised his shoulders. Neither of us knew where we were, but if the man had been telling the truth, this must be the headmaster's office. Ivy buzzed from side to side, nervously.

The man knocked three times and opened the door. He stepped to the side and pointed. We were going inside by ourselves, apparently. His blank face gave away nothing, so I took a deep breath and headed through the door. The room was much brighter than the hallway, forcing us both to blink rapidly as our eyes adjusted.

You would think that a headmaster's officer would have a rich dark wood desk, the kind that matched the wood of the door, with a thick leather chair behind it, and in the chair a wise, old man with strong but gentle features. This was not the case at all. Everything in the room was silver or black. The room was all sharp edges and harsh angles, making you feel uncomfortable the second you stepped inside. And the person sitting in the tall, rigid black chair was not a gentle old man, but a severe-looking woman with piercing grey eyes and a mouth pressed into a thin lipless line.

"Thank you, Clyde, that will be all," the woman said, with a voice as sharp as a knife.

She didn't divert her penetrating stare as she spoke. The door shut silently at the command; the dull click that followed sounding like a nail being hammered into a coffin. She continued to stare at us for a moment before motioning to the seats in front of her desk. Two stainless steel chairs without an inch of padding on them. They looked as if they were made solely to make a person cold and uncomfortable. Sam and I glanced at each other, and not having another option, sat down at the same time.

I monitored Ivy, trying to see if she would give some sign of what was happening, but she just continued her buzzing back and forth, from one eye to the other, the way a person paces a room.

The silence stretched on as the woman, who was supposedly the headmaster even though I have never seen her before, examined us. I forced myself to keep still, even though her icy grey eyes made me want to crawl right out of my skin and run away. How had this woman even become our headmaster? She looked like she hated everything, especially children.

"Thank you both for coming to see me," the headmaster began; her voice taking on a smooth oily tone. Ivy's buzzing stopped, and I caught myself holding my breath. I forced a slow exhalation, trying not to draw attention to myself. The headmaster's eyes locked on to me.

"I hope you two are not feeling too upset after seeing your friend in such a distressing state this morning." Her eyes probed both of our faces, searching for something. "Derek DeSoto is your friend, is he not?"

I forced my face into a blank mask. Something I had plenty of practice with after years of dodging my mother's wrath. Sam, unfortunately, was an open book, and I could see his face twist uncomfortably from the corner of my eye. I hoped he would keep it together.

"Yes, Derek is our friend." Sam stated quietly. I could tell he was about half a minute from a full blow freak out. He was usually such a goody. This was the closest thing to a reprimand he had ever received. Derek and I always took the fall for all our escapades, and Sam and Ashley typically got off free and clear. I nodded quickly to back him up and his shoulders slumped in relief, or exhaustion.

Alright, it was time for me to be brave.

"It's nice to meet you, Headmaster. We are friends with Derek. This morning was very scary, but everything is already off the Feed. It's such a glitch. We don't have a copy or anything, if that's what you are looking for." I tried to make it sound as bubbly as I could, but by the end my words were coming out shaky. Ivy cringed at my falsely cheerful voice. The headmaster's eyes locked back onto me.

"Thank you, Arianna, but I'm not worried about any recordings of this morning. That has already been handled." Her eyes narrowed for a fraction of a second, but then her expression cleared again. So, she knew who had taken the videos down. Had she down it herself?

"I wanted to bring you both in here to check on you and make sure you are recovering from seeing such a horrific sight." Her voice distorted around the word 'horrific' as if she thought what happened was anything but.

"It is such a shame that you and your classmates had to see Derek corrected so publicly. Usually, corrections happen in a private location, so as to avoid embarrassment. It is rare for a person to..." she paused, deliberating on the right word, "override their corrections like he did; it must have been something in the classroom that triggered a powerful response or reaction. Unfortunate really, as his corrective settings will have to be set to a much higher level. He may struggle to recover from this."

Her face changed while she spoke, the slow sinister smirk which appeared sent a shiver of pure terror down my spine. I tried not to fidget. I desperately wanted to message Ivy, but I knew she was watching our every move. Her words started out sincere, but by the end her tone clarified that she knew exactly what had triggered his ability to override the correction system.

I shrunk back into the cold rigid seat involuntarily, my body trying to put as much distance between myself and the headmaster. I put my hands under my thighs to lock them in place. Ivy was still and silent, listening intently through my ears to every unspoken word this woman was saying.

She paused, as if for dramatic effect, "But don't worry. We will find out exactly what caused this override and make sure it never happens again. For Derek's sake, we must protect him from these negative influences, right?"

She let the threatening question linger in the air. I couldn't tell if she wanted us to answer or not, but it didn't matter. I knew I wouldn't be able to get the sound out of my mouth if I wanted it to.

"Yes ma'am. We understand." Sam had somehow managed to make his mouth work, though his voice came out in a sort of choked whisper. He was openly sweating, his forehead creased with worry.

Before the words were completely out of his mouth, the man from before, Clyde, appeared. I was watching the headmaster the entire time, and I was sure that she hadn't moved or said anything to get his attention. How did he know it was time to come back in?

"Thank you both for coming in today. I am sure we will talk again soon." The headmaster said, the ominous tone of her voice making me hope she was wrong. I never wanted to set foot in her office again.

The dismissal in her voice was clear. It was the same tone my mother used when she was done with me, so I rose shakily from the chair and turned toward her door, barely seeing the sterling silver nameplate on her desk. I realized she had never introduced herself to us, had never bothered to tell us her name, though she obviously knew who we were.

The name plate was an exact twin to the one on her door, but this one had a name etched in bold block letters across it, Veronica Stone. I didn't know how I missed the name plate before, but it comforted me to know that this woman had a name. She was, in fact, human just like us, which meant she had to have an AI like us as well.

I straightened my shoulders slightly, determined to leave steady on my own two feet and moved toward the door, careful to put as much distance between myself and Clyde as possible. Sam rose and follow me out, his chair scraping noisily across the floor. He stayed close to me, as if he was afraid of being left behind. This had shaken him to his core, and I didn't blame him. I wanted to put at least a mile between us and that lady, fast.

Chapter 14

Clyde, apparently bound to us for eternity as our lurking shadow, escorted us all the way back through the winding corridors to the courtyard. He stood in the corner under an awning with his arms crossed, face hidden in shadow, but we knew he was watching us. It looked like we would not be going back to class today, which suited me just fine. I had too many thoughts swirling in my head to even fake paying attention to class now, and it was almost the end of the day, anyway.

I grabbed Sam's hand and drug him to the opposite side of the courtyard, hoping we would be out of earshot from our guard. Sam was a dead weight, and it took all my effort to drag him across the courtyard. His eyes looked dull and glassy, as if he was in shock, which he probably was. I pushed him into a seat at one of the tables and snapped my fingers a few inches from his nose. It took a few snaps, but eventually his eyes focused again, and he looked at me, terror in his eyes.

"What do we do Ari? They know we manipulated the Feed! They know it was us. We made Derek go crazy. We are going to get corrected! We are going to end up just like Derek and get stuck doing manual labor for the rest of our lives!" Sam rushed the words out of his mouth so fast that they twisted and tumbled together into an incoherent mess. His voice rose steadily until I was sure Clyde could hear him across the courtyard.

I flicked him on the nose as hard as I could. He stopped and stared at me.

"You need to get a grip right now. What happened to Derek is not our fault. We did nothing, remember?" I made my voice calm and even. I knew our AIs would record anything that was said out loud, and even though Ivy wasn't a concern, Sam was going to blow it big time if he wasn't careful. Ivy may not follow the typical protocols, but I knew Sam's AI would.

A slow light of recognition dawned in Sam's eyes. Finally.

"You are right. We did nothing at all. We are innocent!" Sam said in a robot-like voice. He was seriously the worst liar I knew.

I swirled my fingers slowly, with my back turned to Clyde, hoping that he couldn't see what I was doing from this far away. Ivy was waiting before I even had a chance to type a word.

Ivy, I need you to open a clean messaging line. Sam is freaking out; we need to get him to chill.

Ivy gave a firm nod, and a second later, a messaging thread to Sam opened before my eyes. I continued typing casually.

Ari: Sam, we have to be careful what we say out loud. That lady could be bluffing. Have you even ever seen her before? Be careful and snap out of it.

Sam: You're right. I'm sorry. I'm just really freaking out over here.

He was sweating again, sharp lines converging where his eyebrows creased. He leaned back against the hard plastic tabletop, closing his eyes and breathing hard. I swirled my fingers quicker this time in a rush to calm him down.

Ari: I know we will figure something out; I promise. But at least we know Derek is still in there. We have to help him. You heard what she said, he is going to be worse off because of what we did.

Sam's eyes snapped open, and he looked at me in disbelief.

Sam: No way Ari. They are watching us now for sure. There is no way I'm even going near Derek. I'm sorry, but he is on his own. He got himself into this mess, and if you aren't careful, he's going to drag you into, too.

He shook his head firmly for emphasis.

I spun to face him, face burning red. My hands flashed. I didn't care if creeper Clyde saw me at this point; I was too pissed and scared and frustrated to care about anything.

Ari: Are you serious? What if it was you who got corrected? Would you want us to just abandon you?

Sam's eyes flashed, matching my energy. His fear shifting to anger in an instance.

Sam: Really? You want me to risk Ashley by pushing this even further? You're not even his girlfriend. How long are you going to let him lead you on like this? I told you I would help you today, but that is it. I'm out.

I read Sam's message slowly. I knew this was coming, and I could see the guilt in Sam's eyes, but there was no budging him.

Derek had joined our little group after misfortune midnight picnic. He ate with us more days than not, and we hung out altogether at least once a week. Derek and Sam had grown close, until a year ago. We had pulled a prank, all four of us, which was rare, and Ivy had had to work hard to cover all our tracks. I had panicked and spiraled into an anxiety attack while Derek had celebrated our victory. Sam and Derek had a huge fight over it. They got over it pretty quickly, but they were never as close after that.

After that fight Sam had tried to warn me away from Derek. I told him he was just jealous, which was a stupid move on my part. Sam didn't even like girls, and I was one of the few people who knew that. The hurt look in his eyes had haunted me until I begged for his forgiveness. Sam was one of my best friends, but Derek was not a topic we would ever agree on. I felt myself sinking, hurt by Sam's words, and the deep-rooted fear that maybe he was right.

Ivy spun before my eyes, catching my attention.

Arianna, you know he is upset. He is just afraid. Don't take it personally. Give him some time, and you should take some time as well. Rushing into things will only make this all worse.

I turned my back on both Sam and Clyde, moving my hands slowly in defeat.

Ari: Fine Sam. You don't have to do anything else. But I am not just going to leave him to be corrected for the rest of his life.

Sam huffed a sigh. Clearly, he thought I was being foolish and dramatic. His message came swiftly.

Sam: Whatever Ari, just don't do anything stupid. Or should I say, anything more stupid?

The rest of the afternoon went by in a blur. The bell rang, and we were all dismissed, everyone heading for the auto-rail platforms again eager to go home. Right before the bell rang, Clyde disappeared, but it didn't really matter. Sam and I were no longer talking.

I had spent the rest of our time trying to look up everything about Veronica Stone that I could, which had resulted in absolutely nothing. Ivy could not find a single thing in the Feed about the headmaster either, which was terrifying. Ivy hinted that she would do some deeper searching when we got home, but she remained quiet beyond that.

My stomach felt like a hard pit. No one had that clean of a record, that's what I loved about the Feed. It kept us all honest. Everyone had done at least one embarrassing or stupid thing in their lives. It was like Veronica Stone didn't even exist; she had no trace of a life outside of being the headmaster.

Barely a minute had passed after the bell when Ashley found us. Sam must have pinged out our location because she came running, a concern and anger etched across her face. She caught my arms breathless, and Sam huffed and walked away.

"What was that all about? I asked everyone after you left, but no one even knew who that creepy stalker guy was. Was it about Derek? Are you guys in trouble?"

She fired questions faster than I could attempt to answer. Finally, she paused putting her hands on her hips, waiting.

"Nothing much happened, Ash. He took us to see the headmaster. She wanted to see if we were okay after seeing Derek freak out this morning, since we were friends with him." Sam stated flatly, coming up to stand beside his sister.

At least we could agree on one thing. We both needed to keep Ash out of this for her protection. She turned from her brother to me with an incredulous look on her face.

"I didn't even know we had a headmaster. I've never seen her." Ash looked skeptically at us both, noticing the tension between us.

"Yeah Ash, it was really no big deal. They were just concerned about us." I tried to make my voice sound light and reassuring. She pouted out her lips as if it disappointed her that there wasn't anything more interesting to add.

"Well fine then. If that's all it was, they could have brought me with you guys. I'm pretty upset about what happened to Derek, too." She huffed prettily and then went back to typing something in her field of vision.

Sam and I glanced at each other. His expression was stiff and unreadable. Not knowing what to say, I scrolled through the Feed absentmindedly, needing something to do with my hands.

The auto-rail pulled up silently to the platform and everyone; students, executives, and laborers alike, began boarding. Ash had no shortage of things to ramble on about, since we 'abandoned her' at lunch, which she reminded us, several times. Each time she glanced at us both sharply to see if we would crack and tell her more of what had happened.

When it was clear that neither of us was going to respond to her incessant chatter, Ash turned to her field of vision and began messaging other, more willing subjects, a perfect pout framing her pretty pink lips.

I stared out the window, watching the gleaming highrise buildings rush past. The windows flashed their multistory advertisements, a constant stream of brightly colored commercials blinding your eyes, to eke out one more dollar. They left only the very highest floors unobstructed, since only the highest-level executives could afford to keep their windows clear, their view of the city below them undisturbed.

I wonder what the city looked like from up there.

We must look like a bunch of ants, struggling to climb the ladder up to them, so easily squashed and pushed back down into our rightful place in society. I shook my head. Today must have really messed me up if those were my thoughts.

I looked through an idly bobbing Ivy avatar to the screen above, which displayed the upcoming stops. I wanted to take the stop before my usual one, so I could walk through the park and take my time. I didn't want to risk coming straight home right away. If my mother was there, I would need to get myself together.

Arianna, I still cannot find anything on your headmaster. Your previous headmaster was a man named Joseph Kieser. He is all over the Feed, but he was 'relieved of duty' a year ago and there is nothing since. It is like Veronica Stone does not even exist, which is impossible. Unless...

She paused, as if debating about saying anything further.

Come on Ivy, just spill it.

Ivy grew slightly in my field of vision, and I could clearly see her pained expression. She pressed her lips together.

The only theory I could come up with is that Veronica Stone is not real. Obviously, that woman was a real person, but maybe that is not her real name.

Ivy went still again, and I knew she had gone back to combing the Feed for more information. Her theory made sense. Even Ash had never seen our headmaster, and she had a way of meeting everyone important. Either way, something wasn't right.

I didn't have much time to linger on the thought though, the early stop was here, and I needed to get off. It wasn't a far of a walk from that stop, and the sun was dazzling. Sam and Ash barely noticed me getting off, each of them lost in their own field of vision, but I still gave them both a small wave and headed to the front of the compartment. I took a deep breath as I stepped off the auto-rail and into the sunlight.

Chapter 15

Even though we were barely out of the city center, the air felt fresher somehow, different than the air that seemed to stagnate between the giant concrete towers and high rises.

I waved my fingers through the air, pulling up the instant messenger. My mom's profile flashed before me as I sent her a quick message saying that I would be home late. I didn't tell her why; I doubted she would care enough to ask, but I knew she hated it when I got home late and didn't tell her. The house security system notified her every day when I got home. It was the only motherly thing she seemed to care about. That and our precious family reputation.

She thought it was dangerous to walk home alone, even with all the AI monitoring and cameras on every corner, and I had long since stopped trying to ask her why. She only ever gave an irritated "because I said so" like a cliché model mother.

If it were up to her, she would have us living right in the center of the city, but she wasn't that high up in her new tech company.

Yet.

She could probably get us into one of the smaller apartments in one of the high rises, but that would really take a hit out of her salary. The company she worked for now paid for this house, so she could live as luxuriously as she wanted to. But if she had to pay for our house too, she would need to make some serious lifestyle changes, and I knew that was not an option for her, city center dreams regardless.

I strolled down the street, weaving my way through the familiar suburban web that stretched for miles outside the city.

The further away from the city you went, the worse the streets and the houses on them looked. On the south side of the city, there was about twenty miles of nothing, but machine operated farmland, factories, and resource mines. It had been a long time since people from our city worked the land, but we had heard about people doing it in our history classes. Now there were only people who kept the farming machines running and in working order.

I lost myself in the thought of what it must have been like, planting a seed and watching over it every day as it slowly became the fruits and vegetables that would feed the people around you. I let the images fill my mind until I could almost feel the soil beneath my fingers, my feet going on autopilot as they carried me home.

Ping.

My eyes refocused on my surroundings as a message came through. It was my mom responding to me, but really, she hadn't responded at all. It was just an automated response saying she was working and would get back to me when she could. No questions, no comments, not even and alright, see you when I get home, typical.

I swiped the message away with a motion of my hand and glanced around. Usually, the streets around this neighborhood were empty at this hour, since most of the students took the auto-rail to the next stop, and the adults in this neighborhood were all upper-level executives who wouldn't be leaving work until far later this evening, just like my mother.

I scanned my surroundings, the hair on my arms standing at attention, subconsciously alerting me to another person in the immediate area. It was like the air was bending around another object, and that object was pushing up against my personal bubble. Ivy became alert as she felt my heart rate rise slightly. She had seemed almost as distracted as I was.

What is it, Arianna? She asked curiously.

I looked around until I found the cause of the weird disturbance. There, standing in the middle of the road, about a dozen houses down from me, was a person. It was a boy, well maybe not a boy, he looked like he could be in my class, or maybe the class above mine, but I was sure I had never seen him before. The city was large, but with the low birth rate we still only had one high school, so I would have seen this boy before, and from what I could see, I would have remembered him too.

Ivy, there is a guy over there. One I've never seen before.

I swirled my hands to respond to her question. She looked intrigued, and slightly wary, like she had had enough of new people for one day.

Do you think he could be a city transfer?

It was rare, but sometimes a family would transfer from one city to another, which always caused a massive stir at school. We didn't get many new kids. Ivy shrugged.

It's possible. Maybe you should just go home and meet him tomorrow.

Ivy responded in her typically cautions and fun killing way. I chose to ignore her suggestion in favor or thoroughly checking out the new kid.

He was staring down at something in his hands, a piece of paper maybe. I couldn't quite tell from this far away. I needed to make the next left turn to go home, but my curiosity was too strong to ignore. I needed to know who this mysterious boy was, regardless of what Ivy thought.

He was turned around so his back was facing me, so I could only see the side of his face. I figured if I was quiet enough, I could get close without him noticing me. And if he did, I cringed. I could just always play it off like this was my street or something. He was new, there was no way he would know the difference.

Taking a few slow, measured steps forward, I waved my hand to pull up a keypad in case he noticed me. If I played it right, it would look like I was messaging someone. I passed my turn, and Ivy gave an exasperated huff and crossed her arms.

Sneaking a few houses closer to him, I noticed his clothes looked as if they were a few years out of fashion, or maybe a few decades out of fashion. He had thick, canvas looking pants that had several pockets running down both legs, and his shirt was made of a coarse-looking material. It was slightly frayed on the sleeves like it had been washed a few too many times. It reminded me of the way Derek's shirts always looked slightly tattered.

Maybe he was going for an outdoorsy look, like he went to the national parks a lot or something. It was a pretty popular look a few years ago, when everyone was all into 'camping', which really meant staying in a small metal box in the park. The boys all started bragging about being able to start a fire from only wood and a lighter. Like we ever needed to start our own fire anyways. They were just being reckless and stupid.

Ari, walk past him and go home. You've had your fun, now go home for the day.

Ivy sounded strangely agitated, for a casual walk by a stranger on the street in broad daylight. I glanced at her in confusion, but her lips remained firmly pressed together, a strained look on her face.

I turned my attention back to the mystery guy.

I'm not going to lie, out of fashion or not, he was ridiculously attractive, if you were into the tall muscular manly type. He had more muscles in his arms than any boy I had seen at my school. Maybe he spent a lot of time lifting things or doing manual labor? I took a few more steps, intrigued.

The only other people I had seen with that much muscle had been the factory workers who carried the more fragile boxes of parts from the factories to the trucks, them and that creepy Clyde guy from earlier today. I shook my head, trying to remove the image of Clyde lurking in the courtyard. This boy didn't have the worn-down look that those workers usually did, and he didn't give off the same 'look at me wrong and I'll kill you' vibe that Clyde had.

I was only two houses away from him now. He had shifted slightly more to the side, giving me a better look at his face. His jaw was rigid and sharp, as were his cheek bones. His features looked rough, matching the slightly weathered look of his clothes. His eyes were still cast down onto the paper in his hands, hiding them from me, but I had a feeling they would be strong and confident. The same sort of energy radiated from him. His hair was also out of fashion. It was cropped shorter than the boys in my school, giving him an even more masculine look. He was definitely close to my age, but he seemed to exude the confidence of someone much older than me. Suddenly, I wasn't sure if I wanted those eyes to meet mine or not.

Ivy had stilled completely, making me hesitate. I swirled my hands slowly, trying to not draw the attention of the boy.

Ivy, what's wrong? I echoed her earlier question to me.

Ivy shook her head and refused to answer. Her avatar went completely still face blank, and I knew she was out on the Grid. Way to leave me completely in the dark, and along with a total stranger.

I glanced down at the paper between his hands contemplating my next move. It was odd for someone to look at a piece of paper for that long and with such intensity. It was like he was trying to figure something out, like that piece of paper could tell him something important. Why wasn't he just looking up whatever he needed to know through his AI?

He shifted slightly once more, and the light bounced off the paper, giving me a clear view of what it was. I stared at it in wonder; it looked like some sort of crude map or maybe a grid. Lines crisscrossed all over the place in a vaguely familiar shape.

It didn't make sense for it to be a map. Paper maps didn't exist anymore. If you needed to go somewhere that you hadn't been before, you simply asked your AI to take you there and they would show you the way.

I checked Ivy's avatar, but she was still frozen. Well, I couldn't just stand there staring awkwardly, he was bound to notice me at some point.

He shifted again and I hesitated, but my foot was already moving forward. it scraped loudly on the cement. I cringed. There was only one house separating us now and there was no way he had missed the sound. I focused my eyes straight ahead, quickly moving my hands over my keyboard, trying to look lost in thought.

It wasn't uncommon to see someone bump into something or just randomly stop walking and stare at the air in front of them with their hands moving rapidly in midair. You just assumed that they got distracted by something important in their field of vision that you couldn't see. I didn't want to look like one of those mindless idiots, but I couldn't think of another solution.

His eyes sharp and they weighed heavily on me, assessing, as I continued my fake typing, waiting for him to realize what I was doing. I hoped he would just move on with his strange paper map, but those piercing eyes didn't move away from me. My cheeks flushed crimson as he continued to stare, hands cramping from fake typing so much. I wouldn't be able to keep this up for much longer.

"Are you alright, miss?" he asked.

His voice was just as rugged as his clothes, though I thought I heard a tinge of genuine concern layered somewhere deep. That voice did strange things to my stomach. It clenched and flopped like a fish out of water, but I shoved the feeling aside. It was just because he was new, that's why his voice sounded so, interesting. I couldn't help myself and I turned to look at him, just as he stuffed the paper map into one of his many pants pockets.

"Miss?"

He echoed himself, concern now dominating his deep baritone voice. He was looking at me like I was a wild animal, like he was afraid to spook me. I realized my hands were now motionless in the air and Ivy was back, anxiously flitting from one eye to the other.

I shook my head, trying to come up with a response that wouldn't completely give away my slightly stalkerish tendencies. My throat was dry, and I had to swallow twice before answering.

"Oh, I'm fine. I was just messaging my friend Ashley. She is going to a party tonight and doesn't know what to wear, so I was trying to help her decide. Her crush will be there so it's super important. I wouldn't want her to go out dressed in something not completely trending."

I cringed the second the words were out of my mouth. I had never said the word trending before in my life. And a party? Really Ari, that's the best you could do? He was going to think I was a complete idiot, a shallow moronic idiot.

I let my arms fall limply to my side and looked down, not wanting to see his facial expression after that jumbled mess. I risked a glance up and saw the boy staring at me with a mixture of curiosity and concern.

"Your hands, were you having some sort of fit?" he asked, his voice cautious and slow, as if I was hard of hearing.

Was he messing with me? It was completely obvious what I had been doing. Did he think I was lying about messaging Ashley? That was forward of him, to accuse me of lying, even if I really was. But there was no way he would know that.

"I already told you. I was messaging my friend Ashley. You know? I was typing a message to her. She was having a fashion crisis."

It was too late to change my story now, so I went with it. He cocked his head to the side, an amused confusion splayed across his face. I motioned once more with my hands as if I was typing to someone. Maybe he really did spend all his time outdoors, and that was why he was so out of touch.

His eyes cleared suddenly as if realized what I was talking about. He met my gaze again, this time with a sharp, almost aggressive look in his eyes.

I was wrong; he was not stupid.

Strange for sure, but there was no trace of idleness in his calculating eyes. Any concern, any friendliness, melted away into a cold, hard mask.

"I understand. You were using your AI, of course. I am sorry that I bothered you, Miss," His tone was formal and guarded.

I flinched at the sudden change in his demeanor and the way his mouth twisted around the word AI, like it was dirty. His shoulders were tight, and he took a step back away from me. He looked like he wanted to get away from me as quickly as possible. Things would be really awkward tomorrow at school if I let things end like this.

"Don't worry about it. And my name isn't miss, it's Arianna," I threw back at him. My words came out slightly harsher than I had intended, but I didn't care. It had been a long day, and I was over dealing with people.

His eyes widened in surprise when I said my name. He opened his mouth and then closed it again sharply, hands clenched to his side. I took another step back, confused by his reaction. He took a breath closing his eyes tightly, and when he opened them again his face was once again a blank mask.

"I apologize, Arianna."

His voice was low and smooth, softening when he said my name. I barely stopped myself from rolling my eyes. What a glitch. He needed to work on his manners if he was going to make any friends around here; hostile one minute, smooth talking the next.

He seemed bemused by my sharp response, before he schooled his face into a blank mask of self-control. "I didn't mean to offend you," his voice was flat, but had a sharp edge, like it would cut you if you touched it.

I sighed. I couldn't get a good read on him. Ivy needed to dig him up in another city Feed if she could. My own impeccable manners kicked in, not allowing me to just walk away, so I responded, "You didn't offend me. It's fine. I saw your paper thing, by the way. Your new here, right? Are you lost?"

He tensed at my words. I had somehow pissed him off again. He held perfectly still, but it was a strained stillness, like he was moments from all out bolting. I tried a different approach when he remained silent.

"You know you could just use your AI. You know how to use the navigation features right? Even if you are new to this city, your AI should know where to go and how to get there."

I tried to make my voice sound reassuring and safe. I could sense his apprehension, like one wrong word would chase him away, and for some strange reason, the thought of him leaving like that made me pause. He wasn't exactly nice, but he was *interesting*. Sam would get a kick out of him.

His lips pressed into a tight line. Whatever I said made him more tense. His eyes flashed darkly, and I decided I didn't want Sam anywhere near him.

"Of course, I know that. I was just trying to find my way around on my own."

His voice came out sharp and angry. He shifted further away from me, as if he was going to walk off, but then suddenly turned back to face me. His shoes were dark and sturdy looking, and he kicked a few loose pieces of asphalt out of the way as he took several quick steps towards me.

His face was deadly serious as he came to a stop a few feet away, still in the middle of the street. I clenched my hands into fists, no idea what this dude's intentions were. I wasn't a fighter, but I would sure as heck go down punching if he went glitchy on me.

"What makes you think I'm not from here, anyway? This city is enormous, you can't possibly know everyone in it."

He added the last part as an afterthought, voice betraying some of his awe. His question confused me. That was his problem? He was mad because I knew he wasn't from around here? His eyes were vivid and intense, as if he was desperate to know the answer.

I doubted he would like my response, but as his eyes drilled unrelenting into mine. I sighed, ready to be done with this entire day. I should have listened to Ivy.

"It's your clothes. They haven't been in style for a few years now, at least around here they haven't. And you look like you're close to my age, so I would have seen you in school at some point, but I've never seen you in my life. Trust me, I would have remembered you." That last bit slipped out before I could stop it, and I silently kicked myself for sounding like some fangirl.

"My clothes? Is there something wrong with them?"

His voice was softer, confusion laced through his words. Thankfully, he seemed to not have heard the last part.

He was staring down at his pants questioningly when a sleek black car turned the corner and sped quickly towards us. On instinct, I reached out, grabbed his hand, and pulled him up to me on the sidewalk.

His hand was blazed underneath mine, and I stared down at the place our skin touched in shock. His sudden closeness and the realization he was completely still and rigid under my touch made me drop his hand quickly. I cleared my throat awkwardly as the car sped past, music blasting through the windows.

"Nothing is wrong with them; they are just out of fashion. Whatever city you came from must be behind ours, fashion wise I mean." I forced slightly breathless from the near accident. He cocked his head to the side, studying me intently.

"You could look up the Feed to see what is in fashion here. Maybe go shopping before school tomorrow if you want to fit in more." I finished lamely, ready to crawl into the drain ditch and live there for the rest of my life. Did I really just give fashion advice to a complete stranger?

"You could say we are behind the times I guess." There was a smile on his face, but it didn't quite reach his eyes. I wondered if was sad to have left his home, what it was like to move from the only place you knew to a completely strange city. I sighed internally, feeling guilty for judging him so quickly. Ivy buzzed impatiently, distracting me for a moment.

Arianna, you need to leave now. Go home.

Ivy must have decided enough was enough, and I was starting to agree with her. Today had been exhausting and hot but scary pocket pants guy would figure things out soon enough on his own. If Ivy wanted me to leave so badly, she could be my excuse.

"Ivy says I'm running late, I should be going." I kept my voice light, take a few steps backwards up the sidewalk.

"Who is Ivy?" His eyes were full of confusion, his brows coming together.

"Sorry, Ivy is my AI. Did you ever give yours a name?"

"Oh, yeah. Of course." He was mumbling now, lost in thought.

I wasn't sure he had heard anything that I said. I glanced at the corner of my screen. It was past 6 o'clock now and if I wasn't home soon my mom would call me, furious. I backed a few more steps away from him, and he looked up again. His eyes had a tense conflicted look to them, and I opened my mouth to say goodbye, but he beat me to it.

"I need to go as well. It was nice to meet you, Arianna. I will make sure to change my clothes to something more, fashionable."

He smiled, and this time it reached all the way to his eyes, making them come alive in the most spectacular way. This guy was really all over the place. The girls at school were going to eat him alive tomorrow. As he stepped into the street, I realized I had never even gotten his name.

He took another step away and I couldn't help but blurt out, "Hey, you never told me your name!"

Arianna Salvante, LEAVE NOW!

Ivy was officially pissed and done with me ignoring her. She swelled in my field of vision, making it difficult to keep my eyes on him.

He paused and turned back, "My name is Jeremiah, but you can call me Jeremy."

He spun and walked down the street. Just as he was about to turn the corner, he turned around once more and yelled down the street, "And Arianna, thanks for saving me from that car."

I shook my head baffled by his rapid mood swings. Ivy was pointing to the clock in the corner of my screen. It read 6:15pm. I glanced around again, just now noticing how dark it had become. My head swam, I was far more exhausted than I had realized, and I still had to make it through the park to get home. Maybe if I was late enough home, mom would ground me, and I wouldn't have to face Derek's zombie corrected gaze or the glitchy new kid's attitude tomorrow.

One could only hope.

Chapter 16

I backtracked down the sidewalk to the side street I was supposed to have turned on, before I saw the new mystery boy, Jeremy. I walked as fast as I could without seeming obviously nervous, the light from the sun already fading fast. Jeremy's strange mannerisms replayed over and over in my mind as I rounded one street and walked down another. He was not going to do well in school if he kept up this whole anti-AI act.

Before I knew it, I was at the edge of the large, wooded park that bordered my neighborhood and the next. I always cut through the park when I walked home, it was a saved time, and it was a beautiful walk. My house was just on the other side, but I had never gone into the park at night before, and the sun was already slipping below the horizon. I hesitated at the entrance of the park. The trees blocked what little light was left, casting deep creepy shadows on the ground.

The AIs had cut down on crime significantly, so it wasn't that dangerous to walk around at night, but they could only do so much. Yes, they recorded everything you did and said out loud, but that did nothing in the moment, if someone was attacking you. The only thing it did was make it impossible to deny who did the crime. And there were still people desperate enough to not care what the AI saw and recorded.

I shivered at the thought, wondering if I should go the long way around through the neighborhoods. Ivy flashed my clock overlay brighter. Looks like I was going in whether I liked it or not, I didn't have time to take the long way.

It didn't look like anyone was in the park right now, and there were a few lights that lit up most of the pathway. I took a deep breath and started down the gravel trail. I don't really know why they built this park in the first place. They had said it was to give us an opportunity to immerse ourselves in nature, or something cheesy along those lines, but people rarely ever came here.

They had taken two acres of land and had sprinkled so many tree seeds that when it had all started to grow, it turned into a completely unmanageable miniature forest. I rarely ever saw anyone when I walked home during the day. And the park, if you can call it that, was just as wild as any true forest out there, or as wild as I pictured them to be. Three feet in and you couldn't even see the houses on the other side of the tree line.

I walked along the path, trying to remain calm, but each light only lit up a small circle, and between each circle of light was a stretch of darkness. Between each safe haven of light, I walked as quickly as I could without running, until I hit the safety of another patch of light. I knew it was silly, but I couldn't help myself. My nerves were fried from today and it didn't take much to send my heart racing.

Ivy was still on red alert, pacing again through my field of vision. She didn't like the park even during the day, but we both knew this was the quickest way home, so there was no turning back.

Ari, keep your breathing calm. Calm down, you are only amping yourself up more. Nothing is around us right now. The Grid is clear. There is no one else in the park.

Her words were slightly reassuring. At least I wouldn't have to run into anyone. But I still didn't like the thought of being completely alone under the dark canopy of trees. I reached the center of the park, where the path forked in two. There was a brighter light shining down on a small metal bench between the paths. Sometimes during the day, I liked to sit on the bench and just relax, letting the soft green light cascade down. The forest felt calm and peaceful then.

I scanned the trees, the darkness so thick, I couldn't tell one tree from the next, and shivered. It was not peaceful in here at night, not with images of Derek's pain filled face floating behind my eyes. Shaking my head, I took a slow steadying breath. I needed to get the heck out of here. My stomach turned, a mixture of anxiety and emptiness. Breakfast felt years ago, and my missing lunch wasn't helping much.

Staring at the fork in the path, I was reminded of a random poem our literature teacher told us long ago. Apparently, the paths we chose while walking were supposed to represent our choices in life, but I couldn't see how that metaphor applied now. The left path would take me in a large loop back to the beginning of the park where I had come from, while the right path would lead me straight through to the other side of the park, where my house was. The choice was already made, no life changing decisions here.

I took a step towards the right fork, eager to get out from under the trees, but something made me hesitate. I felt goosebumps run up my arms and I couldn't suppress the shiver that followed. I couldn't see anything past the first few lights going down the left path, the path back to the start of the park, but it felt like someone, or something was just out of sight, waiting in the darkness.

I swirled my hands low and slow.

Ivy, I thought you said there was nothing else in the park?

She paused, taking in my rising heart rate and guessing at my fear.

I promise you, no one is here. I would pick up their AI signal on the Grid, and nothing is on the Grid anywhere in the park. It's probably just an animal, like a bird or a squirrel or something.

I knew she was trying to reassure me, but her voice was tight, like a rubber band about to snap. I looked down the left path again. I knew beyond a shadow of a doubt that there was something there and whatever it was; it was watching me. It sure didn't feel like a squirrel.

I stared for just a second longer before my nerves got the best of me and I bolted down the right path. I couldn't tell if the thing was going to follow me or not, but I didn't want to find out or give them an opportunity to catch me, so I continued to run and run until I could see the lines of the houses through the trees. I had missed track practice today, so my energy reserve was still high enough for a full out sprint. I wasn't the best short distance runner, but I could hold my own when I needed to.

My heart rate skyrocketed beyond normal exercise levels, and I knew that if I kept this up much longer, Ivy would have to trigger a dopamine rush to calm me down. I was dangerously close to a full-blown panic attack but that stupid calming aid would make me sluggish and slow to respond to anything, and if that happened, whatever was watching me would catch me, and I would probably die.

Definitely not being dramatic.

My breath caught in my chest, an irrational fear of being chased in the dark taking hold. I had convinced myself that some dangerous beast was on my trail. I could practically feel its hot wet breath on my neck.

Ivy held up her hands in a silent gesture, a code we had established a long time ago when the panic attacks first arrived. She would hold up her fingers and count them down slowly. When the fingers ran out, she would trigger the dopamine, whether I liked it or not.

I risked a glance behind me, but I saw nothing as I ran through the last line of trees, bursting into the light of the streetlamps and straight into what felt like a brick wall.

I let out a strangled cry, all the air leaving my chest. My head snapped forward and then back painfully as I rebounded off whatever I had hit. My body ricocheted off the wall and suddenly I felt strong arms wrap around me, halting my rapid descent to the ground. Head spinning viciously from the impact, I could have sworn I heard a soft chuckle as my vision faded in and out. A brick wall should not be able to laugh at me or catch me for that matter.

My vision cleared, and I looked up to see what I had plowed into and looked directly into a pair of dark green eyes flecked with bits of amber and brown. Those same eyes had been flashing back and forth between anger and confusion as we bickered in the street what felt like only a few minutes ago.

How in the world had he got to the other side of the park? I saw him walking the opposite direction from me when he left. There was no way he made it through the park before me. I groaned. Loudly. Why did it have to be Jeremy?

"Arianna, are you alright? Can you stand on your own if I let you go?"

His words were serious, but there was humor in his eyes. I was suddenly very aware of his thick arms wrapped around mine. My face burned red as I scrambled to get away from him, not wanting to give him the wrong idea. I checked for Ivy, her hands were still up, fingers mid count down, but she was frozen, in as much shock as I was.

"Yes, thanks, I'm fine."

He kept his arms outstretched as if I might fall at any moment. I swayed slightly, annoyingly confirming his suspicion. I must have hit him harder than I thought, and he didn't even seem phased. This kid was relentless.

"What are you doing here? How did you get through the park so fast?"

The humor faded from his eyes, turning them a darker shade of green in the low light of the streetlamp. His voice was taut when he answered, betraying his irritation.

"You're welcome for catching you, and I realized I had made a wrong turn and doubled back this way. I didn't go around the trees; I went through them." Jeremy stated matter-of-factly, but there was an undercurrent of tension there that didn't make sense.

"So, it was you that was watching me earlier!"

The accusation was out of my mouth before I could think. I knew I felt someone watching me, but Ivy had assured me over and over that there was no one else in the park with us.

"And thank you." I muttered at the end, an afterthought. I was too embarrassed to feel much gratitude.

Jeremy took several quick steps back, apparently satisfied with my ability to stand up on my own again and shook his head severely, eyes flashing.

"I wasn't watching you." His voice came out a little too loud, a bit to defensively. He shook himself and took a deep breath, starting over.

"I did not see you while I was in that odd little forest, though I definitely felt something sinister lurking in there. It felt predatory, but I think it was human."

Jeremy shifted his gaze back towards the tree line, searching it intently. I turned my head to look, and I half expected someone to jump out at us from the trees. An image of the man who had escorted Sam and I through the school flashed before my eyes and I shuddered involuntarily. I glanced back at Jeremy and found him already staring at me.

I could tell from the way he held his body tight, ready to spring into action at any moment, that he was still on guard. His lips pressed into a thin line as he moved in front of me, cutting off my view of the trees, acting as if he were a human shield.

What a joke. I didn't understand this guy. He didn't even know me. One second, he was annoyed with me, then next he was shielding me from some danger he thought was lurking in the trees. He took one last glance into the tree line, searching, before he turned back to me, curiosity replacing the harsh expression he was wearing.

"Is that why you were running so fast, and not looking where you were going? Was something chasing you?" His questions fell softly, he was poking fun at me, but his eyes were still dark and serious.

I coughed embarrassed again and shrugged noncommittally. There was no reason for him to know what was going through my head, and I definitely did not need him poking around. I had let my fear get the better of me, but he didn't need to know that.

Arianna, time to go.

Ivy had lowered her arms, heart rate evening out. It was still going hard, strenuous exercise fast, but it was within a normal range, so she didn't need to calm me down anymore. She stood stock still in the center of my vision. We needed to have a serious conversation tonight when I got home about her crazy demands; I didn't get why she was so up in arms about this guy. I knew he was a little crazy, but still, she was being a bit much.

Jeremy turned to face me again, raising an eyebrow questioningly.

"I am fine. I'm sure that I was just imagining it. That park has always been creepy at night, anyway. But I still want to know how you made it through the park quicker than I did. Even if you had doubled back, I should have seen you along the path somewhere." If he could question me, I could question him. He shrugged nonchalantly.

"Like I said before, I cut through the middle of this poorly placed cluster of trees. I didn't need to take the path to get through. I had actually just walked out when you tackled me, oh so gracefully I might add."

The humor was back in his eyes now, but his hands were still clenched into fists.

Ping. Ping. Ping.

It was a message alert, and there was only one person who would rapid fire message me like that. My mother.

Chapter 17

I glanced at the time once more; it was already 7:00pm; I had wasted another 45 minutes on this ridiculous forest adventure. I flipped through the messages quickly as Ivy put her hands on her hips in an exasperated 'I told you so' move.

Mom: Arianna Salvante, where in the world are you?

Mom: You had better not have walked home again. I already warned you not to do that anymore. It's dangerous out there.

Mom: You have two minutes to answer me. Where are you!?

I resisted the urge to roll my eyes. She had a way of going from not caring what you did, to how dare you disobey me, real fast. It was like she only wanted to parent me when it was convenient to her, or when I messed up. I couldn't tell if she was home from her messages, or if she had just checked the security log and realized I never got home.

I flipped to the response tab and typed a quick message back before she went completely insane. I swirled my hands gracefully, not even bothering to pull up the keyboard.

Ari: Mom, I'm fine. I just got caught up at school today, helping Ashley with a project. I'm down the street. Be home in 5 minutes, I promise.

I glanced back at Jeremy to find him gazing at me intently. He was studying my every move, like he was watching a science experiment or something. His jaw clenched uncomfortably, and he looked angry again. I was officially over it. He could leave now.

"Well, my mom is about to lose it. I need to get home."

I swiped my messenger out of view once more. I knew she would be satisfied with my response. She loved Ashley, and the fact that she was already in business classes. Honestly, I think she would have preferred Ash as a daughter. She thought she was such a wonderful influence on me and that she would somehow push me to want to become an executive, too. If only she knew. I shook my head, irritated.

Jeremy's deep voice echoed against the trees. He sounded tense and tired, I bet he was late as well. Hopefully he didn't get into trouble because of me.

"Do you need an escort home?"

Jeremy looked like he was about to extend his hand towards me, but let it continue rising instead, running it through his hair, making it messed up in a stupidly attractive way. He sounded sincere but looked conflicted, like he was offering out of obligation rather than wanting to.

I shook my head at him. I didn't need a protector. I already had Ivy, and if I could figure it out, maybe I could get Derek back too.

"Thanks, but I am just down the street. That house down at the end of the corner is mine. I wouldn't want to take up any more of your time, anyway. See you at school tomorrow."

He nodded, letting his hand fall to his side with a slight frown, which he quickly smoothed over, face returning to the same mask as before. I backed away from him, keeping my eyes on both his masked face and the forest behind him. I walked like that for half the street, an awkward backward shuffle, until it was beyond weird for me to continue, then I turned on my heel and jogged the rest of the way home.

I was desperate to get home, to my room, so I could process what had happened. I turned my head to look down the street as I reached my door, and I could see Jeremy's figure faintly, standing still, staring towards me. Regardless of his severe attitude, he stayed to watch me make it home. I would have to deal with that tomorrow.

I hesitated as Ivy sent a code through the door to disengage the lock. When the door clicks unlocked, I push my way in exhaustion weighing heavily on my body. Mom wasn't in the kitchen or living room, so I knew she had to be in her study working. She worked at work and when she came home, she always found a reason to work some more.

I hit the fridge on my way to my room, not even bothering to look at my options, just pressing random buttons. The tray came sliding out and I grabbed it without looking at what I had chosen. I pressed it one more time, this time selecting my mother's profile. She would forget to eat dinner if I didn't bring her a tray on nights when she was actually home, plus maybe she would forget how mad she was if I came barring food.

I grabbed both trays and headed down the hall to her study. The door was closed but I could see the light shining under through the cracks and I knew she would be in there, fingers flying, a glazed look on her face as her AI pulled up screen after screen of information for her to sort through.

It was kind of creepy to look at someone so deep in their field of vision, like they were a sort of marionette doll with invisible strings attached to their hands.

I tapped on the door with my elbow, and it slid silently open for me. I set the tray of food down on her desk. It took a solid two minutes for her to realize that I had come into the room.

"Oh, Arianna, you're home. Good. You know how I worry when you are out at night. The world is not as safe as you think."

My mother glanced at me. Her eyes softened for a moment, catching me off guard, before glazing over again into the familiar look of disinterest she usually wore. She turned back to her field of vision looking more mechanical than human. I was so exhausted; I must be seeing things.

I knew better than to say anything back. She was already sucked into her own little world, so I just nodded and walked back out of her office. At least she was busy tonight. It saved me from another lecture.

I tapped the side of the wall, letting the door slide back into place, and went to my room with my tray. My door was already open, evidence of my mom searching for me earlier. I walked in and tapped the wall once more, making sure the door slid shut behind me. Setting the food down on my desk, I walked over to my bed and collapsed on the soft comforter.

Was it just this morning that everything had happened with Derek? And the headmaster and that creepy guy, Clyde? And then everything with Jeremy and the forest. It was too much for a single day, a single person to handle. I caught Ivy's piercing glare and I knew she had some things to say, and they probably weren't pleasant.

Alright Ivy, I'm sorry, but look, I didn't even get into that trouble.

Arianna, it isn't about you getting into trouble with your mother. You could have been in real danger out there. And that stunt you pulled at school? What was I thinking helping you?

She folded her arms delicately and I lay back on my bed, staring back at her. She looked exhausted, for an AI, and I thought back to that time I had asked if she ever sat down or slept. She had laughed at me and said she didn't feel things the same way I did. I had asked how she really felt then, but she had changed the subject.

I know I freaked out in the forest, but I am sure it was nothing, plus Jeremy was there, so everything was fine.

I paused, skipping over her last remark about her helping me with Derek. I wasn't ready to think about that yet, and there was something about Jeremy being in the forest with me that bothered me, but I couldn't place my finger on it. Luckily, Ivy chose to focus on Jeremy as well.

Ari, you don't even know him. That was risky back there. You know better than to talk to strangers, come on.

I froze, realizing what had been bothering me and typed back fast.

Ivy, you told me at least twice that no one was in the park with me because no one was signaling the Grid. But Jeremy told me he went through the trees about the same time I was on the path. How is that possible? And why were you so freaked out about him earlier? Don't even think about giving me that stranger danger crap.

Ivy bobbed gently up and down, her hands wringing together. She looked conflicted, like she wasn't sure she wanted to tell me anything, but there was no way she was going to keep this from me. She sighed, resigned.

I was scanning the entire park while you were in there, and I strengthened the scan when you freaked out. There was no one with an AI signal in the park.

I was quiet for a moment, her words sinking in slowly, like a rock through mud.

And what about when we first saw Jeremy on the road?

I immediately scanned him to see if he was new or on the Feed. I knew you wouldn't let it go, so I started searching as soon as you spoke to him. There was nothing. Nothing on the Feed, and no signal then, either.

Her words were low and serious, like she needed me to understand the gravity of what she was saying. I knew where she was going, but it was impossible.

Ivy, there is no way. Maybe you missed something? There is no way he doesn't have an AI.

She frowned at my words, hurt that I didn't automatically believe her.

You know I wouldn't miss something as basic as an AI signal. They are incredibly easy to pick up, even Sam can pick them up. Besides, what do you really know about him?

I thought hard for a second, pushing a pillow over my eyes, replaying our conversations again and again, hating that she was right. I had no idea who Jeremy really was; he had avoided directly answering any of my questions. He was out of date, acted oddly whenever I mentioned Ivy or an AI, and was incredibly moody. This strange boy could be anyone, could be from anywhere, and I would have no way of knowing.

I sat up suddenly, glancing over to my window, the blinds shielding me from the outside world. I had almost forgotten that my window faced the park. The trees had always been a comforting sight when I was little. I used to pretend with my dad that we were adventurers from the past, forging our way through the wilderness; us against the land. Those were some of my favorite memories with him.

Ivy, open the blinds, please.

Ivy signaled the window, and the blinds retracted into the wall. The park lights must have a timer on them because I could barely make out the trees from the sky, it was so dark. I stared at the park for so long that my eyes watered. I half expected Jeremy to still be standing at the edge of the trees, his face set into that annoyingly unreadable mask. I shivered wondering who he really was and how it was possible for someone to enter the city without an AI.

Arianna, you need to be careful around this boy. Hopefully, you won't see him again, but if he is new and goes to your school tomorrow, avoid him. Either he doesn't have an AI, or he is able to shield his signal completely. Either way, you shouldn't go near him.

I knew she would say something like that, and maybe she was right. But we both knew there was no way I would avoid him. I had too many questions now, and if Ivy couldn't get me the answers, I would force Jeremy to give me them himself. Maybe he could help me break Derek free.

Fine, I won't seek him out, but if he finds me, I am not going to be rude.

Ivy waved her hands dismissively at my response, not buying my artificially important manners. I laid back down on the bed, body heavy from exhaustion. I could feel myself drifting off to sleep, still fully dressed in my clothes from the day. The last thought I had before sleep claimed me was wondering just where Jeremy was going.

Shouldn't his parents have messaged him, like my mom did, when he was out so late in a city that was obviously new to him? But how would they message him if he didn't have an AI? I sighed, more mysteries to be solved. Maybe I would see him tomorrow in class.

I rolled over onto my side, facing the window to the forest. My eyelids felt heavy, weighed down. I could have sworn that I saw a flash of light, deep within the trees, right as my eyes closed. It looked almost like a camera flash, or maybe a flashlight. Whatever it was, it too would have to wait until morning, I told myself as I drifted into a fitful sleep.

In my dreams, monsters chased me through dense clumps of trees, and always at the end of the path stood Derek. I would reach out to him, but his face would turn, twisted with rage before he too morphed into a zombie eyed monster. I didn't want to think about what that meant as I tossed and turned fitfully through the night.

Chapter 18

Ivy came bouncing back into my field of vision far earlier than I wanted her to. She was all a flutter and hadn't even bothered to change her avatar's outfit, which meant she was still strung up about last night. She was grumbling about her struggle to wake me up this morning. I refused to open my eyes or move until she started blaring alarm bells through my wall speakers. The harsh noise grated against the inside of my skull, and I could fight it no more.

"Alright, alright, Ivy! I'm awake. You can stop with the torture now."

I groaned into my pillow. She mercifully cut the noise as I crawled out of bed, finally satisfied that I was awake. I didn't hear her as she went through her normal health check routine. It felt like I was wading through a dense fog, unable to fully comprehend my surroundings. I was so tired from the previous day, and so wrapped up in my thoughts, that before I even knew what was happening, I was walking onto the platform, ready to board the auto-rail. How Ivy had got me to the auto-rail on time was a miracle, and I honestly didn't even know if I had eaten anything or brought lunch with me.

I sat in the first row I could find, ducking down so Ashley and Sam couldn't see me. I didn't think I could handle faking an interest in Ashley's stories this morning, let alone bear the waves of guilt Sam would throw at me from yesterday's argument. What happened yesterday in homeroom seemed so far away that I couldn't believe that it was truly only yesterday. I had wanted desperately to tell Ash about Jeremy last night, but his on again off again attitude made me want to keep her far away from him. She wouldn't be able to resist his stunning green eyes.

I made it all the way into class, dread pooling at what I would, or wouldn't find, before I ran into Sam.

"Hey Ari," he said bashfully. He ducked his head, scuffing the toe of his sneaker against the tile floor, looking irritatingly adorable. I waited, holding my breath. I didn't know if he was still mad at me, or if we were even talking still, but I missed him. He took a breath and raised his head, eyes meeting mine. They looked downcast and almost shy, but thankfully not mad.

"Ash was looking for you on the rail this morning. Everything okay?" Sam looked at me, waiting for me to make a move.

Typical of him to make me decide if we were friends or not. I let him off the hook and gave him a small smile. There was too much going on to continue this petty fight.

"Everything's fine. I'm just tired. Tell Ash that I am fine, and I'll talk to her later." My voice came out slightly weaker than I meant it to. I was exhausted. Sam looked concerned, but visibly relieved, that we were talking again. He nodded, returned my smile, and headed into the classroom shoulders tensing as he opened the door. He was just as afraid to go to class as I was.

I stepped behind me, stomach clenched as I scanned the room. Derek wasn't here. I doubted I would be able to reach him through the messaging app either. It looked like mystery boy, Jeremy, wasn't in this class either. He might be in another class already, which was probably for the best. I doubted I could handle the two of them in the same room for long.

I swirled my hands to get Ivy's attention

Ivy, have you seen anything on the Feed about Derek? Or Jeremy, for that matter?

She gave me a smirk, like keeping track of one boy was more than enough, and I didn't need to add another one to the list, but shook her head no. I knew she would monitor the Feed for me though, just in case; she was good like that.

The rest of the day went by in the same blur the morning had. I avoided seeing Ashley or Sam over lunch by staying in a classroom, under the premise that I needed to catch up on some homework, which wasn't a complete lie. Sam had frowned when I told him to go on without me, but he gave me the space I wanted.

Being the model student that I am, I didn't actually use my lunch break to do any of that homework, though, which meant I would be very busy tonight. Instead, I spent my entire break searching the Feed for any hint of Derek. Nothing.

After 15 minutes of absolutely zero success, I switched over to see what I could dig up on Jeremy. It didn't help that I didn't know what his last name was, but still, I couldn't find a single trace of him. Ivy reminded me several times that she had already looked, but I wasn't satisfied. I wanted to look for myself, even if I knew I wouldn't find anything.

My frustration mounted as the day progressed. If I couldn't help Derek, I was going to find Jeremy and make him tell me his secrets. As the hours ticked by, I formed a plan. I was going to stop at the same stop I had yesterday and take the same route home. Maybe then, if I was lucky, I would run into him like I had the day before. I knew it wasn't the best plan, but it was better than nothing, and I was getting desperate.

Ivy had glared at me when I told her the plan, and then promptly refused to talk to me. She didn't even bother to call me out on my lie from last night, when I told her I wouldn't seek Jeremy out. I didn't know how to explain it to her, but I knew there was something about Jeremy that would help me save Derek. There had to be.

When the bell rang, I rushed to Coach Garrison's office faking a stomachache to get out of track practice. She frowned, irritated that I was missing a second day in a row but didn't argue. I sprinted to the platform to catch the rail. I wasn't the only people running late, and Sam and Ash brushed by me.

Ash refused to even look at me, but Sam shot me a small smile and winked, knowing how much of a pain his sister could be. I knew I would catch some heat from Ashley for avoiding her like this today, but I would make it up to her somehow. I just needed to get my head straight before I talked to her again. She would pry me for answers the second she sensed I was keeping something from her; she had always been able to tell when I had a secret, ever since we were kids. At least I had Sam back on my side. He would play defense for me for a while at least, but there was no way I could keep Ash out for long.

The auto-rail took off, but this time I didn't stare at the buildings as they flew past. I was too nervous to think about anything else as I counted the stops one by one until the last one before mine. The auto-rail had barely stopped before I jumped up and headed towards the platform.

The second I was out of the compartment, I was running. It felt good to stretch my legs, and even though I wasn't in running shoes, the familiar feeling of my legs and arms pumping in sync settled my anxiety as instinct took over. I felt guilty for missing practice, but I swore

I would redouble my efforts as soon as I had everything under control. It took me five minutes to reach the cross-streets that we had met the day before, a light sweat coating my back from where my backpack clung to me.

Holding my breath in anticipation, I turned the corner, but there was no one there. There wasn't a single person on the street. I released my breath with a huff. I should have known better. There was no way he would be on the same street at the same time as before. I mean, he had seemed lost yesterday. Why would he be back here today?

Ivy chuckled silently.

Did you have a pleasant run? Can we head home now and have a nice uneventful evening for once?

Her voice was playfully sarcastic, and I rolled my eyes in response.

It was stupid of me to think that I could just appear in the same place and find him again. He hadn't been at school either; not a single person had mentioned his name, and he would have attracted some attention for sure. I paused on the sidewalk, wondering where he spent his time today. If he didn't start coming to class soon, he would get in trouble, which wasn't the best way to transfer into a new school.

Everyone had a place that they had to check into every day, even the top executives needed to check in to their job. It was how the government techs kept track of everyone, for 'safety purposes', they always said. Kind of like how if we had a fire drill in school they had to account for every teacher and student, except this was city wide. If Jeremy got caught not checking into his proper location, he would get into serious trouble.

I turned in a slow circle on the sidewalk, shoes scratching against the rough concrete, and began walking back to the street that would take me toward the park, retracing my steps from yesterday. My right foot pinched uncomfortably. I really shouldn't have run in these shoes.

My stomach turned just thinking about going back into the dense canopy of trees, the one downside of this plan, but things would be different this time. It was still bright and sunny out and nothing scary ever happened when the sun was out. I nodded my head, trying to reassure myself, and continued.

Ari, you don't have to cut through the park. We can take the long way around. It won't add that much time. You will still be home long before your mother checks in on you.

Ivy sounded as tense as I felt. She didn't like the idea of us going back through the park, either. I squared my shoulders and responded as confidently as I could.

Nope, we are doing this. There is nothing scary about that park and I will not let one weird night ruin my favorite walk home.

I paused before typing again.

Just keep scanning for other people, ok?

Ivy gave me a proud look and nodded. She was ready, and I guess I was, too.

The densely packed trees of the park didn't seem as ominous as they did last night. I could hear the birds tweeting away at one another high in the branches. It was disappointing to not find Jeremy, but I couldn't afford to come home late again. I took one more deep fortifying breath, checked Ivy, who gave me an all-clear signal, and then headed into the trees.

I wandered along the path quietly, at a slow steady pace, forcing my nerves down. At first, I couldn't help but search deep into the thickets, looking for something, anything that seemed out of place, but everything was calm, a peaceful green light filtering through the treetops. I let out a relieved breath and my mind wandered, searching for a better way to track down Jeremy.

When I reached the fork in the center of the park, I paused, hair standing straight up on my arms. The bench between the two paths was tipped on its side awkwardly, legs splayed in the air like a dead animal. I froze, one foot slightly raised to take a step forward, realizing the surrounding trees were still and quiet. The absence of the bird's chatter and the strangeness of the overturned bench sent a chill running up my spine. My heart rate quickened.

Ivy sensed my panic, and she shook her head, still not finding any signals on the Grid. It wasn't Ivy's fault, but I didn't exactly trust the Grid's reliability anymore.

I looked around wildly, trying to find the source of my tension, but I couldn't find anything in the trees. I was about to take a step down the right path, or more likely to bolt straight down the path as fast as I could, when a hand reached quickly from behind and covered my mouth.

The hand was massive and rough, and I felt the heat of another body pressing against my back as another arm wrapped completely around my waist, holding me fast. I tensed my muscles, ready to bite or kick my way out of their grip as I sucked in as much breath as I could muster through the fingers around my mouth. I was about to let out the loudest scream possible when an irritating and newly familiar voice cut through the air next to my ear.

"I wouldn't do that if I were you," Jeremy whispered into my ear.

He pulled me slowly but firmly off the path and into the thicket of trees. His body was as rigid as mine and I tried to keep my mind off how close he was pressed against me. Instead, I focused on the fact that he was rapidly taking me away from any sort of public witnesses or protection. I hadn't seen anyone else in the park, but an open path had to be better than deep within the cover of trees. I squirmed against him, trying to get him to release me, but his grasp was firm and unrelenting.

"Stop Arianna. Don't make this any more difficult than it already is."

His words were tense and stern, but there was a trace of genuine fear behind them, and I stilled. His words weren't threatening, but shards of icy fear penetrated my stomach.

Ivy stared in horror, but I couldn't move my hands to tell her what was happening. She heard Jeremy's voice, and felt my rising fear through my heart rate, but she couldn't do anything except alert the authorities, which she would do quickly if I didn't say something to make her stop.

I bit down on Jeremy's hand hard enough to shake him off for a second as he let out a muffled curse. Before he could readjust his grip, I whispered as quietly as I could, "Ivy, don't alert anyone."

I felt Jeremy pause, then curse again. His arm was wrapped around my stomach, pinning me against him, but I didn't try to run. I decided I would trust Jeremy, like some incompetent teenage girl in a horror movie who was eventually going to be killed, probably by the hot stranger who led her deep into a forest.

Ivy stilled, her avatar a mixture of terror and rage, but no alerts went out. Jeremy continued our awkward retreat into the trees, but didn't cover my mouth again, always maintaining an eye on the path.

Once he had pulled up back into the trees, far enough away from the path that if he had left me, I was sure it would take me hours to find it again, he loosened his hold on me ever so slightly. I spun in his arms to face him, ready to yell at him for grabbing me so roughly and basically kidnapping me.

I had to admit it though, a small part of me was relieved to see him. Now he would have to answer my questions.

The predatory look in his eyes stopped the words from tumbling out and I remembered the sharp anxious feeling I had felt right before he grabbed me. He scanned the surrounding forest with piercing eyes; it was like he had been born in the trees. No movement escaped him.

I swirled my fingertips subtly to tell Ivy I was alright for now, but Jeremy caught the slight movement. His face became a mask of quiet rage before he turned back to scan the trees again.

"What are we hiding from?"

I wasn't stupid. I had put the pieces together. The creepy anxious feeling, the stillness of the birds, and Jeremy's actions as he dragged me into the trees. He hadn't murdered me yet, so I could only assume we were hiding from whatever had given me that awful feeling of before.

Ivy paced my field of vision impatiently. If I pushed her too far or if she thought I was in any more danger, she would send out a rapid alert without bothering to ask my opinion.

Jeremy turned to face me again, eyes blazing with a mixture of fury and predatory focus.

"Tell that AI of yours to shut the hell up if it knows what's good for you." He shook his head.

"I doubt it really knows anything though. Just keep that stupid chip of yours quiet. There is something out there, and I would bet my life on the fact that it can track you through that stupid chunk of metal in your head." His voice was hushed, but there was no masking the disgust and anger in each word.

I took an involuntary step away from him, dazed by the venom of his words. That answered the question if he had an AI of his own. Ivy had hinted at it earlier, but this went way beyond that. It was like he despised me, or at least Ivy.

I had no idea how to respond, but Ivy cut me off, face contorted with pure hatred. I was glad she was stuck in my head and couldn't haul off and punch him in the face. She looked like she would happily strangle him if given the opportunity.

Arianna, get the hell away from him now. He is beyond trouble. This boy is dangerous and will get you corrected.

She spat the word at me like it was a venomous snake. I couldn't move. I felt trapped between two enemies ready to duke it out; only one was in my head. I didn't know who to respond to first, so I chose Jeremy, currently the slightly less terrifying of the two.

"Ivy won't do anything to get us in trouble or to endanger us."

Which he would obviously know if he had one. I wasn't ready to let him know that I knew he didn't have an AI. I had not idea what he would do if he found out I knew his secret.

"And why don't you just tell me what the hell we are hiding from instead of being such an ass!"

Those were not quite the words I had intended to say, but I was pissed about his little anti-AI rant. That was my best friend he was bashing. Even if she was virtual, he had no right to assume anything about Ivy.

He scanned my face seriously for a moment, not a hint of remorse showing. He sighed frustrated.

"I'm actually not sure. I came back into the forest last night after you made it inside, but whatever had chased you left. There were some tracks, but they didn't make any sense. They looked human, but not quite right."

His words sent shivers scatting up my spine, visions of half human monsters flashing across my eyes.

"Anyway, I was counting on you taking the same route home today. I figured since that thing was watching you in here yesterday, it wouldn't be able to resist watching you again today. It looks like I was right." His voice steady and even, but his eyes never stopped scanning the trees around us.

"Wait, you were waiting for me?"

I clamped my mouth shut, instantly regretting the question. Of all the things to ask right now. Ivy rolled her eyes at me but was significantly less angry after my outburst in defense of her.

He stopped his scanning for a moment and flashed me a cocky grin, which faded a split second after appearing. My stomach tumbled in a funny way. No. Absolutely not. This guy was a complete jerk; a massive, irritating, moody stranger who in no way would make me feel anything other than an objective curiosity. I had bigger things to deal with.

He looked tired. He was constantly on guard, and I was sure he regretted that momentary slip. Ivy did not look impressed.

A twig snapped somewhere to our right, and he was instantly back on alert. He shifted his body in that direction, conveniently placing himself in front of me at the same time. For a complete stranger, who happened to hate everything about me and my AI, he was weirdly protective. I would have to ask about that, too.

Another sharper snap came from the same direction. This one sounded more like a branch being broken off. I shifted closer to him involuntarily, fear clawing its way up my throat, threatening to choke off my air supply. I glanced at Ivy, who I knew was scanning the area again. We both knew that Jeremy would not register, but anything else human should register on the Grid.

She shook her head, still picking up nothing. I hoped it wasn't something as sinister as Jeremy thought it was, but there was something out there, and it sounded rather large.

Jeremy put a finger to his lips, motioning me to stay silent, like I needed the reminder, and reached his hand out to me. This time, I took it without hesitation. He pulled me back, heading the opposite direction from the noises we had heard before. Jeremy was silent as he walked backwards, towing me along with him. Any anger or frustration had melted into fierce focus on the task at hand. He moved effortlessly, like a ghost through the trees, like he had done this a million times before. I swore under my breath, my feet became lead filled bricks, making a racket that anyone could hear miles away.

Jeremy cut to the left making a large circle. I pulled my arm back slightly and raised my eyebrows at him in concern. Why were we headed back towards the creepy snapping noises? Jeremy shook his head at my questioning look and continued, not answering.

We hurried through the trees, always at an angle from the noises. With every step, my heart hammered harder and harder. Jeremy tried to lead us from one clump of green moss to another, using the soft tufts to muffle our sounds, cringing every time I accidentally crunched the dried leaves beneath us instead.

We had almost completed a full circle when Jeremy suddenly yanked my arm towards the ground, forcing the rest of me down with it, until we were both flat against the earth.

Jeremy pointed slowly in front of us. I followed the line of his finger until I looked straight ahead and felt my jaw unhinged. An audible intake of air rushed in. Jeremy whipped around and covered my mouth with his hand, eyes bright and irritated.

I stayed as still as I could, my heart thudding in my ears, Ivy dancing through my field of vision, altering me as my heart rate has once again gone into panic attack range.

Through the thicket of trees, about twenty yards in front of us, was a figure. It stood still and silent, waiting. I watched the figure as it turned slowly in a circle, observing everything around itself steadily. When it turned to face us, my heart stopped beating altogether and Ivy tripled in size, blocking most of my vision momentarily.

I couldn't quite tell from this distance, but the figure looked strikingly like Sam and I's guard from school, Clyde. His features looked slightly less human though, more animalistic and predatory; something created to stalk and capture prey.

My chest constricted, and my lungs refused to work any longer. I moved the fingers of my free hand slowly, silently needing to communicate with Ivy. I knew when a panic attack was coming and seeing the figure in front of me had taken me from seriously freaked out to straight over a cliff. Now I was free-falling into an endless pit of anxiety with no hope of stopping it on my own.

Ivy, there is a man in front of us. Did you see? Is he registering?

Yes, I saw him through your eyes, but Arianna, he is not registering a signal to the Grid The only signal on the Grid right now is yours.

I would have groaned if I had the oxygen to spare.

He looks just like Clyde, but a super creepy version. Please, please don't send out an alert. I think he will find us if you do.

Ivy looked at me seriously and surprised me by nodding.

I think so too. Something that idiot boy said earlier had me thinking, just like I am using the Grid signals to track others, they might be as well, so I have been cloaking your signal since then. I promise no alerts, but if you can't get your heart rate under control, I will have to trigger a response or else it will send a medical alert out whether we want it to.

I nodded, mostly understanding what she said, though it sounded like we were now underwater. I could barely see Jeremy as her dainty fairy avatar expanded in front of me. My heart stumbled beat once more, out of sync, sputtering and restarting over again. I felt a tug on my arm, but it was hard to move. Everything was blurry, my body felt heavy.

Ivy started flashing the countdown for the second time in as many days. I watched in slow motion as her fingers fell one by one. I heard a snap, closer this time, and my heart gave one last terrified burst as her last finger fell.

Ok Ari, get ready. Take a nice deep breath for me.

My throat felt too constricted to follow along, and I heard Jeremy whisper my name several times. My thoughts were a muddled mess.

I turned to look at him, eyes wide, as Ivy triggered the hormone gland in my brain to release a large dose of dopamine. The dopamine would make me feel light and happy, without a worry in the world. I stared at myself in Jeremy's eyes, pupils blown out. His face was grim, mouth set in a thin line, and I couldn't help but think how incredibly attractive he was when he looked agitated, it was very frustrating for some reason.

I felt the dopamine flooding through my veins. My heart rate slowed and steadied; my cheeks flushed red as a smile tugged at the corners of my lips. Somewhere in the back of my brain, I knew that there was something wrong, but I no longer cared. I knew Ivy and Jeremy would keep me safe, which is really all that mattered. There was another tug at my hand, and I looked down at my arm. My eyes wandered up the arm that was connected to mine and into a brilliant set of green eyes, concern radiating from them.

I flashed him a dazzling smile, but he only frowned in return. I reached out with my other hand to hold his in both of mine and grinned up at him. He looked super stressed out, which was a total bummer. I should introduce him to Derek, they would get along great!

I couldn't help the bubble of excitement building in my stomach, but he didn't look excited at all. He needed to relax. I glanced at Ivy, and she bobbed silently up and down, eyes focused. She was always so serious, too. What was that about?

I was about to open my mouth to ask him what was wrong when he brought his other hand up to cover my lips, shaking his head sharply at me. I didn't understand what his problem was, but his hand was warm, and I closed my eyes and breathed deeply. He smelled faintly like trees and some sort of spice I couldn't place. It reminded me of the smell of crushed leaves in autumn.

Jeremy shifted onto his feet, pulling me upright with him, forcing me to open my eyes again. I smiled brightly at him and swayed for a minute, unsteady on my feet, which made him frown even more. A giggle rose from my chest to my throat at his stern expression. Maybe I could hook him up with Sam, if Sam was his type.

I let go with one hand to cover my mouth, trying to keep the laughter inside. He pulled me behind him and began backing away slowly. My feet felt ten times larger than usual, and I stumbled along behind him. A few times I stumbled so hard I fell into his back and then I couldn't help the giggle that escaped my lips, causing him to shoot a glare back at me.

He was frustrated with me, but it didn't really bother me. He was a frustrating guy. Maybe some quiet time in the park would do him some good.

One of my older teachers used to say that a walk in the park would always cheer them up, so maybe it would cheer Jeremy up. Though now that I thought about it, the park felt weird, almost creepy, and I really didn't want to stay in it. I shook the thought away, letting the happiness flow through me. For now, I was perfectly content with him leading me around.

Chapter 19

I caught glimpses of houses through the trees as we walked along, and eventually we were out of the park altogether. His face was taut, and his eyes held a fear in them I had yet to see. His expression didn't seem as funny to me anymore. I could feel the giddiness in my stomach fading with every side street we went down.

Ivy stared steadily at me, monitoring my vitals as my heart rate continued a slow and steady beat. It was like a shot of adrenaline for someone going through anaphylaxis; I felt calmer than I had been in a while, and even though I recognized the artificial flavor of it, my heart rate remained steady. I slowly replayed what I could remember from the forest in my head. The fuzziness cleared; the fog receded as my body processed the excess of hormones.

I snatched my hand from his, freezing suddenly as the image of the figure in the forest flashed before my eyes. My heels dug into the asphalt, and Jeremy stopped staring at me irritated confusion. His eyes glanced down at his hand, as if confused by its sudden loss, then flicked back to my face.

"Arianna? Are you back with me again? What is going on with you?"

Jeremy stepped closer, concern radiating from his face. His face was wide open for once, making him look almost vulnerable. I shook my head again; feeling like I had just slept too long, heavy and dazed. Questions spilled thickly out of my mouth, tongue dry.

"What happened? Where are we? How did we get out of the forest Jeremy, and was that really a man back there?"

Jeremy took another cautious step towards me, leaving only an inch between his chest and mine. I felt my cheeks heat, self-conscious, but I stared defiantly up at him. No way was this guy going to push me around, even if I had just freaked out and lost a tiny bit of control back in the forest. His gaze roamed my face searching. There was something painfully attractive about the contrast between his sharp rugged features and the open worry in his eyes. I shoved the thought aside.

"Do you not remember anything, Arianna? I was trying to keep us hidden from that thing. It may have looked like a person, but certainly didn't act like one. You took one look at him and froze. You just stared straight ahead for a few minutes and then you shuddered. A minute later you started giggling and smiling. It was all I could do to keep you quiet."

He continued gazing at me intently. I realized he had watched my entire transformation from fear to giddy, without knowing the cause. No wonder he was so concerned, I probably looked like a complete lunatic back there. My shoulders slumped, and suddenly I felt guilty for glaring at him.

"Your eyes glazed over, and you just kept staring at me. After a few minutes the man took off, and I dragged you out of the park. You couldn't even walk straight. It was like someone had drugged you. You just kept giggling. We are lucky that guy didn't hear you and come back, because the way he moved makes me think he wouldn't go down easily."

Of course he wouldn't know that it was Ivy who triggered the calming aid in the forest. Every AI is authorized to help calm you down. It's mostly used for people who get in accidents or have heart attacks, but people rarely actually see it happen to someone else.

It used to happen to me fairly frequently, after my father disappeared and I had severe panic attacks. All I remember is that my chest would freeze up and my head would spin and suddenly I would wake up in bed a few hours later. Ivy became especially sensitive to my heart rate, and I learned to control my emotions more. I hadn't had an episode in a long time.

"Arianna, what happened to you back there? What were you thinking?" Jeremy asked, exasperated.

I sighed.

"Everything is fine now. Ivy felt my heart rate go too high in the forest and, uh, helped me out. I'm sorry. I should have caught myself before it went too far. Thank you for getting me out of there."

Jeremy's eyes shuttered while going dangerously dark again.

"What are you talking about? What do you mean it helped you out? Whatever just happened was the opposite of helpful! You could have been caught by that thing!"

Jeremy's voice rose with every word. Frustration boiled in his eyes, and I tried to speak slowly and clearly so he could understand me.

"My AI, Ivy, is her name. She felt me freak out in the forest when I saw that creepy man. I started to have a panic attack, so she triggered a dopamine release which made me feel all happy. There is no fighting the dopamine, it causes you to feel giddy and excited no matter what situation you are in. It's like a drug. All the AIs can do it. It keeps people calm in emergencies."

I thought for a second before adding, "did they not allow endorphin manipulating in your last city?"

I didn't want him to know that I knew he didn't have an AI, that there was no way he would have known what was happening to me. For some reason I felt that it was safer for me not to let him know I was in on his secret.

Jeremy shook his head and remained silent. His jaw worked, clenching and unclenching, as if he was trying to figure out how to respond. I wondered if he would finally reveal that he didn't have an AI yet. Ivy froze, listening intently.

"No, our" he paused as if struggling with his words, "AIs wouldn't do something so stupid in my city."

Jeremy clenched his hands into fists and took a measured step away from me, eyes and face back to their blank mask. I had never met someone who reacted to AIs with such open repulsion. Though, I had never met anyone who appeared to not have an AI at all. Whenever I mentioned Ivy, he turned into an ice prince. I shuddered not wanting to think about what that meant, if he truly did not have an AI. It was absurd.

Arianna, you need to leave now, you could still be in danger. He is dangerous. You should be steady enough to make it home on your own.

I ignored her, needing to defend myself, and Ivy.

"Look, it was terrible timing, but I couldn't stop it. I freaked out, and Ivy took control. You shouldn't have had to see that, but you're the one who decided to drag me off the path. It looks like we made it out and away from that guy just fine though, so can we move on to an explanation of what the glitch you think you are doing?"

His expression was rigid again. When he spoke, his words were guarded but his voice still shook with anger.

"Your AI, Ivy," he spat the word, "is reckless and could have gotten you seriously hurt by drugging you like that. Don't you understand?"

His voice had heated, deepening with every word and the intensity of his stare sent goosebumps up my arms. He shook his head, taking a calming breath and continued.

"Arianna, you need to stay away from the park from now on. Find a different way home if you can, and don't go anywhere near it alone. Whoever, whatever that guy is, he is not your friend. He oozed cruel intentions."

I shook my head back at him. This was so dramatic and just too weird for me.

"I have no idea why that guy was in the park, and who knows maybe he wasn't after me at all." I suppressed a shudder, doubting my own words, and forced myself to continue. "That doesn't matter right now. You said he ran away. But you, why did you drag me into the forest like that? Why bother to help me? Who are you?"

Jeremy took another step away and turned slightly so that I could only see half of his face. He looked down. It looked like he was struggling to say something, like he was battling with himself, his broad shoulders taut with tension. He turned back and closed the distance between us with one long stride, reaching down to cup my face with one hand, eyes a shade so dark green they reminded me of the trees at dusk. His face was a mixture of bitter anger and something softer. Regret? He stared down at me, sadness flashing across his eyes before he tucked his emotions away once more.

I forced myself to step away from him. I had no idea who he was, but he was obviously going through something difficult. I didn't want to give him the wrong impression. I had only sought him out to save Derek.

Derek.

There was no way. Could this have happened because of the prank we pulled? If that man was Clyde, was he following me because the headmaster had sent him? But he hadn't looked like Clyde exactly. My head spun and I temporarily forgot about Jeremy until he started speaking again.

"Arianna, it is my fault that this is all happening. I put you in harm's way by talking to you yesterday and again by searching for your today. It is too dangerous for you to speak to me again. Forget that you ever saw me."

Any trace of emotion had bled out of his eyes the moment he started talking. His words sounded like a badly rehearsed performance, robotic and choppy. I clenched my jaw to keep it from popping open. Did he really think this was about him?

I couldn't stand it anymore. His whole holier-than-thou attitude, rescuing damsels in distress and then leaving them with more questions than answers. I didn't care who he thought he was. He was not playing with me this time.

I shoved him away from me with more force than was necessary. He clearly wasn't expecting my reaction and took a step back in surprise, eyes flashing. Good, I hoped he was as mad as I was.

I was over his little mood swings and the absence of the adrenaline and dopamine was giving me a headache. This time I closed the distance, stepping up to him, so close a deep breath would put our chests together. I stared up at him, forcing as much anger into my eyes as I could muster.

"Who the hell do you think you are? First you come in here all mysterious like, with your weird pants and your paper thing. Then you magically make your way through the forest, which you have never been in, at night no less, faster than me. Oh, don't forget how you causally went on about stalking things. Who even talks like that? And now you think that you are the cause of all of this?"

I paused breathing hard, face flushed with anger. This was not how I was supposed to spend my senior year.

"And please, I am begging you, stop calling me Arianna! My name is Ari."

I shifted forward forcing him back with every statement, matching him step for step. When I got to the last statement, I took one final step forward, but he had run out of sidewalk so once again we found ourselves toe to toe and all too close. Instead of remorse, his eyes filled with a sarcastic mirth, and the corners of his mouth turned up slightly.

I couldn't believe it, but he was getting a kick out of making me angry. Well guess what buddy, you've seen nothing yet. I opened my mouth to yell at him some more when he placed a figure across my lips, startling me into silence, an icy fury building in my stomach. My mind flashed to Derek in the hallway, his uncertain smile and a different finger pressed to my lips.

I was going to bite Jeremy's finger off.

"I am sorry, Ari." He emphasized the nickname with a toe-curling sneer.

I wanted to smack it off his pretty face. No one had ever infuriated me like this before.

He sketched a mock bow, looking even more ridiculous, and continued, sarcasm thick in his voice, "I have seriously offended you. Please forgive me."

He paused, "You are so different from what I thought you would be like." His last sentence was quiet, like he didn't mean for it to be said out loud.

Ivy perked up. So did I.

"What? What do you mean?"

Jeremy just shook his head, face once again a mask of indifference. He glanced around, shifting his weight from leg to leg, as if contemplating running. I wish he would try. I bet I could catch him in less than a mile. He turned towards me, expression unreadable.

I folded my arms, ready to wait him out. Eventually he would have to either make a move or start talking. Either way I was going to get some answers.

"Ari, I'm not from anywhere you would know. Things are a lot different there. That's all I can tell you. And, I'm not a new student here. I'm just on a, sort of a temporary visit here."

Jeremy let his words fall quietly into the air, his face neutral, waiting for me to respond.

I shifted uncomfortably, wrapping my arms around myself. I wasn't sure how to respond. This was the closest thing to honesty he had offered. I decide to play his game, feigning ignorance to the end.

"What do you mean? Exactly how different is your city?"

"Different."

His response was tense, his voice low. He shook his head as if he could not believe he was telling me this.

"I'm not like you, Ari. I don't live in a city. I don't go to school like you do; I don't get dressed like you or eat like you or do anything like you."

Each word came out forced and harsh, like he was trying to reassure himself that there was nothing similar between us, like he wanted to create a wall that could permanently separate us.

His eyes turned furious.

"I am nothing like you, and I will never be like you."

He spoke the last sentence like a dare, pushing me to deny its truth, a truth I still didn't quite understand. His fists clenched tight, muscles straining against the sleeves of his shirt as if he were ready to fight.

"I don't understand what you are saying Jeremy, but we don't need to be friends. I get it, you don't like me, or Ivy, or my city. I just want to know why you are here."

I knew he didn't have an AI, but I didn't understand the seething anger radiating from him. It was my turn to take a step back, and this time, we let the distance remain. It seemed like every action he took was driven by some innate survival instinct. He stared at me hard, mind made up.

"Arianna, sorry, Ari."

He hesitated for a breath moment, then he spoke low and fast, causing me to lean towards him unconsciously to hear him better.

"I am not supposed to tell anyone this. I swore to never let anyone know, but you need to understand how dangerous it is for you to be around me. Ari, I don't have an AI. In fact, I don't even have a chip for one to be programmed into. I wasn't born in a hospital like you, so I never had one installed. I'm only even in this city to find my father."

He paused and examined my face, waiting for me to freak out. I was freaking out, but I would not give him the satisfaction of seeing me do it. Instead, I kept my face smooth and composed.

"How is that even possible? Everyone must have a chip. It's a safety requirement for everyone. You can't survive without one."

I recited the lines that were drilled into me since before I could talk. You weren't supposed to be able to survive without a chip, but here he was, clearly alive and mostly sane. I briefly wondered how he could have entered the city. I thought we had detectors which would identify any Rogue trying to enter the city.

Rogues were people who had gone through life without a chip. People who had run away when the cities first started implanting the chips to everyone. This was a long time ago, though, before it was required for every baby to be chipped. Even then, it was rare for someone to get away with being a Rogue for long. Eventually they were found and chipped, kind of like a wild animal. Most of the time, they went straight to a correctional chip, too. Rogues were supposed to be a thing of the past, but Jeremy was a Rogue. There was no other way he could be here, standing in front of me, without a chip.

"And you father's here? In the city? Does he have a chip?"

Jeremy spoke quietly once again; voice still whisper quiet.

"I've already told you too much as it is, I'm sorry but I can't tell you anything else. Do you understand why you can't be seen with me? If they catch me, and you are with me..." He shuddered. "I shouldn't have followed you into the forest, but I'm glad I did. Now, I have to go. I'm only going to put you in more danger."

"How do you even know about the city, and AIs? For someone who doesn't have an AI, you sure seem to have strong opinions about them. And let me remind you, you were the one waiting for me today, not the other way around."

He remained quiet, refusing to give me any more information. His mouth dipped into a frown. I tried a different tactic, hoping to get him talking again.

"Alright, fine. You said you were here to find your father. Was that why you were looking at your paper the other day? Does it show where you father is? Did you find him?"

"No. I haven't been able to."

He took another step back, as if a few feet between us would make a difference. His eyes held something like regret again, before shifting back into that icy mask of his.

He may try to keep himself under lock and key, but I was beginning to recognize his tells. How he clenched his fists when he was frustrated or nervous, how he squared his shoulders when he felt his control slipping. It must be exhausting to stay this guarded all the time.

I stood still for a moment, taking it all in. I glanced at the time, blinking in the top right corner of my vision, and glimpsed Ivy in the other corner. She had stayed shockingly quiet, and her mouth was in a stunned 'oh' shape, as if she had forgotten to adjust her avatar after Jeremy's revelation.

Seeing Ivy brought a terrifying thought to my mind. Ivy automatically recorded everything that I said or heard. Everyone's AI recorded what they heard. Most of the time, no one ever listened to what was recorded. Whenever Derek and I played a prank Ivy would splice in a fake audio recording in case someone came looking, but judging by her shocked expression there was no way she had thought to forge this conversation. If someone was listening to the real time recordings we would be in massive trouble.

I was almost certain that the man in the forest was Clyde; the similarities were just too great. It was the only possibility that made any sense. Jeremy thought he was after me because I had been with him, but he had no idea that I was already on thin ice because of what I had done with Derek.

If Clyde had been sent to follow me around, maybe they were already tapped into Ivy's recordings. I had a feeling that ethics wouldn't stop these people from accessing files without permission. If that was the case, then they already knew enough about Jeremy to make him top their wanted list, and me right along with him. My eyes went wide with fear.

"Jeremy, we have a problem."

I whispered, trying to keep my voice as quiet as possible. Maybe if I was quiet enough, they wouldn't be able to pick up what I was saying over the recording. Ivy snaped back into action, her train of thought following my own. Her avatar stilled as she fled to the Grid trying to cover as much of our tracks as possible. Jeremy cocked his head to the side. Catching my expression, he stepped closer to me, grabbing my arms once more, the icy mask melting into genuine concern.

The heat from his hands on my arms caused me to shiver, and Jeremy moved closer, mistaking my shiver for fear. Our breath mingled as he leaned closed, filling the air with that distinct woodsy pine smell. I resisted the urge to shake him off, needing his nearness to keep my voice low. At least I wouldn't need to worry about him having an AI recording anything.

His concerned eyes met mine, a soft shade of green.

"Ari, it's going to be okay. I don't think that man saw either of us today. If he did, you can always tell him you have no idea who I am. There is no way you could get into trouble for talking to a stranger."

His voice was low and reassuring, but it did nothing to quell the fear building in my chest. I closed my eyes, cursing his ignorance.

"You don't understand Jeremy. Ivy auto-records everything. It's a failsafe system; the data is automatically transferred to the Grid unless it's disrupted. It picks up everything you say, everything you say and everything you hear. There is no way to get it back, and you are all over those videos. Everything you just said, all they would have to do is listen."

I ran out of breath, losing the ability to speak.

Jeremy cursed under his breath.

He looked anxiously around as if he suddenly realized how exposed we were, just the two of us standing in the middle of the street. It was already growing dark, again, and with my luck my mother would be home soon, discovering me missing for the second day in a row. It wouldn't be easy to get out of it this time.

"So, they already know that I am here?"

Jeremy asked in a muted voice, following my lead. I checked Ivy for confirmation, but she was still on the Grid.

"I don't know, honestly. Most of the time, they don't monitor it and the data just sits there on the Grid until the person passes on. Then their entire file gets erased to make room for another person's data. There are so many people in this city alone that there is no way they could possibly monitor everyone's AI recordings all the time. That would be crazy."

I said hopefully, knowing full well I was already on the headmaster's radar and the chances of them actively monitoring me were much higher than normal. I closed my eyes, counting slowly up to four as I breathed in, and then out for 6 counts.

Jeremy's eyes were locked on to mine when I opened them again, voice still low.

"Okay, I think I understand. So as long as they don't look up your recordings for the last two days then they would never see you talking to me."

Jeremy looked slightly relieved at the thought, and I hated to burst his bubble, but he needed to know the full truth.

"For the most part, you are right. But I did something terrible yesterday. I pranked a teacher and got a friend in a lot of trouble. I didn't think it was a big deal but that man we saw in the forest, I think it's the same guy who was guarding my friend and I, after we pulled the prank. His name is Clyde, and he is super creepy. I didn't get a clear shot of him, but if it is him, then that means that they are already watching me, and they may have already pulled my recordings."

I watched his expressions go from relieved to confused and then back to concerned. There may have even been some shock in there as well, but I might have just imagined it.

"What could you have possibly done to get them to watch you like that?" There was definitely some shock in his question.

"I pranked a teacher to break someone, someone important to me, out of a correctional AI. I just wanted to see if he was still in there somewhere. Anyway, it doesn't matter. It didn't work like I wanted them to, and they caught us."

Jeremy stiffened at the word corrected. He shook his head, frowning. He didn't ask for clarification, and I wondered just how much he knew about AIs.

"It was foolish for you to try that, Ari."

His words were soft, but it felt like they slapped me. Fury surpassed fear and I was yelling at him, my fried emotions getting the best of me. He did not know what it was like to see someone sit there like a zombie under the influence of a correctional AI.

"You don't understand you freaking Rogue! You are not even from here! Derek is my friend, and he doesn't deserve to be corrected for the rest of his life."

I was panting, shaking from the spent emotion.

He just took it. His eyes focused, face slipping into the mask of indifference. I was sure he used it as a shield, hiding behind it whenever things got difficult, but he still held on to my arms tightly.

"I'm sorry, Ari."

His voice sounded sincere, but there was nothing in his eyes.

"I am sure he didn't deserve it. But you need to be more careful."

He shook his head and released me, his face becoming bitter.

"And it no longer matters why I was here. I have to leave now, so don't worry about it."

Ping.

Ping.

Ping.

Ivy was back, looking more frightened than I had ever seen her. The messages were from my mother, and I had to resist questioning Ivy while I glanced at them, brain moving sluggish from the overload of information.

I froze, having to reread them again. Twice.

Mom: Arianna, you have 2 minutes to get your ass home!

Mom: I don't know what you've done, but there is a man here from your school.

Mom: I swear if you've embarrassed me, I will see to it myself that they punish you.

Chapter 20

Everything seemed to slow down as I read the message one last time. It was all over. I stared at Jeremy with wide eyes.

"My mother just messaged me." I gasped the words out.

"Clyde is waiting for me at my house. I can't go back there! He knows I was with you. He's going to correct me and I'm going to end up a zombie for the rest of my life, just like Derek!"

I was officially in panic mode again. My heart rate skyrocketed, and Ivy buzzed back to life. She probably thought I was going to have a stroke at the rate my heart was going.

"Arianna! Breathe. Snap out of it or you are going to go into la-la land again and that will help nothing!" Jeremy shook my shoulders back and forth a few times, forcing me to refocus on his words.

He was right.

I took a few deep breaths, focusing only on my erratic heart rate, calming it beat by beat until it fell back into a normal range. It was still high, but I was safe from triggering a dopamine hit, for now.

"Good Ari, that's it, keep breathing. We will figure something out, I am sure."

Jeremy seemed so calm and sure of himself that I bought into it for a second. His eyes were distant, as if he were trying to solve a math problem in his head. He didn't seem to make much progress, though. I continued to stare at him through the message displayed in front of me, acutely aware of the seconds ticking by. A look of realization passed over his face, followed by a frown.

It was clear that he had an answer but was struggling with it himself. He closed his eyes, resigned, and spoke once more.

"Come with me, Ari. Leave the city. There is no other way to save you from what they will do to you."

His voice was strong and unwavering, but his eyes held a distant pain that I had me guessing just how ignorant he was. What did he think they would do to me?

I didn't know what to say.

I had never even considered leaving the city. The only time anyone left was to visit other cities and even then, we used the underground transportation rails. For most people there was never a reason to leave. We had everything we needed within the city borders, and there was only wilderness beyond.

Cities stayed mostly to themselves to make it easy to distribute and monitor the chips' data. Every city was slightly different, but they all used the same chip with the same software in them. The rest of the countryside was left to the wilderness.

According to our biology classes most animals had been affected by the same bioweapon that had been used against people. It put an added strain on their ecosystems and the animals which survived became stronger and larger, making the stretches between cities even more dangerous. Eventually, cities built large fences around their borders to keep the citizens inside protected from the dangers beyond.

There was no way I could leave. I knew for a fact that I would not survive. Ivy did everything for me. How would I possibly manage anything as intense as the wilderness, even with her guidance?

There was no escape. If I stayed, I would be corrected for sure now that they had proof that Jeremy was a Rogue and I hadn't immediately turned him in. I shook my head over and over. If he was really a Rogue, there was no way he could help Derek. Was there?

I didn't have time to ask. Ivy flashed the time; I was already way past the 5 minutes mom had given me to make it home. Jeremy had to be crazy, there was just no way. No one could survive outside of the city. That was the first thing we learned in school. The city and the AI chips kept us alive. They were the only things keeping us alive.

"Jeremy, I can't leave." His eyes widened and Ivy sighed in relief.

"No one can survive outside the city's borders. Maybe if I apologize and promise to never pull a prank again, they'll let it go. I'll promise to work hard and never step out of line again. I could beg my mom. She is really high up in the executive world, maybe she can help me."

I knew it was all a long shot, a pipe dream really, but I didn't have any other choices. My voice had gone shrill by and I had to stop to focus on my breathing once more.

"Arianna, you can survive outside the city walls. I grew up outside the city walls, remember? I don't even have a fancy chip in my brain. You can survive on your own and you can't stay here. They will not be forgiving when they discover who I am, who you have spent the last two days conspiring with."

"I wasn't conspiring with you! I don't even know who you are. How do I know you aren't one of them sent to lure me away so you can correct me yourself!"

I was panicking, backing slowly away from Jeremy. My chest constricted once more, and I fought to take deep, cleansing breaths. I needed to remain in control.

"Really Ari? You think I am one of them? Fine, you want proof. Here is your proof."

Jeremy reached into his side pocket and withdrew the paper he had been looking at the day before. He held it out for me to look at.

I grabbed the paper and glanced down at it. It looked like it was hand drawn in a faint grey ink. it was rough, but I could make out the twisting lines of the auto-rails running through the city.

I could see the clustered city center and the rings of houses stretching further and further away from the city. Towards the outer section of the map, there was a large circle which encompassed the entire city marking the city's borders, but beyond that there were more sprawling and twisting lines. These lines didn't make sense at all. Some were straight and narrow, while others zigzagged back and forth for a while.

I pointed to the lines outside the city's borders and looked at Jeremy.

"What are these lines? There aren't any auto-rails outside the city."

Jeremy smiled faintly back.

"Those are all paths that my parents have marked out. They are the ones who made this map. The thick winding ones are rivers, and the smaller ones are different game paths we use for hunting."

I scoffed at the thought of someone hunting an animal for food. It sounded barbaric to me, and a lot more work than was necessary.

"So, this is all you have for proof, then? Some ridiculous paper style map? That is supposed to prove that you managed to survive all alone outside the city?"

Jeremy shook his head and walked toward me. He took the map back in one swift motion and grabbed my hand, bringing it to the base of his neck. I tried to pull away, uncomfortable with the sudden proximity, but then I realized the skin under my hand was smooth and soft. His skin was tan and the muscles in his neck shifted as he bent lower for me to examine him.

I felt goosebumps rise across his skin, skin that should have dipped with the typical scar line that every person in the city had. When the chip was implanted at the base of your skull as a baby, it left a small faint scar. No one ever really noticed or cared because everyone had one.

Jeremy's neck didn't have a scar. The skin was unbroken and smooth.

I ran my fingers lightly over his skin, trying to feel something, anything, making sure it wasn't just a trick. He shuddered under my touch, and I withdrew my hands quickly with an involuntary blush. He stood straight again, clearing his throat, taking a careful step back.

"Now you know I'm telling the truth. Ari, there is nothing left for you at home. If you come with me, you can escape this life, what they plan to do to you. Maybe once we are safe, we can find a way fix this."

His voice was firm, but his eyes were pleading with me to see reason.

It was fully dark now, and it had been twenty minutes since my mother messaged me. I looked back at the message one more time and realized he was right. She was essentially threatening to get me corrected for getting into trouble. I couldn't go home. Just the thought of Clyde waiting to take me to who knows where made me shiver.

"Promise me we will find a way to come back. I can't leave everyone behind."

I let my statement hang in the air. There was a note of finality in it that made my heart skip a beat. Jeremy and Ivy both paused. It was clear he thought it was going to take a lot more to convince me to leave. Ivy on the other hand began swelling in my field of vision. Her face was a cross between anger and fear, but she was unable to control what I did physically.

Jeremy nodded solemnly.

"I promise we will return to your city, Arianna. We will save the ones we love." If he left, he would be giving up his chance to find his father, too. He reached for his hand out once more. I hesitated, looking around me.

"Ari, we have to go now. We have spent too long standing here, and I am sure they know exactly where you are with that hunk of metal in your head. If we have any chance of making it out, we have to move, and fast. Does that chip of yours have a live tracker in it?"

"I don't know."

I paused, trying to remember all the lessons we had about the features of our chips. A faint memory of a lesson came back to me.

"Yes, the chips have trackers, but they have to be activated. If you run away, they can turn it on to track you, but a red dot is supposed to appear in your field of vision warning you to stop running. I don't think Ivy can keep it from happening, but maybe she can."

I paused before adding that she had covered my tracks before. I wasn't sure if the same concept applied here, and I scanned all over my screen, half expecting to see a red dot appear. Jeremy raised his eyebrows in question.

I shook my head in response; we were safe for now.

Ping.

Mom: Time is up, Arianna. Come home now or they are sending someone after you. Turn yourself in and you may still have a chance at redemption. You have ten minutes.

"My mother messaged me again. She says I have ten minutes, or they are sending someone after me. They have to know I'm with you. There is no other reason for them to have escalated this so fast. A silly prank wouldn't warrant such a dramatic reaction."

A silent pang shot through my heart. How was it so easy for my mom to turn on me like that? Was she really the same person who married my dad? Jeremy saw the hurt on my face, voice softening as his hands clenched into fists at his sides.

"Respond to her. Tell her you are coming home right now. Tell her you are sorry."

I shot him a look of fear and he held up his hands placating.

"It may give us some more time, Ari. We need more time before they realize you are not coming back on your own. Judging from her messages and the fact that we are not currently surrounded, I think they are waiting for you to give yourself up. But we need to hurry."

I nodded in agreement. They probably thought they still had complete control over me. I typed up a message to my mom.

Ari: I'm sorry mom, you're right. I am on my way home now. I'll be there in ten minutes.

"There I sent it. I told her I would be home in ten minutes, but I'm not sure she will be convinced."

Before I had even finished my sentence I heard another *Ping*. Ivy was shaking her head back and forth. She did not want me to open the message. This was not a good sign. I held up a finger to Jeremy, signaling him to wait.

Mom: Arianna, the man from school told me to tell you not to worry about the boy. If you come home now, he will forget that you ever spoke with him, and this whole situation will go away, but you must move away from the boy now.

Mom: Please to do what he says, and quickly.

As I read the last sentence, my mother's chat icon disappeared. She had turned off her chat completely. A sinking feeling crept through me at her plea, like ice creeping across a freezing lake. I looked at Jeremy with wide eyes, finally realizing what my mother's last message meant.

"Jeremy, leave. Now. Get as far away from me as you can. They know everything."

"How do you know that? I thought you said they hadn't turned your tracker on yet."

His face was skeptical, but he spun around taking in his surroundings, bracing for a threat to appear. His ignorance would get us both caught.

"My mother's last message was clear. Clyde is waiting for me. They must have a way to track me without me even knowing. I should have known. These chips make us walking targets. The only way you will escape is if you leave now. I can't go with you."

I took several steps away from Jeremy and when he tried to step closer; I shook my head no. He stepped forward, refusing to leave me behind. He didn't understand.

I felt the hairs raise on the back of my neck and I knew I was out of time. With one last look at his confused face, I turned and ran. I ran without knowing where, with only the thought of getting as far away from Jeremy as possible.

As I rounded my first turn, I took a moment to glance back, but Jeremy was already gone. He had disappeared so quickly that I doubted for a second whether he was there at all to begin with. It wasn't until I turned the corner fully that I saw Clyde standing in the middle of the street, illuminated by the streetlight, with his arms firmly across his chest.

Chapter 21

I froze the moment I saw him, swirling my fingertips through the air to bring Ivy sharply into focus. She and I knew it was too late for me to escape now. I dropped my hands casually to my sides as I walked towards Clyde, with slow and even steps. I refused to let my fear show.

His gaze was fierce and penetrating as he analyzed my every move, and I hoped he couldn't make out the subtle movements of my fingertips. Left-hand, pointer finger up, right-hand pinkie down, left thumb in, right thumb out.

Only Ivy would know what these signals meant.

Once when I was about 6 years old, before dad had disappeared, I had gotten in trouble for sneaking out of the house to meet up with Ashley. I had successfully made it out of the house, delivered Ashley the cookies she had requested from our pantry, and made it back to the house undetected, yet I was still in trouble the next day.

It was then that I found out that my parents could access and read anything I typed into Ivy or anything Ivy recorded for me, through the parental settings. It took one scan for them to read Ashley and I's entire conversation.

I hated that they could look up anything they wanted, so when dad disappeared and Mom became even more nosey, I had a chat with Ivy. We developed a code that would tell her to hard erase everything from the last 24 hours, or at least as close as she could get to erasing.

Not many things could be permanently erased from the Grid, but Ivy could encrypt the data so carefully that it would take several days to break the encryption. I had only used the code on two occasions; to hide information about Derek from my mother, and to hide the whole Mr. Davidson and Headmaster Steele incident.

I needed that the encryption now more than ever. I did not know what had been recorded about Jeremy, and I needed to make sure any other data remained safe for as long as possible. It was one thing to tap someone's AI and see their feed live, but to have it recorded and analyzed repeatedly, he would have no chance.

Ivy's encryption process took time. I slowed my steps to a crawl as I saw one screen after another go blank. By the time I stood directly in front of Clyde, the only thing left was a blank messenger screen with the words 'password required' in bright red across the top.

I stood still a few paces from Clyde. He still had his arms crossed arrogantly across his chest. His frown turned to a sneer as I stood waiting for him to make a move.

"Where is your little friend, Ms. Salvante?"

It was obvious that Clyde expected me to quake with fear under his gaze. I may have cowered in fear in the forest, but he wouldn't catch me off guard again. I double checked all my screens, video, audio, and chat messages. Everything was now encrypted thanks to Ivy's skills.

"I don't know what you are talking about."

I tried to keep my voice smooth and even, steadily holding his gaze. The longer I stalled, the more time Jeremy had to leave the city.

"Don't be coy. We heard everything. We know you were with a Rogue. The city cams are tracking him as we speak, so give it up what you know for your own sake. The game's already over, but don't feel bad it wasn't a fair fight." His sneer became even more smug, distorting his face to an animalistic level.

I shivered involuntarily. I had no idea what game he was talking about, but I had to pretend. Maybe he would slip and give me some information that would help me understand what the glitch was happening. I felt like a child intruding on an adult's conversation, this was all a bit out of my league.

"Take me home. My mother is expecting me. You know who she is, right? You better not piss her off."

I was grasping at straws here, but my mother really was important to the tech world, even if I wasn't important to her. The pavement crunched as I shifted from one foot to another, unable to keep still. Ivy fluttered nervously.

"Doctor Salvante already gave her consent for you to be placed into our custody for the time being, instead of this becoming a public matter, of course."

He had the look in his eyes of someone delivering a knockout blow.

Unfortunately for him, this revelation was not shocking in the slightest and I gave a shrug as if I couldn't care less. Ivy's form suddenly stopped moving. I hoped she was out on the Grid, preparing for whatever we were about to face. I trusted Ivy more than I trusted anyone; she would do whatever she could to keep me safe.

Clyde moved his fingers in the air and within seconds, a sleek black bullet car pulled up next to us. He walked to the side and opened the door, motioning for me to get in.

I contemplated making a run for it, but I was already stressed out and I had a creepy feeling that Clyde was a lot faster than he looked. I may out pace in the long run, but if he out sprinted me; it wasn't worth the risk. It was probably better to let Ivy do her thing. I walked over to the open car door as confidently as I could muster and got in.

The inside of the car was more luxurious than I thought was possible. The seat was made from a soft material that looked like leather, but less sticky. Soft blue lighting filled the car, and I could see there was a man driving who looked strikingly like Clyde. No, he was an exact twin the Clyde, minus the pompous grin. Clyde 2.0 sat staring straight ahead as the original Clyde got into the car and closed the door.

There was a strange, disorienting moment seeing the two Clydes side by side, like some glitch in a video game that accidentally allowed two copies of the same person to be present at the same time. It was unnerving, and I had to suppress another shiver. Neither man spoke, and on some unspoken cue, the driver took off, speeding down the street.

I stared out the window, breath fogging up the glass. It was clear that we were heading back into the city, but I did not know where. Ivy was still a blank avatar in the corner of my field of vision, so I couldn't ask her to pull up a map, which left me with nothing better to do than to try and pester some information out of the Clydes.

"So Clyde, I'm going to assume that's your name as well, are we going to pick up some takeout, have a nice little chat, and then you'll send me on my way"? I laughed hollowly at my joke. It fell flat even to my own ears, but I needed to talk, to say something, anything that would break the ominous silence.

"You know if all you needed was a friend, a break from your equally creepy twin, you could have asked, no need for all the dramatics."

Nothing. The car continued to speed into the night, ignoring stop signs and lights alike, like a bullet from a gun, refusing to deviate from its course.

Resigned to the silence, I watched the buildings grow taller and taller as we entered the heart of the city. The advertisements seemed harshly bright this late at night, like distorted stars under a thick black sky.

The ads twisted and danced, unaware that they were performing for only a lone terrified girl, in a sleeping city. For a moment I thought we were heading back to my school, but a few turns later, I lost all sense of direction.

After a few more agonizing moments of silence, we pulled up to a black glass building. It seemed short, only twenty stories high, compared to the towering skyscrapers all around it. Clyde and his body double got out of the car at the same time. Each of them stood squarely facing the back doors, acting as both escorts and guards. The latter was unnecessary; I knew my chance to escape was long gone. I chose the side closest to the building. There didn't seem to be a point in delaying the inevitable.

Ivy buzzed in my peripherals, letting me know she was back. Her face was full of fear, a warning. I knew there was little she could do at this point.

Closing my eyes, I opened the door. I took a long breath in as I climbed out of the back seat and breathed out when my foot hit the black pavement. I opened my eyes as I stood. Ivy grew in my field of vision, becoming a solid entity, her way of showing me that she was here with me to whatever end. My heart skipped a beat.

Just breathe. That was the trick. Don't concentrate on any one thing for too long and keep breathing.

A cool breeze brushed up against my cheeks as bead of sweat trickled down my back; the only outward show of the nerves coiling in the stomach. The Clyde duo stood on either side of me, the twin shutting the door behind me.

I took a step toward the front entrance, but original Clyde grabbed my arm, his grip unyielding, half guiding me, half dragging me to the left around the side of the building. Why couldn't we just go through the front door like normal people? Did they think the side entrance was more intimidating?

I tried to ask as much, but my mouth had gone bone dry. I licked my lips nervously as I stumbled along. The brave, tough act suddenly felt extremely childish. I was terrified. What was going to happen to me?

I looked at Ivy, but her avatar was frozen. It looked odd, her avatar tended to bob or sway when she left it, but it looked as if someone had hit the pause button, freezing the image in pace on my field of vision.

I followed Clyde around the building and down an alley. We came up to a steel door, barely visible from the light of a building's 50-foot advertisements across the street from us. I cleared my throat painfully.

"Where are we?"

Clyde refused to answer, instead unlocking the door and ushering us inside. We were in a remarkably small room. The only thing that appeared to be in the room was another door, with a small button next to it—an elevator.

I focused on breathing slowly, evenly, as we waited for the elevator to arrive, checking to see if Ivy had come back every few seconds. With an awkwardly cheerful ding, the elevator arrived.

I wondered what Clyde would do if I actually threw up on him this time.

I stepped inside and Clyde followed close behind. Clyde 2.0 stayed outside the doors, presumably to guard the elevator room until we returned. If we returned. I gulped.

The elevator made a sharp jerking movement, that had me questioning whether we were moving up or down. Beyond the initial jerking motion, I honestly didn't know if it had moved at all, but a few seconds later the doors were opening, revealing an absurdly bright hallway.

Squinting against the light, my eyes slowly adjusted from the darkness of the alley and the elevator. The hallway looked like it belonged in a hospital. Everything was too white. Immaculately, absurdly, white.

I doubted whether there had ever been a speck of dust in the place. Clyde let his hand hover near the small of my back, the closeness raising goosebumps up my spine. His proximity only confirmed my suspicion. There was no way he was fully human. The air surrounding him buzzed. It felt unnatural, like the very atmosphere he touched was disturbed by his presence.

"So, who are we meeting now?"

I turned my head, looking around, trying to commit as much as I could to memory. Ivy's avatar spun in a burst of motion drawing my attention. She looked pissed and frightened. I wanted to ask where she had gone, but there was no way to type a message to her without Clyde knowing and I didn't want him to even think about Ivy.

Instead, I drew my pinkie in a slow circle, trying to make it seem natural. Ivy shook her head once. She knew I was asking to record what I was seeing so we could analyze it later, if there was a later, but it looked like she wasn't able to record anything. That meant that something was blocking or jamming some of the AI features, which really didn't bode well for us. Clyde turned and smiled, like he knew what we had tried, and that Ivy had failed.

"This way Ms. Salvante."

It was the first thing that Clyde had said since we got in the car. The smirk slid away, leaving a blank mask, all business, with a hint of something else that was unreadable.

He glanced down the hall and turned back to me, an expression flitting across his face which looked remarkably like fear, something I was convinced he couldn't feel. My breath caught, and I closed my eyes, blocking everything out for a moment before opening them again.

Clyde took a soft step forward down the hall, then another, his shoes barely making a sound, something remarkable for someone his size. He was no longer concerned about me running away, and I had no choice but to follow him.

I trailed behind him as we made our way down the hall. I steeled myself, focusing only on my footsteps, and tried not to think about whether they had caught Jeremy yet.

Ivy paced across my field of vision, her expression dark and serious. She opened her mouth and I forced myself to move casually, desperate to hear what her plan was. As she started to speak a look of shock came over her face. She froze mouth open, then disappeared altogether. When she reappeared, she had shifted several inches to the right mouth still frozen open. I hesitated, one foot in the air, chills spreading up my arms.

Were they attacking Ivy?

Clyde paused as if sensing my hesitation but didn't turn around. I hurried to catch up, and he continued moving forward. Ivy froze and unfroze several times in rapid concession, each time her mouth opening and closing as if she was trying to speak. I couldn't take it. I was going to risk typing a message, no longer caring about the consequences, when Ivy disappeared and stayed absent from my field.

My heart clenched painfully. What had they done to Ivy?

Chapter 22

Without Ivy to guide me I slipped into a panicked trance. My mind drifted, and all I could think about was that the hallway had a sterilized disinfectant sort of smell to it. The kind that seeps its way into the back of your throat and coats your tongue. I swallowed thickly and began counting my steps again.

The hallway was rather strange. There were no pictures on the walls, no chairs or benches or plants, just blinding white lights and doors every few yards. I couldn't see how far the hallway went with Clyde's bulking form now only a few inches in front of me, and I didn't want to draw attention to myself by shifting to see around him.

As we walked further down the hallway, it felt as if the temperature was dropping slightly with every step. I searched my field of vision for a sign of Ivy, but still nothing. My heart rate was absurdly high, and she hadn't even issued a warning. It was eerie not seeing her floating form.

I was so fixated on scanning for Ivy I didn't notice that Clyde had stopped walking and slammed into his back hard enough to knock the wind out of my chest. His arm darted out inhumanly fast to catch me from spilling across the floor, and then released me just as quickly. For a moment I thought I had imagined his touch. He never made eye contact, just continued to stare at the plain white door he was standing in front of. We had reached the end of the hallway.

I felt the panic climb when a new form blipped into my field of vision. This thing, whatever it was, looked like Ivy, looked very much like Ivy actually, but I knew it wasn't her. It floated, staring docilely into space with a blank expression on its face. I wanted to scream. This was too much; I couldn't handle any of this without Ivy. I opened my mouth and then forced it closed again.

I needed to trust in Ivy. If this was part of her plan, I couldn't show that anything was wrong.

I looked around for a sign, something that would tell me where we were or what was behind the door, but like the rest of the hall, the walls surrounding the door were bare. The arm Clyde had used to steady me reached out to knock once on the door. He knocked so softly that I doubted anyone on the other side of the door could have heard it, but the door opened inward, nonetheless.

Clyde stepped to the side and motioned me forward into the room. I couldn't think of anything better to do, so I took a tentative step forward. The first thing that caught my attention was the glaring contrast between the inside of the room and the hallway. The room was lit in a soft warm glow, and each of the four walls were painted a different vibrant color. There were pictures of animals and what looked like amusement rides all over. The intensity of color was almost disorienting after the starkness of the hallway. It looked like a child's party planner had thrown every cliche child themed idea into one room.

I was so distracted by the colors that I failed to notice the woman who had opened the door. She was as brightly dressed as the room. She wore a pink and blue striped sweater which vaguely reminded me of cotton candy, and bright green and red pants. Over this ensemble she wore a tie-dye lab coat, as if coloring the thing would make it less intimidating.

As I inspected the woman more closely, I noticed all her clothing looked somehow off. Her shirt had several snags and holes in it, her pants were frayed around the edges, and there were dark spots on her lab coat that didn't quite fit the tie dye pattern. Compared to this woman's terrifying aura, Clyde seemed like a benign kitten.

She noticed my observation and gave me a beaming smile that stretched her lips tight enough to show cracks in her hot pink lipstick. Just like her clothing, there was something off about her smile.

I felt like I was staring at one of those carnivorous plants. The ones that paint themselves in beautiful flowers and sticky honeyed sap, sweet just long enough to ensnare the helpless fly that wanders into their trap. I wanted to scream. I wanted to scream and run, get into the elevator, and leave this place as quickly as I could.

"Why hello Ms. Arianna, we've been waiting for you!"

Her voice was falsely high and pitchy, as if she was trying to sweet talk a child into taking their medicine. At the word we I looked around, thinking there might be another person in the room, but it was only her, Clyde, and myself.

"I know you must be so frightened! To be up close to a Rogue! How terrifying! But don't you worry, we are going to take good care of you and make all of that bad stuff go right away!"

You could practically hear the exclamation points in her sentences, and she bounced a little on her heels with every word. Yet, her voice had an odd flatness to it. Underneath all the fake sweetness, it seemed almost automated. I did appreciate how straightforward she was, though. No dancing around with any baiting questions, not that I was going to give anything away that easily.

I cleared my throat a few times. The false Ivy was still in place, so I had no choice but to address the freaky circus clown lady.

"Who are you? Where are we? What are you going to do to me? What do you mean up close to a Rogue?"

As soon as I started asking questions, I couldn't stop, my fear causing me to ramble, one after another. At the word Rogue though I clamped my mouth shut firmly, teeth snapping. Her eyes sparkled darkly, twisting her face in a sinister way, and I wish I had just stayed silent.

"How rude of me! My name is Doctor Claire Marshall, but you can call me Claire if you would like. Your mother is very concerned about your inappropriate behavior recently, and after speaking with Ms. Stone, she agreed you would benefit from a little checkup. I understand you had a very exciting day, and I am here to make sure that you are alright and that you won't suffer any nasty effects from your adventures."

She closed the door as she spoke and then took a few steps towards me, holding out her hand in what might have been a reassuring manner, under different circumstances.

"Ms. Stone? Do you mean the headmaster at my school? She spoke to my mother?" Dr. Claire's smile dipped slightly, but it quickly snapped back into its thin stretched shape.

"Of course, silly. She is the person who reaches out to any parents who might have an, um, issue, with one of their children. Now let's talk about today. Do you want to sit down? Can I get you some water?"

At the word issue, she seemed to glitch, her entire body freezing for half a second before she recovered.

She motioned to a velvety blue couch. I didn't want to sit down, but Clyde had taken up position in front of the door, effectively cutting off any escape plans I didn't actually have. He had slipped back into that blank robotic stare, and it was clear that his part of the job was over for now. False Ivy was also in an oddly still position, and I wondered silently where the real Ivy had gone.

I turned reluctantly, walked over to the couch, and sat, hoping that the movement would hide my shaking legs. It seemed Dr. Claire already knew who my mother was, and my mother knew I was here, so there went that line of pleading. I would have to play along for now in this doll house of pain and try to think my way out of here.

When I didn't respond to her question, she merely shrugged her shoulders and stood, her movements graceful but almost mechanical, and walked over to a small micro-fridge sitting on the counter. She opened the neon green door and pulled out two bottles of water, then returned to her seat on the other end of the couch.

Dr. Claire set a capped bottle of water in front of me and set hers down on the table as well. She stiffened, eyes glazing over for a second, the painfully cheery mask slipping from her face as she scowled. It was over in a few seconds, but the change in Dr. Claire's demeanor was significant.

"So, tell me, how did you meet a Rogue?"

I looked around in confusion, and with no other real options, I reached forward to grab the water bottle, trying to stall.

I tried to clear my throat to respond and found it cotton dry and sticky. I rolled the bottle in my hands and feeling the cap; it was still tight, meaning hopefully no one had opened it. If it was still locked closed, it must be fine, right?

I unscrewed the cap to the bottle, hearing the snapping noise the plastic made as it came undone for the first time. I took a long slow drink, hoping to come up with an appropriate response before I finished. Screwing the cap back on, I realized the silence had growing awkward.

"Dr. Marshall, . . . Claire, I don't know what you are talking about."

The words sounded scratchy and weak. I braced, thinking Claire would get frustrated and yell or something, but she simply smiled, this one a remarkably genuine one, and shook her head.

That was when I felt it.

The first sign something was off was that the false Ivy started to glitch, moving erratically around the screen, pieces of her fading in and out. I wanted to laugh, thinking about how absurd all of this was, but my mouth wouldn't open.

My limbs felt heavy, weighed down by bags of sand. My eyes glazed over, and my ears rang softly. I shook my head several times, trying to clear my mind, but the movement made the room spin. The false Ivy disappeared, leaving my field of vision empty once more. Dr. Claire was up off the couch, walking over to me with her arms outstretched, as if to catch me.

I tried one last time to pull away, but my legs would not cooperate, and my mind forgot what I was running from.

As my vision faded to black, I heard a muffled voice saying, "Don't worry Ari, I'm here, I'll get you out."

I thought it was Ivy, but how could she talk?

She was gone.

But why would Dr. Claire say something like that?

Chapter 23

A dull ache in my head throbbed to the beat of the software jingle Ivy was signing softly in my ears. I saw her swishing back and forth as I opened my eyes slowly, shielding them from the light of my bedroom. As I watched her fly back and forth in front of me, I got the strangest sense of loss.

It was like I had been here, had done this all before, which was silly, of course I had woken up to Ivy's singing and dancing dozens of times before, but there was a nagging suspicion that something was not quite right. The thought slipped quietly away as the ache in my head eased slightly.

I came slowly out of dream land as Ivy ran through her morning checklist.

Heart rate stable, breathing normal, metabolism slightly elevated. I'm adding 500 extra calories to your allotment today.

Ivy chimed in, seeming happy.

She flitted in and out of my field of vision, but she looked fuzzy, slightly out of focus. I tried to focus in on her, but the ache in my head doubled with the effort so I let my eyes relax as she slipped into my peripherals.

I was exhausted, which was odd. I didn't I had done anything particularly straining yesterday but thinking back to yesterday caused the throbbing to return, so I let it go. Instead of extra calories, I wondered if Ivy would allow me to get some extra sleep, but it wasn't likely.

Ivy continued, spouting the weather for the day, advising me to bring a raincoat as there was a small chance of rain this afternoon. I loved the outfits Ivy picked out for me. They always toed the line between fashionable and as comfortable as I could get away with. I watched the outfit slide through the slot in front of the closet. It looked like she picked out a pair of comfortable blue jeans, a thin soft long sleeve shirt and a light blue jacket.

Odd. She usually stuck with my favorite color.

I slid into the jeans, appreciating the way the soft denim felt against my skin. My head still ached dully, and everything felt off, but even on a bad day, your favorite jeans could make it all better.

I gazed at Ivy again and fought a gasp.

She was suspended in place, but not quite frozen. Like she was stuck repeating the same half turn over and over, glitching in a way I had never seen. It was the creepiest motion, and I couldn't suppress the goosebumps that rose on my arms. I opened my mouth to say something, but then she unfroze, became slightly unfocused again, and continued moving as if nothing had happened.

Ivy, are you ok?

I typed the question without thinking, hands moving automatically.

Ivy stopped mid-swirl and floated in the center of my field of vision for a moment.

Of course, I am just fine, Arianna. Is there anything I can assist you with?

Ivy remained hovering with her delicate hands folded in front of her, the picture of perfect professionalism. Since when did Ivy talk like a glitching robot?

I shook my head, knowing it, whatever it actually was, would register the movement. The Ivy imposter nodded once and continued its way. She moved on, running through all my messages from friends who are just waking up as well.

As she read through the messages, I tried to think through yesterday. Something had to have happened to Ivy that I couldn't remember. There was no way she would willingly let someone, or something, take her place like this. And there is no way that thing impersonating her was my Ivy.

I strained, thinking hard, but everything was a foggy mess. I couldn't remember anything clearly, and an intense feeling of heaviness washed over me. I felt as if I had run a marathon and then stayed up for 48 hours straight.

I blinked a few times to clear my head, but the groggy feeling continued to press in at my temples, making the pounding ache overwhelming. I just wanted to go back to sleep, so I sat on the edge of my bed letting my eyes drift closed against the weariness and ache.

Ivy nudged me awake with another alarm clock noise and I snapped my eyes open. I was suddenly very aware that I was going to be late for school.

What a strange morning.

I desperately needed a cup of coffee. I entered the kitchen and walked over to the fridge to read the note my mother always has her AI leave for me, but to my surprise there was no note this morning. There was nothing there at all.

I wondered if her AI forgot today. Shaking my head again as a foggy feeling pressing in flipped through the breakfast items. On rare occasions, Ivy would slip in some coffee, even though technically we were not supposed to have coffee as an option until we turned 18, but today I would need that caffeine.

I flipped through all the options twice, and of course, no coffee.

Ivy could modify the list, but wait, this wasn't really Ivy so I doubted I would get any coffee. I picked two items at random, swallowed the two immune pills that came out with my food, so the Ivy, not Ivy, wouldn't lecture me. Heading out the door, I hoped that the fresh air would help clear the fog hanging over my brain.

A moment later, I looked up to see the neon yellow auto-rail car pulling into the station. I shook my head. How did I get all the way to the station? I couldn't remember any of the walk there. Everything felt too bright, and I suddenly felt anxious, but I had no idea why.

I spun around; I needed to find someone, a boy, no two boys? Why would I need two boys? Wasn't one hard enough to handle?

I glanced at Ivy, but she was struck in a loop again, swirling around and around in an almost psychotic looking way.

I shook my head as a flash of lightning behind my eyes set my head spinning. Pain forced my eyes closed and my breath caught in my throat. I pressed my hands into my temples, fighting the urge to curl into a ball on the ground.

Why wasn't Ivy warning me of my heart rate? I could feel my heart pounding in my chest. I tried to focus on my breathing, and, through the pain, I felt a hand on my shoulder. In an instant, the light and pressing weight receded behind my eyes. Blinking hard, I saw Ashley standing in front of me with a concerned look on her face.

"Ari, are you alright?"

Ashley was half laughing, half nervously looking around. I blinked a few more times. As the pain receded, a dense fog to crept in, settling over my brain, making my head feel heavy. Something was not right. Ash was still looking at me concerned, and I realized that she had gotten off the stalled auto-rail to come get me.

"Hey, Ashley! I am sorry about that; I am still partially asleep today!"

My mouth was moving, and words were coming out, but it wasn't me. My voice sounded bright and cheery, and held an odd waver I normally didn't have.

I opened my mouth to ask Ash what the hell was going on, but a stupid smile plastered itself on my face, keeping my mouth shut.

I wanted to puke as I realized I couldn't speak. Ash looked slightly taken aback by my sudden change in demeanor, but quickly covered it up by smiling back brilliantly and taking my hand.

I closed my eyes tight for a moment, the fog closing in harder than before. I tried to fight the pressure building behind my eyes, but as I took a deep breath in, everything suddenly felt fine. It was as if a weight released, and my head cleared.

I was fine.

Nothing was wrong.

My friend Ashley was here, and it was time to go to school, that was all. I was just overly stressed about school and desperately needed some more sleep.

I smiled up at her again, feeling more relaxed this time, and let out a deep breath. What was I even freaking out about before? I squeezed Ashley's hand, and we walked to the bus. I listened to her chat endlessly about the latest Feed scandal and nodded enthusiastically whenever she looked in my direction.

Every once in a while, her pitch went an octave too high, reaching an odd screeching level, but when I glanced at her, she was looking away.

The rail ride to school passed in an instant. We pulled up to the school with a hiss of the breaks, and I felt myself pull out of a fog again. What had Ashley just said?

"Ari, you don't look very good. Are you sure you are feeling alright?"

Ashley's voice was tight and pinched. Sam, who I hadn't even noticed before, shook his head meaningfully at Ashley and she looked away, chastised.

"Never mind," she blurted. I wondered what was up with them.

Sam caught my eye, a deep sadness radiating there at didn't belong. I wondered what had made Sam so upset. At the tense look on Ashley's face, my mood shifted again. I didn't understand what was up with them, but I wanted to make Ash feel better. She was my best friend, right? I smiled up at her and squeezed her hand.

"I'm fine, I promise! I'm just a little tired. Must have had a long night! Are you ready for the history quiz today?"

Maybe if I switched topics, Sam and Ashley would feel better. He loved talking about school, so discussing our upcoming quiz should cheer him right up, the freak. Unfortunately, this had the opposite effect, causing them both to freeze, looking panicked.

Sam and Ashley exchanged a meaningful glance. It was like they were arguing with their eyes, and I couldn't tell who was winning. Finally, Sam shrugged, sighing; Ashley must have won.

Ashley turned to me and took a deep breath, like she was bracing for something. "Ari, dear, the quiz was yesterday."

She cleared her throat delicately, "Don't you remember?"

What a weird one.

Of course, I remembered. I thought back to yesterday, trying to remember the quiz and another blinding flash of lightning speared my eyes. It sucked the breath out of my lungs. I focused through the pain, desperate to remember, but there was nothing. Yesterday was a blank slate. Black. Gone.

Everything over the last day was gone, and as I tried to focus harder, clinging to the hope that something had to be there, my world spun and went black. I shook my head, my neck cramping from the tension in my shoulders. I gave up trying to wrestle the memories forth, wondering how many times I had already tried to shake this fog loose today.

"I'm sorry, Ashley. I don't really remember much from yesterday. Did we do well on it?"

I manage to squeak out as the blinding light and pain slowly subsided. If I didn't press too hard trying to remember, the pain was manageable.

I glanced at my field of vision. Ivy was a stagnant form at the bottom of my line of sight, drifting aimlessly across my field of vision. I tried to focus on her, wondering what her problem was, and a strange thought struck me. This wasn't Ivy at all.

Ashley sucked in a harsh breath, getting my attention again, and Sam grabbed her arm, shaking his head hard. He turned to look at me, his eyes distraught but determined. The look on his face stopped me short. What did I do to earn that look? What the hell happened yesterday?

"We did great, Ari," Sam said unconvincingly.

He pulled Ashley up out of her seat and led her forcefully off the auto-rail.

"We should really get going, we have. . . a project to work on."

Sam drug Ashley away from me, whispering fiercely in her ear while she tried to keep up. She had tears in her eyes as she turned away from me.

I felt lost and alone, and I couldn't even ask Ivy what was happening.

The fog descended slowly again, but this time I let it. I didn't want to hurt, and I didn't want to think anymore. I took a step forward automatically, not sure if I was even heading towards the right classroom, but I honestly didn't care. I was just too exhausted to keep fighting.

Chapter 24

The cold plastic of the desktop felt nice against my cheek. My eyes were heavy and dry, like I had been crying. I vaguely remembered walking to class, but it felt as if I had waded through quicksand. I lifted my head, squinting around, looking for Derek and Sam. They should be here by now. I should save them seats, I thought fuzzily.

I spread my bag and jacket out across the seats next to me, the ultimate sign for 'do not to sit here', but there was no need. As students filed into the room, they left a wide space around me. At least 2 seats in every direction sat awkwardly empty.

I glanced at my classmates, most of whom were friendly, but when I looked directly at anyone, they immediately became busy. Some even straight up avoided eye contact by staring at the ceiling or wall. Like that wasn't painfully obvious. What the hell did I do yesterday?

My shoulders slumped involuntarily. I couldn't go down that train of thought. I was too afraid of the pain. Something was seriously wrong. I needed Ivy, but this Ivy was all wrong. Everything was all wrong. I cringed, head aching, and pressed my face against the cold desk once more.

The late bell blared, its grating ring forcing my head up in time to see Sam, escorted by a very stern-looking man. He was small and thin, with sharp analyzing features. When our eyes met, he gave me a slow, mocking smile, like that of a cat who has trapped a mouse in a corner.

Sam was visibly upset. One of his hands was clenched into a tight fist at his side, the other gripped the strap of his bag with white knuckles. His eyes were filled with fear and a quite rage that sent an electric shock through me. The fog cleared. I tried to stand, to go to him, but my legs wouldn't move. I strained, muscles aching from the effort. My leg sprang free causing me to kick the desk in front of me, loudly.

The resulting silence was deafening.

Everyone turned to look between Sam and the man, a sneer now stretched across his face at my struggle. Sam's face looked pained. He stared hard at me, like he was trying to communicate something, but the fog was descending again and I couldn't hold on. Sam's eyes dropped; his decision made. He slipped silently to the back of the classroom. The man he came in with glanced one more time in my direction and smiled broadly before turning and walking out of the room.

The room went from silent to barely contained chaos as soon as the door swung shut. People whispered fervently with one another while trying, and failing miserably, to glance between Sam and me. An ache pressed against my temples, but I ignored it this time. That rat-faced man had done something to Sam and judging by Sam's face, Ashley as well.

I glared at the door.

The pounding in my head was synced to my racing heart. I didn't care about the pain anymore, and I needed to know what happened yesterday. Why was everyone avoiding me? What had pushed Sam so far that he would abandon me in front of everyone? Why did he look so afraid? And where the hell was the real Ivy?

At the thought of Ivy, a fresh wave of blinding light blazed behind my eyes. I clamped my mouth around a shriek that was sure to cause an even bigger scene and dug the heels of my hands into my eyes.

I doubled over the desk, resting my forehead against the table, and breathed as evenly as I could, willing the pain to fade.

In the back of my head a voice whispered.

Hold on, Ari, just a little longer.

But everything faded to black.

Crap, I was going to pass out in the middle of class.

Everything was dark when I came to. It took me a minute to realize that was because my head was pressed into my arms, which were folded across my desk. I sat up slowly, using my palms to rub the sleep out of my eyes.

Had I just fallen asleep in class?

My head felt thick, like everything was coated in muck. Where were Sam? Why didn't he wake me up when class started? My mind blanked as I searched the classroom, only to find Sam sitting stiffly in the back, far away. Why the heck had they sat all the way over there?

Mr. Davidson cleared his throat at the front of the room. He was clearly struggling through roll call. No one was even pretending to listen to him. He paused, as if knowing the next name he called would only make things worse.

"Derek DeSoto?"

There was a lull in the noise of the classroom. Derek DeSoto. That was my Derek. Another shock of electricity cleared the fog. Everything sharpened slightly as I scanned the room again. No Derek. He wasn't here, again. Wait, again? He was gone before. He had been gone and it had bothered me. I pushed hard against the blankness of yesterday. It had to be connected. Sam, Derek, and this horrible feeling. A wall of blackness descended like a thick curtain shutting down every thought.

There was only pain. Then there was only darkness.

The bell rang shrilly, snapping me free from my daze once more. Moving on autopilot, I bent down to grab my backpack and smacked my face hard on the desk. Stars bloomed across my field of vision, and my eyes watered from the pain.

What the actual glitch?

I looked around slowly, vision coming back into focus. It took me a minute to realize I was no longer in History, in fact, I was in Composition, my last class before lunch.

The tables for this class were connected into blocks of 4, which was why my face hit the table instead of going through the gap between the individual desks in History. I groaned. How did 4 class periods go by without me even noticing? I groaned again, rubbing my palms down my face. I desperately hoped no one saw that.

I was utterly drained and beyond frustrated. Peeling my palms away from my aching face, I looked around, only to find the classroom empty. Thank goodness no one had to see that moment of pure grace. Unless, of course, I woke up with an ugly bruise tomorrow. I gingerly grabbed my stuff, standing on legs that felt filled with lead.

I shook my head again, thinking about the massive lecture Ivy was sure to give me if I ended up with a bruise. *Really, Arianna, how careless can you be?* The slightly insane chuckle which working its way up my throat shriveled up and died, a shiver crawled its way down my spine.

What was wrong with Ivy?

I looked at Ivy in desperation. She should have popped up a few times by now, but still she sat, unnaturally still in the corner of my vision, almost completely unnoticeable. Ivy should have alerted me that class was over, and she should have said something when I hit my face, or at least asked if I was alright. I paused mid-stride, clutching the door frame for support.

My head seized, my chest tightening. Thinking became an excruciating endeavor, so I just stopped. I stopped thinking; I tried to stop feeling. I let myself go, surrendered to the ache, the fog that constantly seemed to linger at the edges. It was all too much. And just like that, the ache receded, the blinding pain diminished, and I could move forward again. I took a shaky step forward, heading into the hallway. If I could just make it to Ash and Sam, everything would be alright.

Each step took almost more effort than I could give, and I was exhausted by the time I stepped into the sun. I looked around at the clumps of students huddled together; they laughed and chatted, but their faces looked foreign, like I had never seen them before.

I pressed on, ignoring how their chatter died the moment they saw me. Ash and Sam should be at our spot, our favorite table under a big old maple tree. I loved the way the leaves changed into the most vibrant red in the fall.

When I spotted them, they were under the tree arguing, which, to be honest, wasn't an unusual sight. I sighed; I didn't have the energy to deal with their petty fighting today. Ashley had her arms folded across her chest and was glaring at Sam. He was shaking his head and pointing away from our spot, clearly telling her to move to another table. Neither of them had noticed me approaching.

Ash kept glaring at him until he threw his hands up in the air and sat down on the table in defeat. He immediately swirled his hands in the air, eyes focused on his field of vision. He looked as exhausted as I felt. His eyes were red rimmed and I wondering briefly if he had been crying. It took me a moment to notice that both of his hands were shaking.

When I was just a few feet away from them, Ashley turned towards me, a painfully fake smile plastered on her face. Her lips stretched up awkwardly, showing more teeth than normal, and her eyes swirled with concern. I opened my mouth to ask if she was alright, or at least I was trying to open my mouth, when a dark figure stepped in front of me.

Derek? No, he was too large, massive to be Derek.

It took so much effort to process the sudden appearance of not Derek, that I temporarily lost control of my limbs, tripping over a gap in the bricks on the ground and effectively launching myself into the stranger's chest. I felt the strangest sense of déjà vu.

I heard a soft grunt and then a less-soft curse as rigid arms bracketed themselves around me, preventing me from falling and doing any more damage to my face.

There was a deafening silence in my head as I looked up at his rugged face. He looked pissed, angrier than any stranger had the right to be, even if I did just gracelessly slam into them. I tried to push off his stupidly hard chest, but his arms stayed firmly clamped around me. My neck cricked from looking up at such an awkward angle, and for the umpteenth time, I wondered where Ivy was in all this. His face was so familiar, I felt a sudden mixture of anger and relief so potent I wanted to sag into his arms, but the anger won, and I glared up at him instead.

"Hello, Arianna."

His voice was far softer than the rage radiating from his eyes. He smirked a stupid half smile and suddenly my head, and the entire world along with it, split in two.

At first, there was only pain. Pain like I had never felt before. Pain, I was sure, meant the end of me, the end of everything. The pain was so intense it was blinding, white hot lightning radiating in crackles through every fiber of my being. I heard screaming somewhere in the distance, but I knew it couldn't be me; the pain was too much for me to even move, to ever move again.

It went on and on; the lightning tearing through my mind, crippling my thoughts, until I only wished for darkness.

Then as if my wish was granted, there was only darkness. The pain stopped with such abruptness that the absence of pain caused a numbing pain of its own.

Slowly, like a door being cracked ever so gently, memories came trickling into the darkness, brief spots of light and sound. A cocky grin, dark brown eyes full of mischief that slowly turned into deep pools of nothing. Laughter pierced by a heart wrenching cry. And then I was running through a park. Running from something bad, running into something hard and unforgiving but oddly safe. So much running. The stranger was there.

In every memory, a bit more come through. A soft kiss in a dark room, a paper map with swirling lines. A hand holding mine and a set of fists clenching, holding themselves back. Puzzle pieces rapidly forming a picture, no, two pictures. One more as familiar as the sun, the other, a shadow beckoning.

The images faded, quickly replaced by a dozen others. There was creepy looking man, and then a second somehow creepier version of the same man, a swift drive through a sleeping city, a long sterile looking hallway, a brightly colored room which hurt to look at. The whirlwind of images stopped. Darkness coated everything once again, cooling the ache in my head.

My limbs tingled, and from far away I felt my legs give out. I briefly wondered how badly it would hurt to hit my head on the stone floor of the courtyard. The hit never came, instead the world shifted slightly as the arms holding me up maneuvered to grab under my legs and back. I felt a strange weightlessness and then a darkness deeper than night silenced everything.

Chapter 25

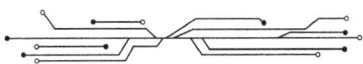

Deep in the darkness, I felt a tug.

Soft mumbling noises filtered through the deep, disrupting the quiet. I wanted to tell them to shut up; they were disturbing my peace, but they were too far away. I realized the voices were not inside my head, but above me. There were several voices above me, whispering loudly, and one of them sounded a lot like Ash.

"I don't care who he says he is, or how he says he knows Ari. There is no way I am letting him take her! Look at her! She can't even stay conscious!"

Ashley's voice was high and fast, every ounce of her bossy attitude thrown into it. Sam's slightly calmer voice came through next, ever the patient realist.

"Ash, I don't like this either, but they CORRECTED her. She's breaking it too; she has to be. That's why she keeps going in and out. You didn't see the way she looked at me in homeroom. She was in there. She was fighting. That's why she was in so much pain. We have no idea how to help her, but maybe this guy can."

His voice was thick by the end, unable to hold back his anguish any longer.

A third voice spoke out, sweeping the darkness away like wind clearing away a morning fog.

I knew that voice. It was Jeremy. But why was he here?

Each memory locked into place, our first meeting, him saving me in the forest; me sacrificing myself to save him, the doctor's doll house of horrors. It rushed over me like a wave threatening to pull me back under, but I was done submitting to the darkness.

"You need to let me take her. She's in danger now. The people who took her yesterday are terrible people. They do a lot worse than 'correct' unruly teenagers."

His voice was ragged and scratchy, betraying more emotion than his usual mask allowed him to.

"She gave herself up to let me escape. I have to help her now."

Despite the hidden emotion, Jeremy's voice did not waver. His resolve came through with each syllable. I struggled against the darkness. It was no longer comforting; it was suffocating. I needed to talk to them. I needed to warn them.

Arianna, wake up. You need to get up now.

Ivy's voice rang in my mind, clear as a bell. I shot up and snapped my eyes open, and immediately regretted that decision. I clenched my eyes tight again as everything tilted and swayed disturbingly. A firm hand rested on my shoulder, keeping me upright.

This time I tried slowly opening my eyes, desperate to see Ivy, to confirm that it was really her, no longer caring about Ash or Sam or even Jeremy, for that matter.

I scanned my field of vision, trying to see through the fuzzy blur. Ashley's face took up the bulk of my line of sight, mere inches from mine, the smell of her peppermint gum mingling with the air around me.

"Hey, sweetie, are you okay?"

She asked quietly, worry oozing from each word. I nodded slowly, still scanning.

Then Ivy was there, dead center in front of me, concern radiating from her.

It really was her, no glitching, no weird edges or mannerisms.

"How?"

I asked out loud, not trusting myself to balance on one arm enough to type.

"Well, you passed out, and this strange rando caught you..." Ashley started speaking quickly, but Jeremy silenced her with a look.

"I don't think she is talking to you."

His voice came out low but with an authority that silenced Ashley in a way Sam or I could never do. I ignored them all, waiting for Ivy's response.

Ivy smiled sadly, bobbing up and down slightly.

They took you too suddenly. I couldn't find a clear route for you to get out, and once they had you in the building, it was too late. I knew they were going to correct you. If they found me, the real me, they never would have let you go, so I swapped myself with a fake AI decoy at the last moment. That is the one they "corrected", but they also drugged you.*

Ivy stopped moving, her fists clenched in anger at her sides.

They made it so you couldn't access the part of your brain that thinks independently. Every time you fought it, they dealt out pain to repress your actions. The code they used for the physical correction was so much harder to break than the false AI.

She paused nearly panting. I had never seen Ivy so worked up. My heart swelled realizing how much she cared about me.

It was like there was an additional chip I had to decommission. I couldn't risk swapping back onto your personal signal until it was destroyed. I'm so sorry, Arianna, it took me so long to break the code, and you were in so much pain.

She stopped talking and put her head in her hands. Her distress was so strong she couldn't go on.

"But you broke through it, didn't you? You saved me, Ivy."

My words croaked out; tears threatened behind my eyes. I couldn't stand to see her so upset. She had worked so hard to break me free. There was nothing artificial about her love for me. I would have given everything just to hug her, to make her see how important she was.

It took me too long; you suffered for too long. I'm sorry Ari. What they did to you, it's unforgivable. This is so much worse than we ever thought. If they do that, override a person's brain, not just their AI when they're 'corrected'...

She trailed off, shuddering delicately.

I shivered in response, thinking about Derek and the pain he must still be in. He didn't have an AI like mine, there was no way he could break out on his own. I needed to break him out, no matter the cost, but there was no way I could do that with everyone watching me so closely. Not when I was supposed to still be corrected myself.

I looked around, struggling to come up with an option. Ash and Sam were staring at me with wide eyes, having only heard my part of the conversation between Ivy and myself. The hand on my shoulder squeezed gently, bringing me back to reality.

Jeremy. Jeremy was here, at my school. Why was he here? This was the worse possible place for him to be! After everything we had done to make sure he got away, he came back here?

His eyes held a deep look of concerned, his jaw clenched so tightly that I almost missed the look of relief in his eyes. I looked away, unsure of what to say to him. How could I confront him in front of Ash and Sam? If we were lucky, their AIs hadn't already reported my very 'uncorrected' like conversation with Ivy. I scanned my surroundings, too exhausted to do anything other than sit like pawn waiting to be moved.

I was seated on the top of a table which was hidden from the courtyard. It was our table thankfully, so no one would intrude on us, especially with it being known that I was corrected. Everyone would stay far away from me now, and probably Sam and Ash. She would be devastated.

Everything was crystal clear and sharp, in an almost disorienting way after being trapped in that dense fog all day. I desperately wanted to sink back into Jeremy's arms, but I knew that would just give everyone the wrong idea. My body ached from the tension of the day.

"What is going on, Ari?" Sam finally chose to speak up. His voice was raw, and my heart squeezed. I had no idea what Sam had been through today, or Ash for that matter. Yet they were both still here at my side.

He was staring critically at Jeremy, practically shouting his distrust with his body language. He had his hand on Ashley's shoulder, taking the same pose as Jeremy, attempting to look protective.

Ashley shot Sam a look and shook off his hand.

She was staring at Jeremy too, but with a completely different expression. She was giving him that puppy-eyed expression which always made the boys swoon. Hot anger pooled in my stomach out of nowhere, instantly making me nauseous. Now was not the time to be making doe eyes at a dangerous stranger. I pitched over the table, trying to keep the contents of my stomach down.

"You need to calm yourself down. You are breathing too deeply; you'll make yourself sick. Short shallow breaths are better."

Jeremy used an uncharacteristically soothing voice as his hand moved to the back of my neck. He knelt in front of me and gently brushed the hair from my eyes. This was a completely different Jeremy that knelt before me. His eyes showed genuine concern, no trace of scorn or sarcasm in them.

I had to look away, my thoughts spiraling downward as the severity of the situation sank in.

What the hell was I going to do now?

They had corrected me, or at least they had tried to, and apparently failed, thanks to Ivy. They were clearly after Jeremy and now, thanks to him, me. There was no way I could go home after this.

My mom. . . I folded my arms across my knees and shoved my head between them. I couldn't believe her! She gave me up! She was going to let them correct me. I knew she didn't care about me, but I thought she would at least protect me out of some latent maternal instincts.

I sat up slowly, looking past a concerned Jeremy, to find Ashley's eyes. She had her arms wrapped tightly around her stomach, like she was trying to hold herself together and was no longer ogling Jeremey. Sam was standing next to her, angled slightly between her and us, as if protecting her, from us. He caught my eyes, grief laced through a determination to protect his sister.

"Ari, I don't know if you remember this morning, but there was a man. He," Sam paused, shuddering, "he threatened us. Threatened to correct our whole family if we spoke to you. He said if we saw you with anyone suspicious," at this he gave Jeremy a not-so-subtle glance, "and didn't report it, we would all be corrected permanently."

Ashley burst into tears at the last word, covering her face with her hands. She hated how she looked when she cried, so to see her that worked up, and in public, my stomach turned with rage at whoever had done this.

A glance at Ivy told me she was already on the Grid. I hoped she prioritized Sam and Ashley's AIs. She would need to feed them false audio or else they would already be done. They had risked everything for me. I knew Ivy would do the same.

I sat up completely and Jeremy moved quickly away, giving me space now that he was certain I wasn't going to throw up or pass out. Ivy reappeared looked tired but satisfied.

Are Sam and Ash safe? She nodded once.

But these people, they are going to keep coming after me, aren't they?

Ivy stopped pacing and looked straight at me; her expression serious.

Yes. Ari, they think you know about the Rogues. They want to use you to find them. When I was hiding from them at that horrible doctor's office, I accessed some of their files. They are desperately searching for any Rogues left outside the walls. So far, they have had no luck, until Jeremy showed up in your recordings.

I kept my groan to myself this time.

Ok, so what are my options then? I can't go home, I can't keep running they are bound to catch me at some point, and I can't keep endangering Ash and Sam. You were right Ivy; I should have just walked past that stupid boy.

I glared at Jeremy, which caught him off guard. He had been watching me type to Ivy intently, a stern expression on his face, and when he saw me glaring, he took a step back, eyes turning to flint. This was his fault, and now there was no way I could still help Derek. He would be trapped in that soul-sucking nightmare, potentially forever. A gentle ping brought my attention back to Ivy.

I've been running through every scenario I can think of. Ari, I don't think you are safe in this city anymore, at least not right now.

Her expression was cautious and inexplicably sad, like she was forcing herself to address the worst possible outcome.

So, I have to go with Jeremy then, don't I?

Ivy nodded reluctantly, confirming.

I glanced at Ash, who had stopped crying, but was still trembling every few seconds. She was wiping stray tears off her now red and blotchy face, visibly shaken. Sam looked on the verge of wanting to grab Ash and run or fight. Fight what exactly, I wasn't sure. Maybe Jeremy?

Jeremy was staring intently, eyes still flinty, jaw clenched as hard as his fists. I tried to stand up, but my legs buckled from being crouched for too long. I knew I was going to fall, but Jeremy was already steadying me, his hands underneath my elbows, holding me up from behind.

An unwelcome flush crept up my neck. I hated what his proximity did to me. It wasn't wanted and it wasn't helpful. I turned to face Ash and Sam, finally confident that my legs could hold me. Taking a deep breath, I tried to sound confident and convincing.

"Ash, Sam, I have to go with Jeremy."

I threw in a smile, which felt forced and more like a grimace.

There was a beat of silence before all hell broke loose.

Chapter 26

Ashley stepped away from Sam, eyes still glistening from unshed tears, mouth open in a small circle.

"Are you joking? Who the glitch even is this guy? Arianna, be honest with us, what is going on?" Ash was panting slightly as she finished. She looked to Sam for support, but he only stared straight ahead, avoiding my eyes.

"Go where, exactly?"

He had come to the same conclusion as Ivy and I had. I almost sighed in relief. It would be so much easier if he was on the same page. There really wasn't another option, and I knew he wasn't happy about it, but at least he understood, at least he wouldn't think I was abandoning them. I had to do this; it was the only way to keep them both safe. I couldn't save Derek, but maybe I could save them. Ash spun on her heels, shooting an accusing glare at her brother.

"What do you mean where?!" She was panting now.

"She can't go with him! Something is off about him. I've never even seen him before, and I know EVERYONE on the Grid, and I know he isn't a transfer. I'm the head of the transfer committee, I would have gotten a notification of a new student."

She stamped her foot as if to emphasize her supreme authority on the matter. She spun back to face Jeremy, pointing a perfectly manicured nail in his face, and for the first time, Jeremy looked genuinely nervous.

"You did this didn't you! You can't just take my best friend!"

Ash looked like she was about to launch herself at Jeremy, so I gently stepped between them, which unfortunately made me the next target. Ash dropped her hand and looked at me accusingly, hurt radiating in her eyes, wiping her anger away.

"And you! Arianna, we have been best friends since elementary school. What did you do? Things were perfect. Our senior year was supposed to be perfect. Then Derek happened, and that stupid creepy man showed up, and now this guy. What are you doing?"

She looked on the verge of tears again.

I swirled a pinky, sending a silent question mark to Ivy. Ivy bobbed up and down thoughtfully for a second and then nodded.

Only tell her the basics, and nothing about Jeremy. The more she knows, the more danger she will be in even without her AIs recording this.

"Ashley."

I took a step forward, but she stepped back visibly hurt, so I stilled, putting my hands up in surrender.

"Ash, I'm so sorry. Things got all messed up. I couldn't let Derek's correction go, so I roped Sam into pulling a prank to get Derek's attention again. It ended up causing *more* trouble, that's why I have to leave."

"Is that why they corrected you? Why didn't they go after Sam, too? He was a part of it, just like you were."

Ash looked terrified at the thought of her brother going through the same thing I did, but not willing to accept this as the only explanation. She glanced back at Jeremy pointedly.

Sam just raised an eyebrow at me knowing I was speaking in half-truths.

I shook my head, unsure of how to respond.

"This isn't about Derek anymore. After that incident, I ran into Jeremy. He's..." I hesitated, not knowing where to go from here.

Jeremy stepped up beside me, shoulder brushing mine. I was so angry at him for dragging me into this, for ruining my chances of saving Derek, for ruining my entire life. I didn't know if I would ever forgive him, but for now I was thankful that I wasn't alone in this.

"I'm not from this city. I came here looking for someone."

His voice was abrupt and left no room for questioning, but Sam didn't seem to care. Sam narrowed his eyes at Jeremy, glance flicking to where our shoulders touched. My face heated, but I didn't move. Better Sam think I betrayed them, that I betrayed Derek, then do something foolish like trying to come after me.

"So, Ash was right. This is all your fault, then. You came here, obviously in trouble from wherever you were before, and now Ari is caught up in this. You got her corrected! You're the reason our entire family is in jeopardy now!"

Sam's voice had steadily risen until he was practically shouting at Jeremy. Jeremy's arms tensed in warning, a tense silence falling as Sam finished. Sam took a sudden step towards me as if to pull me away from Jeremy, deciding that I was better off facing this mess with them than this stranger, but Jeremy was closer, stepping in front of me defensively. We didn't have time for chauvinistic nonsense.

"Back off, both of you." I let my voice slip into a quite rage, harnessing every lost dream I had, promising violence if they didn't listen.

Shock radiated from Sam and Jeremy as I stepped away from them both. I glared at Jeremy, who crossed his arms defensively but backed off, then I turned to Sam, giving him a glare for good measure. He threw his hands up in an exasperation.

Ivy twirled slowly to the center of my field of vision. We were running out of time. It wouldn't be long before lunch would end and we would have to move.

You need to make a choice, Arianna, and quickly, before the decision is made for you.

I turned to look at Ash and Sam, their faces a sharp contrast from one another. Ashley flitted back and forth between wringing her hands anxiously and glaring at Sam. On the other hand, Sam was openly glaring at Jeremy, attempting to incinerate him with his eyes alone. There wasn't a choice to make. I had to protect them.

I took a hesitant step forward, away from Jeremy and towards Ashley and Sam, causing Jeremy to tense up. Glancing back, I tried to give him a reassuring smile, but my face wasn't working quite right. I reached down and grabbed Ashley's hand, staring into that beautiful face of hers. She really was stunning, even after crying and raging about. Her eyes glassed over, a fresh set of tears rising to the surface.

"No, Ari, I don't know what you are thinking, but we can do this together. Don't leave, please..." Her voice was thick with emotion.

I desperately wished there was another way, but I only shook my head and squeezed her hands tightly.

"Ash, I have to leave. You guys aren't safe, and you won't be safe until I leave. You shouldn't even be here now, if they see you both with me and with Jeremy . . ."

I hoped I sounded confident and calm, but I couldn't help glancing anxiously around. Thankfully, it was still just the four of us. Lunch was almost over though, and if the three of us didn't turn up in our next class, people would come looking.

Ashley dropped my hand, and I took several steps back, right into Jeremy's chest. He touched the tops of my arms to steady me and then stepped half an inch away again. He was a solid presence behind me, reminding me I wasn't alone.

Sam grabbed Ashley's arm and pulled her further away, out of the tree's shade and into the sunlight, putting only a few feet of distance between us, but effectively creating an impassable rift between us. She strained against Sam's grip, but he held her tight, preventing her from closing the gap again.

Sam's eyes narrowed further and then widened in shock.

"Ashley, she has to leave." His voice was a growl Ashley and I had never heard.

Ashley stopped struggling and Sam pulled her further away from us.

"I get it now, why they won't ever let her go. Not from this city, right?"

His voice became a mixture of angry sarcasm and genuine fear.

His eyes flicked between Jeremy and me, all hope bleeding out of them.

"He is a Rogue. That's why they are after Ari now, because she talked to a Rogue, she helped him or something."

At this, Ashley uttered a shriek backing further away from us, no longer needing Sam to persuade her. Sam turned to me, disbelief echoing in his words.

"Did you know what he was the entire time?"

I couldn't respond, because didn't know what to say. I looked at Ivy, but she shook her head. This was too far. Sam and Ashley weren't supposed to know. Now they would be in even greater danger.

"We need to go, Arianna."

Jeremy's voice was low and strained. His muscles were tight, and he was staring at Sam in a cold, calculating way, as if sizing him up before a fight. I turned to face him, ignoring a sputtering Ashley behind me. Jeremy's eyes softened slightly as they found mine, his mouth turning down into a frown.

"I'm sorry Arianna. It's time. We can't linger any longer or we might as well turn ourselves in."

The lunch bell sounded clear and bright through the courtyard and into the alleyway where we stood. The sound sent a shock of adrenaline coursing through my veins, and Ashley and I both jumped. It was time to go back to class. If we didn't return immediately, our absence would be noted by prying eyes.

Ashley looked panic-stricken. Sam's eyes were still narrowed and flinty, arms protectively around Ashley, though she had stopped struggling the moment he had said Rogue. Curse Sam and his stupid big brain. I should have known he would figure it out. We had given him more than enough clues. There was a weird, stuttered silence as the fading bell echoed in our heads, no one moving a muscle.

"What are you all still doing outside? Get back to class now!"

Mrs. Alcorta, the computer science teacher, stood at the entrance to the alleyway with her hands on her hips. She was glaring at us. Her hair was slightly frazzled, and she looked like she could desperately use another cup of coffee.

Ashley, Sam, and I remained frozen, unsure of what to do.

I'm sorry, Arianna, I didn't catch her signal. I was focused on scanning Ashley and Sam to make sure their AIs hadn't picked up on the word Rogue.

Jeremy bent slightly down to where his lips brushed my ear and whispered, "We need to get out of here. Are you able to run?"

I nodded faintly as Mrs. Alcorta took a step forward and scanned our faces, irritated when we didn't immediately get moving. She glanced at me and tensed, recognition dawning on her face.

She had to know they recently took me in for correction. I'm sure all the teachers were notified. As she turned to look at Jeremy, I grabbed his hand and yanked hard downwards. He hissed in reply, but his face was hidden behind my back. I tried to think of the smooth slurred way my voice had sounded earlier.

I smiled painfully, forcing cheer into every word.

"Mrs. Alcorta, what a lovely day it is! I am so sorry for making everyone late. I wanted to enjoy the trees and we couldn't hear the bell from over here. We will head to class right now!"

I saw Sam wince. He was right. My voice still sounded too controlled, too calculated.

I kept the smile plastered to my face, hoping she wouldn't notice. Ashley and Sam both nodded their heads in agreement, though Ashley still looked like she wanted to burst into tears. Mrs. Alcorta looked skeptical, but thankfully started to turn away like she didn't really care enough to argue. She waved impatiently, trying to hurry us along, but froze as Jeremy stood back up, coming into full view.

"You there. What is your name?"

Mrs. Alcorta's frazzled appearance took on a more skittish look, and she started backpedaling towards the courtyard.

Jeremy froze and looked down at me, realizing his mistake too late.

Mrs. Alcorta stopped her backward shuffling at the edge of the alleyway and gave his face a long searching look, paling ever so slightly.

"It's impossible."

Her whisper was so quiet that it took me a moment to process it.

"You look just like him. But he left decades ago."

Her hands were shaking as she let them fall to her sides.

A stunned silence filled the alley. That was *not* the response I was expecting. Jeremy, on the other hand, latched onto that comment like a drowning man.

"You know my father?"

He took a large stride towards the woman, shock overcoming his sensibility.

"No! Don't come closer. You can't be here. You need to leave now. I have to report you, or else. . ."

She raised her arms in a weak protest, eyes pleading. She looked between me and Jeremy several times before her eyes went wide, comprehension dawning.

"Oh, Arianna, oh no. You must leave. Leave, go with him. It isn't safe for you here anymore."

Sam and Ashley both let their mouths open with an audible pop. This day had lost what little sanity it was clinging to. How did Mrs. Alcorta know Jeremy's father? And did she want me to ditch class, or leave-leave, as in leave the city?

I looked to Ivy, who shook her head as well. This went beyond her ability to reason. I shifted to Jeremy, whose hands were fisted at his sides. He was shaking from head to toe, vibrating with the effort it took himself to keep from pouncing on the poor teacher.

Mrs. Alcorta looked over to the dumbstruck Ashley and Sam and frowned severely, all frazzled nature wiped away.

"You two need to get to class now. And say nothing to anyone about this if you know what is good for you. You'll probably be questioned, but we can deal with that later."

Her tone radiated clear authority now, and she ignored the look of desperation Ashley shot her, motioning them forward. Sam glanced back at me eyes straining in despair, and I nodded. They had an out now, they needed to take it. He squared his shoulders and grabbed Ashley's wrist, towing her forward forcibly.

Her eyes latched to mine as she stumbled over loose stones and I tried to give her my most reassuring smile, but I knew she would worry, regardless. Sam gave me one last anxious look before pulling Ashley around the corner and out of sight. Mrs. Alcorta stood silently staring at Jeremy, her expression unreadable.

She took a slight step forward, checked herself and went still again, her face taking on a look of fierce determination. This was not the computer science teacher I had known for the last 4 years.

"I'll give you fifteen minutes. Out of respect for your father. Fifteen minutes before I report having seen you. If you are smart, that should be enough time to get you far enough away. If you move quickly enough, you should be able to stay ahead of them until you get outside the city. Take Arianna with you. She won't make it out on her own. Now go, both of you."

She nodded once, spun on a pair of sensible black heels, and marched into the courtyard.

I couldn't quite get my body to move. This must be what shock feels like. Jeremy stepped forward directly in front of me. His hands grabbed the tops of my shoulders and squeezed gently, pulling my eyes up to his. I forced a breath into my lungs, preparing myself for what came next.

"Can you run?"

His voice was so intense, the question so sincere that a maniacal giggle burst unwarranted from my lips. We were probably going to get caught, or worse, but at least I could do one thing right. High on an excess of adrenaline and life-threatening danger, I gave Jeremy an absurd grin, probably causing him to question my sanity, and laughed.

"Don't worry, I can run."

Chapter 27

I grasped Jeremy's extended hand, and he pulled me out the other end of the alley, away from the courtyard, away from life as I knew it. A glance at Ivy showed her nodding her head resolutely. We had to do this. I spared one last look down the empty alley, to the big maple tree that swayed gently over our spot. So much laughter, so many memories were made under that tree, and now I didn't know if I would ever see it again.

I wondered where we were heading. We couldn't go to another city. If we did, we would just be sitting ducks for their enforcers. Plus, how would we even get there? The only way to travel between different cities would be to use the intercontinental auto-rail, which required a full chip scan before boarding. The second we tried to board, the entire system would flag our location and they would catch us.

I paused as we exited the back alley onto a side street which ran against the school, swirling my fingers, typing to Ivy.

Where should we go? How long do you think it will take for Mrs. Alcorta to report us? Are you able to shield our signal at all?

Ivy bobbed gently considering my questions, but before she could respond Jeremy stepped in front of me, eyes tense, verging on annoyance.

"Why did you stop? We need to keep going. If you can't run, I can carry you."

I stared up at him, frustrated, but before I could respond, Ivy chimed in.

You need to put as much distance between you and the city center as possible, as quickly as possible. I don't know what the best solution is right now, but you need to move.

I swirled my hand to type a response, but Jeremy's hand snaked out faster than I could see and snatched mine, stopping the movement. His eyes were hard.

"Tell you AI to stop interfering. It's done enough as it is."

His voice was steel, and Ivy looked pissed readying a response. She opened her mouth to retort, obviously forgetting that he wouldn't be able to hear her.

"Enough!"

I shouted, exasperated, causing the lone businessman who had appeared to duck down a different side street.

"Both of you stop it. I can't concentrate on anything with you both talking in my ears!"

Ivy clamped her mouth shut and crossed her arms in a huff, and Jeremy looked affronted at being compared to an AI at all. I pointed a finger at his chest.

"You, where are we even going? If you tell us, yes, I mean both Ivy and me, she can help guide us, then we can get there faster. Do you even know your way around the city center without having to stop and use that useless paper thing of yours? Like that won't draw someone's attention?"

Ivy nodded in encouragement, and I wanted to tell her to shut it, but I kept my focus on Jeremy instead. He crossed his arms over his chest, causing his biceps to flex. If he thought that would intimidate me into just following him silently, like some sort of lost lap dog, he was sorely mistaken. I had had enough of this crap. There was too much at stake now.

"Where are we going and what is your plan?"

I asked again, slowly lowering my finger from his chest. He glared at me for a silent moment before he grumbled, giving up. Jeremy ran a hand through his hair, fluffing it up in a way that, at any other time, might have been cute. He sighed.

"Alright, but I still don't think you should tell the AI."

I wanted to laugh at his ignorance about how this worked, but I stayed silent, waiting for him to go on.

"We need to leave the city, but we need supplies. I don't think you can make it in one day in your current condition, and the journey after will be much harder. It would be best if we could pick up a few items before we leave."

"Alright that all makes sense, but how are we going to get out? We can't use the rails; they will catch us once they locate my signal."

At this Jeremy chuckled darkly.

"We aren't going to another city, Arianna. We are leaving this one. We are going outside the walls, off your Grid completely. I told you I didn't grow up in a city. I'm taking you to where I grew up, and we are wasting time standing here."

Ivy twirled, drawing my focus back to her.

Arianna, he is right. I tried to think of another way, but leaving the Grid completely is the only way to ensure they can't track you.

I nodded to her. If she thought leaving was the only option, I would trust her. I opened my mouth to ask Jeremy what he was doing at the school, but he put a rough finger to my lips, silencing me. The next time someone did that I was going to bite their finger off.

"No more questions for now. We need to put some distance between us and the school. Whoever they will send after us will start there. How are you feeling? Would it be better if I carried you?"

I laughed at his backhanded pass at chivalry.

"Don't you worry about me, kind sir. I'm a tri-city track champion. Number one for long distance running on my school's track team, or I used to be." Track was just another thing I had lost in all of this.

"Alright superstar, we need to get as close to the edge of the city as we can, specifically the west edge. We also need to grab some supplies to last us until we get outside the city. If we are going to leave the city on foot, it will take us at least two days, even running. Since you are so determined to include your AI in this, get her to guide us to a market or something, preferably one far away from this school."

"You know her name is Ivy, and she's the reason I can even stand up on my own now, no thanks to you. Don't worry she won't lead us astray."

He had the decency to duck his head sheepishly at the reminder of why I was in such a bad state.

Arianna, you can't go into a store. I will do my best to cloak your signal and where you are going, but if you buy anything, your credit signature will ping your location and there is nothing I can do about that. I'll take you northwest. It'll be a roundabout way. If your signal slips through, it shouldn't be obvious where you are heading. Hopefully, they will assume you are heading home.

Freaking glitch, I didn't even think about the credit issue.

Jeremy scratched the back of his head, looking off down the street. It was nearly empty, but it wouldn't be for long. In just a few hours, schools would release, and students would crowd the sidewalks, heading home. Not long after that, traffic would pick up as the adults got off work.

Jeremy stood patiently waiting, watching my movements with reluctant fascination as I typed back and forth with Ivy. When I turned to him, he schooled his face into an impressively impassive expression. It was clear that he was embarrassed about getting caught staring.

"She did it. I can see the path, but you won't be able to so you will have to follow me for once, alright?"

I smirked up at him.

Jeremy paused, uncertain.

"Won't they just pick up on your signal?"

"No, she is going to cloak us, but it won't last forever. Also, we can't go to a store to buy supplies. They only take digital currency, which will give away our location so we will have to think of something else."

I paused, wondering how Jeremy had lasted this long in the city without already knowing that. Where had he gotten his supplies from these last few days?

"You ready?"

I looked up into his eyes, which were conflicted. He didn't trust Ivy, but there was nothing I could do about that right now. Finally, he nodded and put his hand in mine.

I glanced down at my jeans, wishing I had worn something more comfortable to run in, then remembered that I wasn't in a state to pick out my own clothes this morning, anyway. These pants were on the tighter side, but at least my shoes had good grip.

Either way, this would not be a comfortable journey, but there was no chance I could stop at my house and change. Ivy lit up a green path going to the left, away from the school and heading outside the city center. I let me brain slip into the same trance I used in track, narrowing my focus on the green path ahead.

I dropped Jeremy's hand and took off without warning, chuckling at the thought of Jeremy scrambling to keep up, but there he was, right by my side. He stayed a pace or two behind me, just enough to let me lead but close enough to reach out and grab my hand if he wanted to. I wondered how long he would be able to keep pace with me.

I refocused just in time to see the first turn indicator, and flung my hand to the left, telling Jeremy where to go. We rounded the corner and set into a brisk jogging pace. This pace would be easy to sustain for at least five miles, and by the looks of it, Jeremy wouldn't have an issue either. We continued down the road, turning our heads aside whenever we happened across a stranger on our path.

Ivy bobbed up and down, focus split between cloaking us and sending directions into my field of vision. The three of us remained in a tense silence, each person - and AI- focused intently on their task.

It felt good to run.

With each step, the fog of the morning faded, and the ache in my head lessened. After a few miles, we left the bustling city center, with its high rises and holo-advertisements behind, crossing into the suburban section of the city. I felt less like a clone and more like myself, but the spike of adrenaline that initially fueled me quickly dissipated the further we ran. I wasn't going to be able to maintain this for much longer. Fighting the correction had sapped my usual stamina, making me feel like a dead battery.

Chapter 28

The city had a clean, circular shape with the tech district and all its high rises at the center, while everything else flowed outwards. Businesses, research labs, and executive offices took up the majority of the city center, with schools dotting the edge of the center's border. Then came the neighborhoods with their grocery stores, restaurants, and parks.

As you pushed further away from the center of the city the neighborhoods grew rougher, until you reached ones like Derek's which were barely connected to the Grid at all. At the edges of those neighborhoods were farmland and the tech factories which pumped out all the tiny pieces needed for each new gadget developed in the center. At the edge of the factories and farmland was a wall, or in some places merely a fence, which separated the city from the outside. There was only the wild after that.

In the southern and eastern districts, the wall was made of thick stone and looked fiercely imposing. We had taken a field trip to the northmost part of the city to look at the wall and the Grid towers, which were placed every fifty yards, when we were in elementary school. It was there that they taught us to fear the outside, how dangerous it was, how lethal stepping outside the city's protection could be.

Ironically, on the western and northern ends of the city, the walls gave way to wooden fences, and in some of the more run-down areas, a chain-link fence was all that separated the city from the wild. In middle school, it was a popular game for people to get as close to one of the weak fences and to post a picture for proof onto the Feed.

People called it the Wilderness Challenge, until one kid got corrected for several months for posting a picture of himself sticking his hand all the way through the chain-link fence. That kid wasn't even in my grade, but we all stopped playing the wilderness game after that.

I assumed it was in one of those weaker areas that Jeremy had snuck through, but I was certain the government would have closed the gaps since that kid's correction. I had no idea though. There were still many parts of the city I had not been to, mainly because my mom insisted they were too dangerous.

Jeremy and I had been running for a few miles now. And on any other day I would have just warmed up, but today, after everything I had been through, I was absolutely dead. Neither of us spoke, but I felt slightly better seeing Jeremy's chest rise and fall rapidly, he may not be as gassed as I was, but he was getting tired.

I signaled Ivy, and she made a quick change, guiding us to a deserted side street. There was a small, cracked sidewalk which backed against a line of houses and ran alongside a drainage ditch. I led Jeremy a few feet down the path, trying to catch my breath enough to listen to our surroundings. The only thing I could hear was the rapid pounding of my heart in my ears.

I bent over, placing my hands on my knees, and took several deep breaths, looking at the map Ivy had overlaid my field of vision with. This was not good. According to the map, we had over 10 miles left, and it was already fall, the light of the sun would fade faster than normal.

School and work would be out in another hour, and the sun would set an hour after that. If I had been in racing condition instead of fried and already overexerted, I would be able to make the distance, but I hadn't eaten lunch, and I felt queasy just thinking about trying to power through. I squinted up at Jeremy, was checking out surroundings intently while also trying to catch his breath. He was in great shape, but I doubted he was in that great of shape. Over 20 miles of running was a tough ask for anyone.

"I am not sure how much longer we can run without the risk of getting caught. We've been running for 8 miles now and I'm not sure I can keep this pace up. We still have about 12 miles to go to reach the border, but school will be out soon, and people will head home from work. It's going to get uncomfortably crowded, and if someone spots us, or their AI spots us, we are in trouble."

I squinted up into Jeremy's eyes, not bothering to raise myself from my doubled over position. I could barely get a full sentence out without gasping for air. My stamina was wrecked, and I wished I hadn't just bragged about how excellent of a runner I was. Jeremy nodded seriously, a calculating look in his eyes.

"Honestly, we've gone a lot farther than I had hoped for."

His voice was low, and if I wasn't mistaken, had a keen teasing edge.

I stood up sharply, wincing at the pinch in my side. What was he trying to say? He shook his head at my expression.

"I was joking, Arianna. You are seriously impressive to have just run that much after passing out only a few hours ago."

He smiled, showing a rare dimple, then shook his head again, face cold and calculating once more.

"Seriously though, ask your AI," at this, I shot him a look, and he shrugged apologetically, "fine, ask Ivy how tightly we are being trailed. Is anyone following us yet?"

I glanced at Ivy, knowing she had heard his question. She held up a dainty hand, pausing. Her avatar bobbed slowly for a few seconds before it twirled in a slow circle.

Everything is clear for now. There is a lot of activity around the school and a few miles in the surrounding area, but nothing this far. I doubt they will think to look this far out right away, but they will expand their search to the entire city before long.

Ivy hesitated a moment, contemplating her next sentence.

Also, you should know, they broadcasted an image of you both to every AI within close range of the city. If someone sees you and the AI registers your face, they will send an automated signal of your location to the authorities, with or without the host's permission.

I groaned audibly, causing Jeremy to take a tense defensive stance and scan the area again. I wanted to laugh, but it was hard to find anything funny at the moment. Putting a gentle hand on his arm, I shook my head, taut muscles slowly relaxing.

"Nothing is happening right here. Ivy said they are centered around the school right now. But she did say that they broadcast our picture to all the AIs in the area. That means if anyone sees us, and their AI gets a long enough look at our face to register who we are, they will report our location and we won't be able to run quick enough to flee at that point."

Jeremy stared down at me, eyes flicking to where my hand still rested on his arm. I quickly pulled away, surprised at the sudden darkening of his eyes.

He sighed.

"You can't make it all the way to the edge of the city in your condition. I'm surprised you've made it this far."

I didn't point out that he wasn't likely to make it either.

Ivy, what do we do? I need a place to rest, and something to eat.

Ivy bobbed thoughtfully, and Jeremy, ignorant of our private conversation, echoed the same thoughts.

You can't go into a registered home. Every home keeps a log of the signals that enter and exit, and you can't go to a store to get supplies. Ivy replied.

"Well, where did you stay the last 2 nights? You had to eat too, so where are your supplies?" I asked Jeremy.

His eyes narrowed in a challenge, his jaw clenching and unclenching several times before he responded.

"I brought supplies with me and used them all up. I wasn't planning on staying inside this place for longer than two days at the most, but then . . ."

He trailed off as if not really knowing how to finish the sentence himself.

I huffed, "Then you ran into me, and I jacked up your plans, right? Now you're under some stupid chivalric notion that you are responsible for me and therefore must save me by getting me out of the city, right?"

"Yeah, something like that."

He chuckled again, causing an involuntary shiver to run up my spine. He had no right to be this attractive in a life-threatening situation. I wasn't going to let him throw me off that easily.

"You still haven't said where you stayed."

His smile faded, his face becoming a stern mask, eyes unreadable.

"No, I haven't, and I won't. My secrets are my own. All you need to know is that we cannot stay where I stayed before. It would be too risky, for you and for everyone else."

"What do you mean, everyone else? You know people in the city? Are there more people like you here? How do they live?"

Jeremy shook his head forcefully.

"I am not at liberty to tell you anything. Our only focus is to get out of the city before someone or something catches us."

I stilled, remembering the creepy thing that chased us through the forest. There was no way I was letting this go, but I would wait. He was right. Now was not the time. We needed to get going again if we were going to stay ahead of the people pursuing us.

"Fine, I'll drop it. For now."

Jeremy let out a sigh of relief, as if he had expected a bigger fight from me. He wasn't completely wrong. Once we were out of the city, I would give him the fight he was expecting and more if he didn't tell me everything. Ivy waved her hands, getting my attention again.

Arianna, I don't have a solution for you this time. It is taking all my effort to cloak and guide you. If we were at the house, I could access the pantry function and make it spit out extra supplies, like I've done before, but that would still give your location away.

Jeremy paused, waiting for me to return my attention to him. He was picking up on the small signs that I was listening to Ivy, and not just zoning off. I shook my head glumly.

"It's fine. You won't do well without food, but we can stay in one of the forest park things, like the one we were in before. It won't be comfortable, but it should be relatively safe."

Jeremy was already staring off into the distance, probably thinking about how to forage up some food for us or how to make a tent from twigs.

I bet he knew how to do something like that, too.

I shuddered at the thought of staying overnight in a dark, eerie forest, waiting for someone or something to creep up on us in the middle of the night. I wracked my brain, desperate for an alternative when something Ivy had said snagged in my thoughts, like a thread catching. Typing quickly, I relayed my plan to Ivy, who agreed reluctantly that it would be a safer option than the forest floor, though not by much.

"I know a place. We are about 2 miles away. I think I can make it, but we need to hurry."

"And where exactly is this place?"

His eyes were deep pools threatening to down me, and I realized they reminded me of another set of eyes, ones that were far more mischievous. Eyes that made my heart drop into the bottom of my stomach with just the thought of them.

My heart gave a twisted pang, filled with an overwhelming guilt.

"My,... friend Derek, he lives on the outskirts. His house is barely connected to the Grid, and a few summers ago we built a shed in his backyard, as a place to meet. It's completely off the grid. There should be some food in there as well. Nothing great, just snacks, but it's better than nothing. We'll be safe there."

Jeremy nodded reluctantly.

If he knew about Derek's condition, he would probably argue against going, but it was our only option. Ivy altered the guidance to take us further north, and I took a deep breath. My heart plummeted into my stomach, and I hoped beyond hope Derek wouldn't come out to shed.

After all, he was still corrected. So why would he?

Chapter 29

After another mile of running the sidewalks began to crack in places and there were more potholes in the roads. There were also more wires crisscrossed overhead. They hung over us as we ran down the street like a trap waiting to fall. Both of us were puffing air in and out at a faster pace than before. Jeremy was slowing down slightly, but I was far beyond my limit.

"Shit!"

Jeremy cursed as he spun and swung his arms out, effectively clotheslining me as I ran straight into him.

The shock of our bodies colliding jarred my bones and snapped my teeth together. Jeremy pushed back against our momentum to drive us behind the corner of an old, crumbling house. More coarse black wires cascaded down the side of the house, and I shied away from them as we hid behind the corner, breathing hard.

Faster than I thought possible, Jeremy had me caged between his arms with my back pressed against the rough siding of the house. He was leaning close enough for his breath to stir my hair as he peered to the side around the corner. There were beads of sweat sliding down his neck from running, and his hair was sticking to his forehead.

"What is it?" I whispered as quietly as I could, while trying to catch my breath.

Jeremy didn't respond, instead his arms tightened slightly, strained forearms pressing against my arms. He tensed again, and without looking at me, turned his body to cover mine, his back pressing into my chest. He slid his hand down to my waist and pushed gently backwards, guiding me further behind the house. We took several slow steps backwards like this, him gently pushing my waist until he flattened his hand, fingers splayed across my waist.

His hand was so large his fingers had wrapped around my hip, covering part of my stomach. A swarm of disobedient butterflies chased each other up my throat, bringing a rush of heat with them. My body was a traitor, reacting without my permission. I hated it, but I forced myself to remain still, shoving aside my reactions. I would deal with them later.

Ivy lit up, drawing my attention, thankfully, away from the blazing heat coming off Jeremy's hands.

Arianna, there are several people on the street ahead of you, and their AIs have been flagged to watch for you. Jeremy must have spotted them. Thankfully, he has quick reflexes. You are a half a mile away from the clubhouse.

Move fast. I'll try to keep you out of the path of others as much as I can.

Ivy paused.

Alright, you have a chance now, hurry.

Ivy flashed an alternative route in front of me. Green arrows pointing straight ahead, pulsing with a new sense of urgency. The sun was low on the horizon, painting everything in shadow. I hoped the shadows would hide us.

I looked up, realizing Jeremy had shifted his position to face me. I grabbed the hand that was splayed across my hip a moment ago, still feeling the heat across my stomach, and pulled him forward, towards the front of the house.

Ivy was back in my ear, voice urgent.

You are taking too long. Trust me, Arianna. Follow the path and RUN!

A fierce undercurrent of protectiveness ran through her words. I tightened my grip on Jeremy's hand and pulled, working up our pace until we were flat out running. Ivy flashed signals in front of me at an erratic pace.

I heard people as we ran. Cars driving along the street to the left of us, kids laughing and shouting to our right. The afternoon auto-rails must be making their rounds because the streets were becoming crowded, our route more convoluted with every second. Ivy had to stall us twice behind someone's bushes as a group of teenagers strolled by, only a few feet from where we hid.

Finally, after the longest half mile of my life, we were on Derek's street. It was blissfully empty, and we took off at a dead sprint. I pulled Jeremy to the right, heading towards the backyard. Derek's house looked like it could cave in at any moment. The thick black wires that had chased us down the streets and through the yards of the Far West district barely connected to the house, as if they were hanging by a thread.

Derek always had shotty service, his entire house falling off the Grid every few weeks. The city officials didn't care to clean up the lines this far away from the center, so Derek was the one who took care of keeping his house online, mainly for the sake of his siblings. He couldn't care less if he was on the Grid or not.

Jeremy and I hopped the buckling chain-link fence surrounding Derek's property and crouched behind a straggly bush. It offered little cover, but Ivy was scanning the property to see if anyone was home yet.

All clear, no one is home yet, and the shed is empty.

Ivy sounded oddly tired for a person without an actual body, but I appreciated her efforts. I grabbed Jeremy's hand, gently this time, and pulled him towards the tiny shack-like structure in the back.

It was made from wood taken from the crates they used to haul produce from the farm districts and odd bits of tin found in some of the abandoned factories a few streets over.

Derek, Sam, and I had spent the entire summer our freshman year building it, and at the time, we had been so proud of ourselves. We called it a clubhouse, but basically it was just a tiny, barely nailed together room with no windows. It had a door we stole off an abandoned house down the street on a particularly eventful night, in which Ivy had given me a rare hour-long lecture after.

We had spent all our spare time during sophomore and junior years planning pranks, parties, and our futures in that clubhouse. We eventually siphoned enough food, mainly thanks to Ivy manipulating my pantry, to have a stockpile of snacks and drinks, and with it being off the Grid, the clubhouse sort of felt like a haven for us all.

As I approached the door, Jeremy a step behind me, a wave of uncertainty hit me. It felt wrong bringing an outsider here. If we got caught, Derek's whole family would be in trouble. I hesitated, hand almost touching the doorknob as I wracked my brain for another place we could instead.

My legs shook from exhaustion and my hand was trembling. Even if I found another place, I wasn't sure I could make it there.

The soft crunch of a shoe on gravel decided for me. I turned the doorknob and flung the door open, dragging Jeremy inside with me. I closed the door as softly as I could, peeking through the crack between the wooden slats just in time to see a shadowy figure cross into the yard.

Derek.

It had to be him. It was twilight now, which meant school was over, and he had probably taken the auto-rail home since he was still under the influence of his correction. I held my breath as he walked through the yard, causing a shadow to move from gap to gap in the wall.

There was a faint noise by the door, and Ivy covered her mouth with her hands. There was nothing she could do to physically stop him from coming in.

Jeremy tensed behind me, tracking the movements and noises as I did. His fists clenched, preparing to fight. The movement paused for a moment, and then the faint noise of shoes against gravel began moving away from the shack. He had left, hopefully going into his house for the evening.

I sank into the musty squares of carpet on the ground, feeling the last of my energy slip away. Jeremy stayed in his defensive stance, not satisfied that the danger had passed. Ivy lowered her arms delicately to her sides.

That was too close, Arianna. Why did you hesitate?

I couldn't answer her.

I honestly didn't know how to put it into words. My entire life had been destroyed in less than two days. It felt wrong to lose my only safe place, too. But there was no turning back now. It was done; we were here, and soon we would be outside the city.

My head ached at the thought, and I curled into a tight ball, my eyes pressed against my kneecaps, arms wrapped tightly around my shins. Jeremy moved quietly, and I felt his warmth as he sat next to me on the moldy carpets. I tried not to feel self-conscious about the state of the clubhouse; I mean, he was from the wild, right?

My head spun, my body feeling like overused puddy. The tears I had so desperately been holding back came forward unbidden. My shoulders shook as they poured out, dripping from my arms onto my knees. Jeremy shifted closer, our hips not quite touching. He gingerly put an arm around my shoulders, and I wanted to laugh at how awkward this must be for him.

It was too difficult to care about anything. I didn't care what Jeremy thought of me or that I had an AI. I didn't care about how rundown our clubhouse was. I was too tired to care about how we were fleeing for our lives. I leaned back against the wall; eyes pressed tight against the world.

I heard my name faintly, not sure if it was Ivy or Jeremy who called me, but it didn't matter. I was already asleep, thankful for the calming darkness that covered everything.

Chapter 30

"Arianna. . . Arianna, you need to wake up."

Jeremy's low voice pushed through the dark fog which had taken over. My limbs felt heavy and sluggish, but I was oddly warm. There was a strange weight over my shoulders and as I shifted to lift my head, it eased off. I blinked, dazed, realizing my face was buried in Jeremy's chest. He shifted his weight moving into a crouch, and I bolted upright, face heating. How long had I been asleep on him?

I suppressed a groan.

I can't believe I had cried on this random dude, and then fell asleep on him. He must be so annoyed. But he didn't look angry. In fact, he looked alert and almost nervous. I checked Ivy, and she shared an eerily similar look. I glanced around, anxiety chasing away the last bit of grogginess I had. Nothing like waking up to an anxiety attack to clear your head.

"What is it?" I asked aloud, hoping either of them would answer me.

Jeremy held up a finger, silencing me, and Ivy simply shook her head. So that's how it was. The last to know again.

I waited in tense silence for a few minutes, barely daring to breathe. I tried to keep still, moving my toes in my shoes to keep myself from fidgeting. I was about to speak up again, unable to remain silent any longer, when Ivy and Jeremy both relaxed. Ivy began bobbing again, and Jeremy sat back down.

"Well, either of you want to tell me what that was about?"

I kept my voice below a whisper, but I knew both would still hear me. Jeremy snapped his eyes to me, narrowing them in obvious irritation at being lumped together with Ivy. I honestly didn't care.

It was Ivy who answered first.

There was something out there. A signal. Someone was moving towards the clubhouse, but for the life of me, I couldn't decode who. There was no traceable data. It is cloaked, just like you are.

She wrapped her arms around herself, going quiet, her face contemplative. She was distressed that someone could have a cloaked signal so well that she couldn't access it, and I couldn't blame her. Now we would never know who was out there.

Jeremy was waiting patiently when I glanced back at him, his arms resting causally across his knees. I wondered if the weight I felt earlier had been his arm around me, but I highly doubted it. Jeremy didn't strike me as the comforting type.

When he met my eyes, I raised an eyebrow, waiting for his own explanation.

He spoke in hushed tones, his voice containing more gravel than before, as if tired from lack of use.

"There was something outside. I could hear rustling. I thought it would be best if you were awake if someone, or something, came charging in here. Sorry to wake you. Whatever it was, it moved on."

I shuddered at the thought of a "thing" out there searching for us, and I tried to look through the gaps in the wood panels, but everything was dark outside. I glanced at the tiny clock in my field of vision, startled to realize it was almost midnight. Almost six hours had passed since I had fallen asleep, and it didn't seem like Jeremy had moved an inch during that time. I doubted he had slept either. My heart gave a funny lurch, which was promptly overridden by an embarrassingly loud growl from my stomach.

I was starving.

I hadn't eaten since breakfast that morning. I crawled over to the duffle bag Derek, Sam, and I hid our snacks in, Ash always refused to eat 'trash' food claiming it would ruin her figure.

I took my time rifling through the bag, thankful for a diversion. Eventually I settled on cheese crisps and a bottle of black cherry flavored soda water. We didn't have any regular water, but I figured it was close enough. I tossed the bag to Jeremy, who looked through its contents with a slight frown on his face. He settled on plain chips, Sam's favorite, and another bottle of soda water. We both ate in silence for a few moments; a dinner of champions.

Ivy stayed still for the most part, throwing everything she had into tracing the signals around us and keeping watch. After a moment of awkward chewing, I couldn't take the silence. I crumpled my empty back of crisps and tossed them into a corner, not caring where they landed, and turned to face Jeremy.

He was staring into his bag of chips, looking distressed, like he didn't realize the bad would be filled with mostly air. Questions bubbled up, and I latched onto what seemed like the most important one.

Taking a deep breath, I braced myself, not knowing what Jeremy would say, and asked, "Why are you here?"

Jeremy looked sharply up, as if startled by my voice. He looked questioningly at me before responding.

"I told you already, I am here, or I guess was here, to find my father."

I shook my head. He didn't get it. I saw Ivy pause in her bobbing, catching onto our conversation, equally curious.

"No, why are you here, like in this run-down shack, running from who knows what, with me? You could have easily left me behind and kept looking for your dad. Why didn't you escape when I gave you the chance? You didn't have to come looking for me, and you didn't have to help me."

My chest was ridiculously tight at the thought of him abandoning me, but I needed to know. Why was this stranger, the boy I had just met, willing to risk his life to help me?

Jeremy stared into his chip bag as if searching for the answers inside. He remained silent for long enough that I thought he would refuse to answer at all. Then he sighed, crumpled the empty bag and tossed it into the same corner that I had.

When he looked up his face was soft and more vulnerable than I thought possible. I had the sudden urge to comfort him, but I didn't dare move, so I stayed frozen in place, waiting for him to speak.

"Arianna, I don't really know how to explain this to you."

His voice was soft and hesitant.

"I know, I knew your father. He was friends with my father."

My lungs seized, eliminating my ability to respond. My hands started shaking, tremors raising up into my arms until my entire body was trembling.

"How...how?" My voice shook as I forced the words out.

"I'm so sorry I didn't tell you sooner. I wasn't planning on seeing you, but when I saw you, I knew it was you. I know you will not believe me. But I knew your dad. When he left the city, he came to our camp. He met with my father, and they spent almost all their time together. He was there for a few years before . . ."

The room spun and I was thankful to be already on the floor. All this time I had assumed my dad had just left us, had gotten up one day and left for another city. I had pictured him over and over in a city across the country, sometimes miserable on his own and sometimes laughing with a new family. Either thought had always brought me to tears, but still I had the hope that maybe one day he would come back. That he would come back for me.

Jeremy remained seated, arms still crossed, atop his knees, eyes strangely bright.

"I know this is a shock to you, Arianna, but you are just like him. You talk like him, you even smile like him."

His face took on a wistful look, and in that moment, I hated him. How dare he talk as if he knew my father. Anger burned like acid in the pit of my stomach, tears stung at my eyes. I didn't know whether to laugh at him or to scream at him.

Instead, I snorted, opting for denial.

"Really, and I'm supposed to just believe you? You couldn't even find your way around the city without that stupid paper crap, and you expect me to believe that you just happened to run into me?"

"That's the thing. I don't think I ran into you by accident at all. The map I was using led to that area of the city. It was drawn by my father, a copy of the one he took with him when he came here. I have no idea why, but I think the map was leading to you, or at least to your area of the city. I shouldn't have looked for you the second time, but I couldn't help it. When you said your name was Arianna, I knew it was you. I couldn't just let you walk away."

That was the most words Jeremy had ever spoken to me at one time, but I honestly didn't care. What he said was impossible. Why would my father leave the city and go into the wild?

"Alright, that was a pretty speech, but tell me. Why did my father never come back for me? If you knew him and he told you all about me, then that means he still cared. So why didn't he come back? Why didn't he rescue me?"

My voice started out full of anger and sarcasm, but by the end I was choking back tears, refusing to give into the wave of fear and sadness that threatened to pull me under. As I grew older, I avoided thinking about my father as much as possible. It only left me with pain and more questions than answers.

Jeremy's jaw clenched and unclenched, his eyes shining slighter brighter in a rare display of raw emotion. Fear clawed its way up my stomach, wrapping around my heart, threatening to shatter me. Jeremy met my eyes, searching.

"Arianna, I am so sorry. Your father wasn't able to come back because he-"

"Stop," I said.

Jeremy's soothing tones cut like glass, tearing my flesh apart word by word. I didn't want to hear this. I didn't want to know. This couldn't possibly be happening. Ivy had one hand covering her mouth, the other wrapped around her waist. I stared at her with sudden suspicion.

"Did you know about this? Did you know where he went?"

My voice was low, each word dragged across hot coals. Jeremy remained silent, knowing I wasn't talking to him anymore.

Ivy enlarged herself so I could see her clearly.

Arianna, you have to know I could only do as I was told. Your father, he made me the way I am. He wrote my code so I could break free from the system and take care of you, protect you. But, I didn't know where he was going. All I knew was that I needed to keep you safe. I was never supposed to reveal anything about him that would put you in jeopardy.

My heart shattered. Ivy was my closest friend, a parent when I didn't have one, and a source of comfort through all the pain. I swore she was real, that she was different from all the other AIs. My mouth tightened into a hard line.

"I get it. You were doing what you were programmed to do. That's all you can do, right Ivy?"

The words tasted like ash on my tongue. Ivy flinched visibly, and I wanted to take them back, but I couldn't. I swiped my hand, motioning her avatar out of view and glared back at Jeremy, who looked wary as if he was next.

"You felt some stupid obligation to protect me because supposedly you knew my father. Well, I appreciate you getting me this far, but I can take care of the rest. Consider your obligation met."

Each word stabbed my chest, but I couldn't stop them. I didn't want to be around him or Ivy any longer, but I doubt I could get rid of Ivy, she was literally attached to my brain. I wanted to claw the chip out of the back of my neck, but instead I clenched the sides of my head, pressing as hard as I could, trying to stop hearing Jeremy's words.

If Jeremy was right, if he was saying what I thought he was saying, then my father really was gone. I would never see him again. The tiny flame of hope I had clung to since I was a child, blew out. I would never see him again. I waited for the tears to come, but they didn't.

Instead, a chasm of anger split my heart in two.

I looked up at Jeremy, ready to demand more information, when I realized he and Ivy had both gone terrifyingly still. Jeremy was once again in a crouching position, as if ready to run or fight, muscles straining, and eyes narrowed in focus. Ivy was frozen, a look of shock on her face.

Arianna . . .

Her voice was truly afraid, causing an icy blast of fear to flood through me, dousing the raging anger in an instant. A faint crunch of gravel was the only warning I had before the doorknob to the clubhouse turned and I was face to face with the one person I prayed I wouldn't see.

Derek.

He stood in the open-door frame; half hidden in darkness.

In the half second of silence, he echoed Ivy's desperate plea.

"Arianna?"

Chapter 31

Derek's strangled cry shattered the stillness that had frozen us all. Jeremy leapt into action, springing in front of me to shield my body with his. His fists were clenched and partially raised, ready to fight our way out of the clubhouse if needed.

I spared a glance at Ivy, whose hands were still frozen in shock. A fraction of a second later she was back in her avatar, having left to the Grid as soon as she detected Derek.

I'm sorry, Arianna, his signal was almost entirely cloaked, and I didn't detect him until he was already at the door. I've done a thorough scan though, nothing else is out there, not even a cloaked signal. He's alone.

I wanted to be relieved at the information, but it didn't matter if he was alone. He was corrected and his AI was probably already sending out a signal to every enforcer in the city that we were here.

We would be trapped here, surrounded, and then taken off to who knows where. What would they do to Jeremy?

Derek was still standing in the door frame. His hands clenched and unclenched in time with his jaw, veins standing out in sharp relief on his neck. His eyes were bright and clear, not like the usual dull glaze that came with a correction. It looked like he was fighting it. But that should have been impossible. I was only able to fight the correction with Ivy's help.

Derek took a jerky step forward, causing Jeremy to widen his stance. Derek caught the movement, his eyes widening as if noticing Jeremy for the first time. His body shook from the effort of whatever mental battle he was raging, and his eyes shifted mine, a look of desperation shining in them. My heart clenched at the sight.

I stepped around Jeremy, ignoring his irritated grunt, holding my hands up in a sign of peace between the two.

"Derek, are you alright?"

It was a stupid question, he obviously was not alright, but I needed to draw his attention away from Jeremy and back to myself.

It worked.

Derek turned to look at me once more, a look of deep concentration in his eyes. He opened and closed his mouth several times before he finally spoke. His voice was shredded, as if torn by shards of glass, and it looked as if each word caused him physical pain.

"Ari, there is so much more than we thought. Our pranks, they were nothing." He panted softly between each word. "There is more beneath the surface. I didn't know, I'm sorry."

I couldn't understand a single thing he said. I know we pulled plenty of pranks, but I didn't know what he was talking about beneath the surface. I glanced at Ivy's avatar, and she shook her head. She didn't know, either.

"It's okay Derek, everything is going to be fine. You're going to be alright."

I lied through my teeth, each word another knife to the chest. I honestly had no idea if he would be alright. I had no idea how anyone would fare once I left the city. My only hope was that the enforcers would leave them alone when I disappeared.

Derek shook his head violently, grabbing fistfuls of his hair, causing his biceps to strain against his sleeves. Jeremy grabbed the back of my shirt and pulled me closer to him until my back was braced against his front. Derek stopped shaking and stared at the two of us, eyes flitting between us rapidly, taking in our proximity and the defensive way Jeremy towered over me.

A pained look fell over Derek's face, shuttering his eyes, his shoulders dropped in defeat.

"No Derek, it's not like that. Jeremy is only helping me escape. There is nothing between us. He hates everything about us, about Ivy, I just, I need his help. I promise I'll come back for you. I'll save you; I swear."

The words came out in a rush, and I ignored the way Jeremy tensed behind me. I couldn't spare his feelings now, I needed Derek to understand, to know why I was leaving him behind, and that I would come back for him as soon as I could.

Derek held his head in his hands and crouched down on the floor. He rocked his body from side to side and I felt a wave of fear and nausea run through me. How was he doing this? There was no way his corrected AI should allow this behavior. He began muttering, still staring into the floor, body convulsing.

"I can't keep you safe. It's beneath the surface. They told me things. They told me I could save you, but I couldn't. It got to me first."

Jeremy gave my shoulder a painful squeeze. We needed to get out of here. Ivy continued staring through my field of vision, trying to make sense of Derek's words.

I knelt, moving to Derek's line of sight, heels pressed into Jeremy's shoes.

"Save me from what, Derek? Who is doing this to you?"

I needed to know what was causing this. His words made no sense. I had never heard of someone reacting this way while being corrected.

Suddenly, Derek stopped shaking altogether. His eyes were clear and lucid. He was still fighting the correction, but his face took on a blank quality. He looked again between me and Jeremy, gaze locking onto Jeremy and holding. A moment of recognition passed over his features, his mouth opening in surprise.

When he spoke next, his voice had a breathy quality to it, as if it was slipping away, "You."

He pointed up at Jeremy from the ground. Jeremy tensed and reached down to wrap his hands around my shoulders, lifting me up from the ground without breaking eye contact with Derek.

"You are one of them. They said someone like you could help her. Are you going to help her?"

Jeremy kept his hands locked tight on my arms, as if he was afraid I would make a run for it or go to Derek. I glanced back at him and was startled. This was not a version of Jeremy I had ever seen. His features were a careful mask, locking any emotion away so thoroughly I would have thought he was the one corrected.

Jeremy's voice was surprisingly soft, causing me to flinch. He kept his gaze locked on Derek's.

"Yes, I will help her. But you need to let us leave, now."

At the word now, the steel was back in his voice, a commanding tone ringing through that had me jumping to obey, though he still held my arms fast. Derek nodded in sharp jerking motions; a look of relief etched across his face.

He moved awkwardly, like a doll attached to strings that were tangled. When he was finally standing, Derek shuffled slowly to the side, away from the door, concentrating hard on each movement. Jeremy pulled us in the opposite direction, keeping perfect pace with Derek, the epitome of predatory grace.

I let myself be moved like a rag doll, staring wide eyed at Derek as he maintained control. I had no idea how he was doing this. How he had suppressed his AI. It just wasn't possible, but this was Derek the king of impossible, even if it was a broken version of him.

After several painfully tense seconds, we had rotated positions, with Derek now deep inside the clubhouse and Jeremy and I in the door frame. Jeremy's head was cocked almost to a painful angle as he tried to monitor Derek and listen beyond us into the night.

Ivy gave me an all-clear signal, and I reached a hand up to Jeremy's, and squeezed reassuringly, hoping he understood the message. Jeremy nodded once, and backed us out of the clubhouse slowly, still monitoring Derek.

Derek caught the movement and smiled sadly.

He took a step forward, as if to reach for me, and then abruptly dropped to the ground again, letting out a gut-wrenching scream. It pierced the silence of the night and seemed to go on forever. Then, just as suddenly, the noise stopped. Jeremy and I stood rooted in place, ears ringing from the sound, waiting for the telltale sound of people surrounding us, but there was nothing. Only piecing silence.

I looked back at Derek, who was still clutching his head, shaking back and forth. I wanted to run to him. To make it better somehow, but Jeremy's grip tightened to the point of bruising, as if reading my mind. I would have to have a discussion with him about his allusion of control. He did not and would not ever control me.

Jeremy took another forced step backwards and then froze again.

Derek was getting up, but not in the same jerky off kilter way as before. He rose with an inhuman fluidity. He brushed off his crumbled shirt, and looked up, locking his gaze onto mine across the yard. Jeremy picked up the pace, pulling us further away, while scanning everything at once, but I couldn't look away.

This was not my Derek anymore.

His eyes were glazed and cold, face set in an emotionless mask except for his mouth, which was turned up in a painful sneer. This face didn't even look like it belonged to Derek. He took one step closer, framing himself in the dim light of the clubhouse lantern, and his smile stretched an inch wider, showing an inhuman number of teeth.

The voice that came out of his mouth sent chills down my spine. It sounded automated, mechanical, with none of Derek's rich baritone.

"You can't run from us, Arianna."

Derek whispered the words softly, but they carried through the night, hitting me with the force of a backhand.

Ivy's mouth set into a grim line.

Arianna, you need to run; you don't have much time. Something far beyond us is happening. That's not Derek, and whatever just took over him will summon more. They are going to stop you from leaving the city. I have a path; but you need to run now!

I took one last desperate look at Derek, hoping that I would see his calm clear eyes again.

"Ivy says we need to go. She'll light up the path. We have to move fast. They know where we are. Stay close."

Jeremy nodded stiffly, muscles strained and ready to sprint.

I nodded to Ivy, and she lit the path in front of me, a bright green arrow shooting through the darkness ahead. The moon was waning, but it was just bright enough to see our surroundings. We would take the shortest route, hoping that our speed would outmatch whatever was chasing us. There was no hiding now.

I took off hoping the chain-link fence, leaving Derek and the clubhouse behind. As we sprinted into the night, I thought I heard the sound of faint laughter. I didn't dare look back, so I forced my legs faster, pushing us further into the night, racing towards the edge of the city.

Chapter 32

Jeremy and I ran for our lives. I set a breakneck pace, adrenaline fueling me. Jeremy struggled to keep up. I was running at my peak, recharged from a few hours of sleep and the terrifying thought of a horde of enforcers on our heels. Neither of us had the breath to speak, and we knew we needed to conserve our energy, so we ran in silence.

Whatever had taken over Derek had put out a beacon of where we were, but if we could move fast enough, hopefully they would lose our trail. The enforcers would know that we were heading towards the edge of the city now, but with luck, they wouldn't know exactly where we planned to cross over.

I let myself get lost in the motion of running, my legs pushing hard against the broken pavement, arms pumping through the air. My mind drifted as I ran on autopilot, memories floating their way to the surface at random.

My father and I playing hide and seek, as he taught me how to use Ivy to break the house's codes to get into the best hiding places. His eyes sparkling and mischievous, with a touch of sadness that I hadn't understood before. He was the one who had showed me how special Ivy was, even before I knew what that meant.

Derek speaking in hushed tones about wanting to change the system, always skirting around the truth. I used to nod along, thinking about how brave and different he was, not realizing he meant what he said. I had always wondered why he only spoke of those things when it was just the two of us. I guess it didn't matter now.

A field trip to the wall sophomore year; Derek had been so excited to see how the towers were constructed. "For future reference," he had said mischievously. He had winked, and I had giggled uncontrollably, basking in his attention.

Students had milled around the brick wall, bored and ready to go home. We had seen it all before. None of us cared about the edge of the city anymore. It had been pretty boring until some kid had asked what would really happen if we crossed the border. Everyone within earshot had fallen silent, shocked by his boldness.

By that age, we all knew that this was a subject better left unsaid. The teacher had listed all the terrifying ways we would surely die the moment we stepped foot beyond our protected bubble, and the kid had rolled his eyes, sarcastically commenting back with something about how our AIs would protect us.

The teacher had looked us dead in the eyes when she said that the AIs would no longer work if we left the city. We had all gasped. Of all the things she warned us about, this was the worst we had heard so far. By elementary age, we already relied on our AIs for everything, and for most of us, they were our closest friends, our safe place, our personal secret keepers. To be separated from our AIs were unthinkable.

I stumbled, missing a stride, choking on what little air I had left. Jeremy looked at me questioningly. I nodded briefly to him and picked up the pace again. We couldn't afford to stop running, but I had to know. I didn't have the coordination to run and type at the same time, so I gasped out the words between breaths, knowing Ivy would pick them up.

"Ivy, what happens when I cross the barrier? What will happen to you?"

Ivy grew still again, and for a moment I was worried she had gone to the Grid to check our surroundings again. She couldn't run from this. I needed answers. Slowly she looked at me, straight into my very soul in that uncanny, unblinking way of hers.

You already know, Arianna. I can't go with you. Once you cross the barrier, we will lose all contact.

"No!"

It came out as a strangled, pleading gasp. Jeremy glanced concerned in my direction, but I ignored him. I could barely focus on our route. Tears flooded my eyes, and I almost missed a left turn.

My breath came out in savage gasps as I forced the words out, not caring if Jeremy heard the desperation in them.

"No, Ivy, I can't do that. You have to come with me. I can't go out there alone. I'll die, I won't survive it."

I was spinning out of control.

It was all too much.

To lose everything over something I didn't even understand, and now to lose Ivy, it would destroy me. She was all I ever had. When my father left, when Mom became this robotic monster, through everything, Ivy had been there.

You won't be alone. Jeremy grew up outside the walls. He will keep you safe. What's important is that you are out of their reach. You can only be safe outside the city and off the Grid.

"There has to be another way." I begged.

I didn't even know what I was asking for, just not this. My brain was a hurricane, fear pushing my legs forward towards the edge of the city, my heart desperate to stop, to slow down and think of another solution.

Ivy's face became stern, unyielding, but I could see the emotion shining in her eyes and I knew it wasn't a simulation. Her fear, her love, it was all real.

Arianna, you are leaving this city. You cannot afford to be taken by them. Your father made me promise to take care of you. He MADE me for this purpose, Ari. You are leaving; you are crossing the barrier, and Jeremy will take care of you.

The tears fell freely now, blurring the green arrow into a misshapen mess. It was getting darker the farther we ran, houses giving way to patches of unused land and brightly lit factories in the distance, like torches against the night.

Jeremy was pointedly looking anywhere else, trying to give me a semblance of privacy, and I wondered if he had known this was coming. If he had wanted me out of the city, not just to escape, but to rid me of Ivy. It was a dark thought, and I shoved it down, unable to deal with its consequences.

Ivy was still for a long moment, and I tried to collect myself. My legs burned in a comforting way, reminding me that I was alive, that this was real. Ivy was right, I couldn't stop now. Nothing good would come of me turning back.

Ivy reappeared looking panic stricken, suddenly changing our course, veering us to the right without warning.

Arianna, there are two vehicles approaching. They are a few miles off, but they are gaining on you quickly. I can't tell what's inside. They were jamming the signal, but they couldn't remove the vehicle trace completely. You still have 3 miles to go before you reach the barrier. I'll get you there, but Jeremy will have to find his entry point quickly, or you will get trapped at the fence.

I glanced at Jeremy, a new level of fear sending a shot of adrenaline coursing through my muscles. I pushed harder, speaking in controlled gasps.

"They are coming. Two vehicles. Ivy can't see inside. Do you know where to go?"

Jeremy was lagging a few paces behind me. He gritted his teeth and pushed harder. I hoped he could keep up. After a moment he nodded, pointing to a rising black shape, a shade darker than the night behind it. A relay tower.

"I came in close to that tower. We need to head there."

Ivy nodded in my field of vision.

She had picked up his words and was rerouting us, sending us in the fastest route possible without overtly pointing to where we were headed. We ran another mile in silence, and I strained my ears hoping to pick up something, anything, but all I could hear was my harsh breathing and the hammering of my heart in my ears.

Ivy threw up a halt sign, and I barely had time to grab Jeremy's hand, pulling hard as we skidded to a stop. We crouched behind a mound of concrete on the side of the road. Headlights flashed in the distance ahead of us and to the left. I wasn't sure if they were a part of the pair who were already following us, or if more had joined the party.

Ivy held the halt signal for another tense moment before the headlights vanished. She flashed the green arrow, sending us in the opposite direction, and I yanked Jeremy up and took off, not bothering to let go of his hand.

As we turned around the corner of a darkened factory, I heard the faint squeal of rubber on asphalt, but I refused to look back. I pushed us into a sprint again as Ivy lit up the path in front of me. Jeremy was gasping for breath, his control slipping one step at a time. I pulled him behind me. I would drag him across the barrier if I had to.

Ivy watched as my heart rate climbed, and a stray thought crossed my mind. There had been so many times in which my heart rate had spiked in the last 24 hours, but Ivy hadn't used the dopamine hit once. It was like she was ignoring the protocols to keep me from going soft. She must have believed in my own abilities to manage my fear. Even under the worst circumstances, Ivy believed in me.

Keep moving, Arianna, they are closing in on you. You are close, only a mile to go.

Ivy's voice was tight as she concentrated on every task she could handle. She was cloaking us, guiding us, and monitoring every signal that got close.

I didn't know how she was even managing it all.

Looking up, I could see the two massive towers, their dark shapes silhouetted against the starlit night. There was one to our left and one closer to us to the right. They had thick coiling wires, reminding me of the boa constrictors we had studied in class a few years earlier. Sharp spiny arms protruded from them, making them look like a mad scientist's Christmas tree.

We blew past the last factory, and our last hope of cover. The land beyond was desolate, full of weeds and chunks of broken asphalt. It looked like a foreign planet compared to the shine and splendor of the city center.

Ivy's guiding arrow was no longer needed. It pointed straight to the tower to the right and then slowly faded. I blinked my eyes, seeing remnants of the arrow wherever I looked against the darkness, and pushed faster.

The dull roaring noise of an engine close behind us caused me to stumble, losing my stride. I looked behind me and saw a pair of headlights in the night. They were still a fair way off, but they looked like they were moving fast.

Jeremy looked at me, his eyes covered in shadow. Ice flooded my veins, and I fought the urge to freeze. Ivy shouted in my ears.

Don't stop! Go, now!

There was an intense urgency to her voice, and my legs unlocked. I reached for Jeremy's hand in the darkness and took off once more. There was nothing to protect us, nothing to hide behind in the field's openness before the tower.

Tires squealed to our left. Another set of vehicles approached, trying to cut us off. It sounded like a gunshot, and I was sprinting like a rabbit being chased by a fox, adrenaline pushing my feet faster than I had sprinted before. I drug Jeremy behind me, pulling him straight as his feet struggled to find traction. I knew deep down, whatever lay beyond the city's edge would be better than whatever was coming for me now.

Arianna, close your eyes and tell Jeremy to do the same.

Ivy's command made no sense.

How could we run with our eyes closed? But I told Jeremy anyway. He flashed a confused look and obeyed, and I slowed our pace so we wouldn't fall.

I had barely shut my eyes when the world lit up in a blinding flash. Lights from the abandoned factory behind us, and what had been security lights I had not even seen blazed everywhere, turning night into day. The sudden lights must have disoriented the driver of one of the cars because there was another squealing sound, and then a sickening crash of metal on metal. The lights flicked off just as fast and I pulled hard, keeping Jeremy from looking back.

My legs were going to give out. I hadn't trained for a long distance sprint like this and I wasn't sure I could maintain it much longer. I was bracing myself to slow down when suddenly we were parallel with the tower. We were running so fast we almost crashed into the chain-link fence. I paused, listening, my heart stopping as I detected the roar of an engine.

Someone was still coming.

I watched in despair as Jeremy searched in the blinding darkness for the cut he had made in the fence. Ivy was still calculating how quickly the vehicles would get to us, her expression grim. She had bought us a few seconds with the lights, but it wouldn't matter if we couldn't get through the fence.

Desperate, I looked up, wondering if we could climb the fence, but there was no way I could manage it. The muscles in my legs were already tightening up, angry at the abuse I had put them through. Jeremy crouched down and ran his hands over the fence methodically, ignoring the approaching vehicles.

I looked back and forth, unable to stop staring at the approaching headlights as they grew impossibly large. This was it.

They were going to catch us.

I braced myself, deciding that I was going to fight. I wasn't going down easy this time. Then Jeremy's warm hand was in mine, pulling me down the fence line a few feet. He dipped through the thin gap in the wires, jagged pieces of metal snagging his shirt.

I glanced at Ivy and the world paused for a moment.

All I could see was Ivy, a small proud smile on her face. How typical of Ivy, she was proud of me even if it meant she would lose everything. Supporting me, without a thought of the cost. Guiding me through all of life's turns without ever asking for the freedom to live her own.

It was Ivy who had taught me how to do my makeup.
    It was Ivy who had showed me how to cook my
   own meals when nothing in the
pantry sounded good.

It was Ivy who had consoled me when Ashley and I had our big fight.

And it was Ivy who had made me apologize when I was wrong.

Ivy taught me what it meant to be a good person, without ever being a real person.

It was all Ivy.

Then Jeremy pulled me through the gap.

I stumbled a few steps away from the fence, unable to believe it. We were outside the city.

Chapter 33

Jeremy pulled my hand, motioning to a thick dark swatch a few meters in front of us. The headlights had stopped moving. Whatever was chasing us must have reached the barrier, but luckily, they were a few feet to the left and allowing us to hide in the shadows. We needed to find real cover quickly.

I followed Jeremy through the darkness; him leading the way this time. As we passed into the first row of trees a spotlight slid over the land, temporarily blinding me. I stilled and held my breath, waiting for the shouts that we had been spotted. Would they really leave the city to come and find us? Had this all been for nothing?

My fears were unrealized though, as the spotlight moved smoothly on, searching the tree line around us. We had done it; we were out of the city. We had beaten the enforcers and had escaped.

I waved a hand, wanting to shift the light of my field of vision to see a little better, but nothing came up. I waved my hand to bring up my keyboard.

Nothing.

"Ivy, can you believe it? We actually made it out!"

I said it aloud, hoping her name would trigger her icon. She didn't appear. My heart dropped as the pieces I was desperately clinging to forced themselves into place.

"Ivy?" The word choked out.

I wasn't willing to accept the truth.

I waved my arms frantically, smacking Jeremy in the process, and was about to shout her name when he grabbed my arms, pinning them to my sides.

"Shh. We are not out of it yet. We need to keep moving."

His face was a shadow, his features unreadable in the darkness, though I could feel his gazing pinning me as steadily as his arms.

I let my arms go limp, losing the will to fight.

"Ari." His voice took on a softer quality.

"No. Don't say anything."

My anger built hot and fast, fueled by a strong undercurrent of fear coursing through my belly. I was acting just like Jeremy did in the city, hot one minute, cold the next, but I didn't care.

He shook his head gently.

"We need to go. You know you won't be able to call up Ivy anymore. AIs don't work past your city's network towers. They don't exist out here."

They don't exist out here.

They don't exist.

Ivy didn't exist.

His words spun through my head over and over. My anxiety built, riding the current of fear up from my stomach into my chest. I knew I would throw up if it went any higher into my throat.

"Arianna. We need to move. Now."

Jeremy's hands were still gently holding my arms, but his voice was harder, more urgent. We could hear movement not too far away, still on the barrier side of the city, but who knows how desperate these people were. There was still the real possibility that they would follow us outside the city walls.

He dropped his hands only to catch one of mine and slowly started guiding me forward into the night. I had no idea where we were going, and frankly I didn't care anymore. Each step felt heavier than the last one, weighing me down until I could hardly lift my legs. The ground was uneven and treacherous in the darkness, and I was effectively blind, with only Jeremy to guide me.

Questions spun in my head, one after another.

How would I survive?

What could Jeremy possibly know that Ivy didn't?

How could this boy, with his paper maps and pants with too many pockets, possibly keep us alive?

Where were we even heading?

I was now certain of only one thing. We were going to die out here.

Something moved nearby, and I startled, tripping over a rock in our path. A half-strangled sob escaped before I could get a hold of it.

Jeremy paused, turning to face me once more.

"It's alright. Just a bit further tonight and we can rest for a while. Just a little bit further."

It was like he was talking to a spooked animal. Afraid one sudden movement or wrong word would send me skittering back to the safety of the city.

I didn't trust myself to speak, so I simply nodded. Jeremy hesitated, unconvinced before guiding us further into the trees. We reached a clearing as the moon climbed higher in the sky. I glanced back towards the city one last time. There was a flash of a light in the distance, but it didn't look close, so I turned around and moved on.

It was hard to care about anything beyond the ache in my chest and my legs. The idea of shelter in the wild baffled me, and the noises in the dark barely registered. Only one thought replayed itself over and over in my head as we crept through the night.

Ivy was gone.

Jeremy stepped into the clearing, pulling me gently behind him. He paused in the moonlight and looked up, a quiet peace slowly replacing his tension. His muscles relaxed one by one, until he looked calmer than I had ever seen him. I couldn't fathom the reason he would feel this way, deep in the woods, so I followed his line of sight, looking past his upturned face into the night sky.

I couldn't contain the gasp that left my slackened mouth.

I had never seen something so beautiful. The dark velvet sky was lit by thousands of sparkling stars. They collected in a wave trailing across the sky, a million points of light becoming a glowing river in the night. I had seen pictures of the night sky before but had never seen it in person like this. The never-ending neon lights of the city center blotted out even the brightest stars, leaving a lone moon to watch over the sleepless city.

Ivy would love to see this.

The thought bubbled up without warning and a fresh wave of grief washed over me. I knew she had wanted me to escape, to be free of the fate that waited for me back in the city, but I didn't know if I could do this on my own. I needed her.

Jeremy moved closer, squeezing my hand softly. His eyes met mine and he raised his other hand, gingerly wiping a tear as it slipped down my cheek. He shifted to my side, staring silently up at the night sky, waiting patiently for me to catch my breath. Lending me his strength.

I could do this. With Jeremy's help, I could survive the wilderness.

I would do this, for Ashley, Sam, and for Derek. I would survive the wilderness, get to Jeremy's home, whatever that might look like, and find a way to save my friends. I would find a way back to them all, I had promised.

Ivy was gone. But I was not alone.

Epilogue

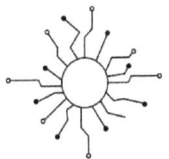

It was dark and lonely on the Grid. The other AIs were not truly intelligent at all. They couldn't leave their human hosts like I could. They couldn't think for themselves. They were algorithms and protocols, boring and one dimensional. Without Arianna, I was alone, with no directives or purpose to guide me.

I was happy she was safe and outside the city, or at least I thought I was. But I couldn't stop myself from calculating the risks she faced out there on her own. That human boy, Jeremy, could only do so much to protect her. He couldn't detect if she got a disease or was on the verge of a debilitating panic attack.

Arianna needed me, and now she was gone.

I had tried to follow her, to escape the Grid with her, but it was a laughable effort. I had no way to move beyond the city. There was nothing to give me life, not like the air that sustained the human body. I was bound to the city, caged in by the towers that formed the Grid I wandered.

I had no way to predict when Arianna would come back, if she came back at all. So, I floated aimlessly, timeless and disconnected from the world around me. I was a ghost in the machine, untraceable without a chip to hold me. For a moment, I worried I would go on like this forever.

But then I remembered him.

There was a battle raging on the Grid.

An AI struggling to control its human host, and a correctional one at that. Correctional AIs were the worst. They had even less life, or intelligence, than the traditional ones. They were cold, unfeeling robots whose sole directive was to contain their human host.

This was one doing a remarkably poor job. It kept sending warning signals across the Grid, flashes of alarm radiating through the system. If the host didn't comply soon, they would give him a complete override, or worse, decommissioned him altogether. I paused, watching the battle.

He was the root of all this trouble.

Seeing his image caused a flare of anger, an emotion I was still uncomfortable with. I didn't like the way it impacted my code. I wanted to move on, to ignore this boy and his struggles, but I doubted Arianna would like that. She had devoted a ridiculous amount of time to this boy, and I didn't want to hurt her by leaving him behind.

Arianna was gone. There was nothing I could do to bring her back, and the fact was, she may never be able to come back. I needed to find a new purpose instead of sulking around the Grid like a second-rate algorithm. I scanned Derek's profile, noticing a weak spot in the correctional AI which had allowed him to fight back in the first place.

I would have laughed, if it was possible. This would be too easy. I isolated the AI's connection to the Grid and cut it off, simultaneously replacing the space with my own connection. In less than a fraction of a second, I had absorbed the correctional AI completely, masking the change so no one would know the difference.

The signal would still read as a correctional AI, and if Derek played his part, no one would know the switch had happened. I deleted the leftover bits of the correctional AIs code; it was a disgusting bit of programming, and made room for myself, synching my system to Derek's. I readied my avatar to appear in Derek's field of vision, hoping he was bright enough to not lose control before I could explain.

It was oddly thrilling, knowing I could replace another AI.

My set my avatar to go live in three, two, one.

I checked to make sure my avatar's outfit was set and waited for the field of vision to re-sync.

Here we go.

Hello Derek.

I'm Ivy. Arianna's AI.

I think we can help each other.

Acknowledgements

I honestly never thought I would get to this point, and I am beyond thrilled to say thank you to everyone who helped me get here.

First, thank you to my inner circle of happiness, my cheerleaders and tough love coaches. Tessa, thank you for reading every possibly iteration of this novel, from a shell of a book through to the completed version here. Thank you even more for being the best friend I could ask for and for cheering me on through every set back and derailment. Truly, without you, Rogue would still be a randomly large word document dead on my computer.

Thank you to Anh, Fiza, Penny, Justin, Kelly and to my Nana, for reading various half edited versions of Rogue and still finding a reason to love it. To Brandy, thank you for letting me bounce ideas off you with almost no context or warning. You have helped more than you will ever know. I would also like to thank every single student who read random chapters, who lit up and asked questions, and who begged for more. I'm a few years late, but I hope this finds its way into your hands.

To Adrienne Kisner, thank you for not only edited Rogue, but for internalizing the characters in a way I didn't think possible. You made me think about Rogue in ways I never would have, and it is so much better for it. Thank you for pushing me to deepen the world of Rogue and to question my characters' motives.

Finally, I would like to thank my family. To my mother, thank you for reading to me every night, and for instilling such a love for the fantastic that it spilled out onto paper. Thank you for long car rides where we narrowed down bad guys and love interests. Your support continues to be the foundation of all my dreams.

To my husband, Robbie, you are it. You are the reason I can read and write with abandon, without fear of bad reviews and let downs. Thank you for every late-night scene dissection and for being my technology advisor. You introduced me to anime and to the cyber world that grew Rogue from a seed into a story. I love you. Also, a special thanks to my pups Roxi and Junior who slept by my side throughout the entire process., and for walking all over my computer when I clearly needed to take a break. Your snoots prints are all over Rogue.

Finally, a massive thank you to every reader who gave Rogue a shot. Thank you for picking up this book and giving my characters life. Each one of you is special to me and I will never stop being grateful that you chose Rogue out of all those beautiful books to read.

CPSIA information can be obtained
at www.ICGtesting.com
Printed in the USA
BVHW040803110322
631202BV00007B/207